"LET ME GET THIS STRAIGHT ...

You haven't made a car payment in three months? How is it that your car hasn't been repossessed until now?" he asked.

Silence. "I kind of went out with the repo man," Cecy finally admitted.

He choked. "You were sleeping with the repo man? Do you have any standards at all?"

"I never slept with him!" Cecy shouted. "And who the hell do you think you are, lecturing me when I don't even know your name?"

He sat very still for a moment. "I'm sorry. You're right; I was out of line. I've just never met anyone quite like you before." He held out his hand. "I'm Chas Buchanan."

Cecy smoothed her hair and tucked it behind her ear. "It's a pleasure to meet you, Chas."

"Of course it is—I just paid your doctor's bill." Chas seemed grimly amused. "And if you think giggling over a few margaritas is going to wipe out your debt to me, you're mistaken. I'm no sex-starved repo chump."

"No, you're a self-righteous jerk," Cecy muttered under her breath.

KAREN KENDALL

Something About Cecily

AVON BOOKS
An Imprint of HarperCollinsPublishers

This is a work of fiction. Names, characters, places, and incidents are products of the author's imagination or are used fictitiously and are not to be construed as real. Any resemblance to actual events, locales, organizations, or persons, living or dead, is entirely coincidental.

AVON BOOKS
An Imprint of HarperCollins*Publishers*
10 East 53rd Street
New York, New York 10022-5299

Copyright © 2001 by Karen A. Moser
ISBN: 0-380-81852-3
www.avonromance.com

First Avon Books paperback printing: May 2001

Avon Trademark Reg. U.S. Pat. Off. and in Other Countries, Marca Registrada, Hecho en U.S.A.
HarperCollins® is a trademark of HarperCollins Publishers Inc.

Printed in the U.S.A.

10 9 8 7 6 5 4 3 2 1

This book is dedicated to my husband, Don, who has redefined for me the whole concept of love.

So many other people deserve recognition for encouraging me along the way. Thanks to my critique partners and friends in GRW, a warm, generous professional organization that has no equal.

Thanks to the "Raiford gals" and the other supportive friends I'm so lucky to know. To Charlotte Hughes, for her kindness. To David Burke, author of *Street French 3: The Best of Naughty French*. To Claudine Chatigny, for her corrections to my abominable use of the language. And to Micki Nuding, my editor, and all the folks at Avon Books and HarperCollins who are part of the magic that creates a first novel from a pile of manuscript pages. Last, but not least, I want to remember my late mother, who said I could write a novel. You were right, Mom, and I'll love you always.

1

Cecy Scatterton tried not to let the curled lip of the Neiman Marcus manager bother her. Why had she ever splurged and bought a dress here? Tears wiggled their way under her lashes, and she blinked furiously, trying to keep them at bay. She produced her most genteel Southern smile.

"I'm afraid that store credit just won't do," she told the manager. "I'd like a cash refund."

"Store credit is more than generous under the circumstances, Ms. Scatterton. The only thing identifying this dress as ours is the brand name. You have no receipt, no attached tags." The manager folded her arms and stared Cecy down. "Our return policy is clearly posted throughout the store."

"But—" Cecy began. *But what? You see, Ms. Ice Queen, I've been hopelessly irresponsible with money and my life in general, but today I'm turning over a new leaf?*

"Ms. Scatterton, do you really want to push this? I could point out that this dress smells of perfume and hair spray. There are deodorant marks inside it. And the bag you've chosen to bring it back in is of last year's design."

Cecy thought about her entirely empty refrigerator, the one last packet of dried soup in her pantry, and Barney, her orange cat. His breakfast had consisted of an unlucky cricket and some crumbled saltines. She thought about her rent bill, which had been racking up ten-dollar-per-diem late charges since last Friday. Her tears loomed closer.

". . . store credit, Ms. Scatterton?" The manager was saying.

"Yes," Cecy said quickly. "I'll take it. Thanks." She signed the bottom of the required form. "Where is your gourmet section, please?"

Barney licked his crooked little chops and twitched his tail in gratitude. Imported foie gras and chutney were evidently more to his liking than crispy cricket à la saltine.

Cecy dunked the last chunk of a chocolate-dipped biscotti into black French coffee she had flavored with honey. It tasted wonderful, and she savored the food down to the last crumb.

Then she picked Barney up and snuggled him under her chin. As she kissed him he protested amiably and wriggled up over her shoulder, hanging his paws down her back. The snooty gourmet section of Neiman's had filled their growling stomachs, if not their nutritional needs. And, Cecy thought, trying to look on the bright side, it hadn't cost anything, strictly speaking. She'd gotten them imported food of the finest quality without passing so much as a nickel over the counter. Of course, there was that silly matter of the twenty-two percent interest on her store charge card, but what did it signify? If she couldn't pay her rent, she had no hope of paying her charge cards. She had to eat, however, until she found a way out of debt.

She walked with Barney into the living room and sat on the sofa, scratching his belly. As he writhed with pleasure, she looked about her.

Knickknacks sprouted from every available table, shelf, and crevice. Seven Lladro figurines fought for air across the mantel. The china cabinet bulged with small crystal animals. The left wall crawled with costly porcelain plates, fifty-six of them. The right wall stood awash in a sea of small but original watercolors and oil paintings. A series of vases lined the hearth. Cushions and throws smothered her furniture. The room, Cecy reflected honestly, was way too small for all this stuff.

And then there was The Box. The Box lurked

under her fancy scrolled coffee table, covered with a heavy brocade cloth. She shuddered at the thought of its contents.

But just as her thoughts began to turn gloomy again, Cecy's doorbell rang. It had to be Leo, her UPS man! What had he brought her today? Was it her order from Bloomingdale's, or the nightie from Victoria's Secret? She shivered with excitement and sprinted for the door. The familiar consumer's high warmed her cheeks and upped her heartbeat. She loved opening packages. Adored it. Lived for it, in the six months since her brother Brock had passed away.

As she reached for the doorknob, her feet slid and flew out from under her. Cecy's thoughts were suspended for a moment, then knocked out of her along with her breath as her nose, pelvis, and knees connected with the tiled floor. She'd tripped over a stack of glossy catalogues.

With a howl of pain, she let her tears flow. When she opened the door holding one hand over her bloodied nose, even the sight of Leo's friendly face wasn't much comfort. Nor was the lovely satin nightie in Passionate Peach—she had no one but herself to wear it for.

Cecy sat in the emergency room, stoned on a handful of Midols and a minibottle of champagne from the Neiman's gift basket. It was all the painkiller she'd had in the apartment, and her nose still throbbed.

Across from her sat a man—actually two of him—with coal black hair, almond-shaped dark eyes, and lips that curved to trigger a woman's darkest fantasies. His long, rangy body was gift-wrapped in cowboy boots, denim, and a pressed cotton shirt. One of his large hands was band-aged, the middle fingers taped to a makeshift splint.

Cecy was holding a bag of ice to her nose and wondering muzzily what he'd look like in only the boots when the nurse on duty stepped out and called her name.

"Cecily Scatterton?"

Cecy stood up, wobbly, and said, "Tha's me." She took two steps, then stopped—she'd forgotten her pocketbook. Turning to get it, she swayed and stumbled over the toe of a cowboy boot. For the second time that day, the floor rushed toward her, but this time it stopped. A steel-like arm encircled her waist and set her firmly back on her own feet.

"Watch it, sweetheart. You okay?" His voice was deep, lazy, without accent. It made her liver quiver. It made her heart stop.

"Mmmmm," she managed. Her blood began pulsing again after its momentary hiatus, and she stared into those depthless dark eyes. Her rescuer had a wildly sexy five o'clock shadow on the lower half of his face, and she desperately wanted to burn her own skin on it. Everywhere.

"Ms. Scatterton?" the nurse repeated.

"Yer," Cecy said stupidly. "I mean, uh, coming." She retreived the bag of ice from the potted plant it had flown into and held it to her nose once again. Stumbling past the booted god, she turned her head back toward him, then murmured, "Thanks."

"No problem," he said. He smiled, then yawned, causing Cecy to gasp for breath. Those lips, those even white teeth, caged a lithe, prowling tongue, and she feverishly imagined it assaulting her body.

Cecy blinked, shocked at herself, and decided never to mix pills and alcohol again. She might attack the man if she didn't snap out of this.

The nurse looked at her strangely, took her arm in a vise grip, and after hustling her to a private room decorated with a blue giraffe motif, asked her point-blank if she'd been drinking.

Cecy, eyeing the giraffes surreally, said she had, but added that she really thought it was the pills that had pushed her over the edge.

Alarmed, the nurse pushed her onto the cushioned examination table and demanded a full accounting of what she had ingested.

Cecy swung her legs and crackled the white paper under her. "About eight Midols," she announced solemnly, waggling the appropriate number of digits in the nurse's face. "Couple glasses Verve Klee-co. Tha's all."

The nurse's lips tightened. "Young lady, did

anyone ever suggest to you that it's unwise to mix pharmaceuticals with alcohol?"

"Yes," Cecy said baldly. "But s'also unwise to fall on face. Did both. Whad'ya know?"

The nurse, her face impassive, grasped Cecy's ankles and swung them up on the table, pushing her torso down at the same time. "Stay," she ordered brusquely. "I don't trust you not to fall off, if you try to sit. The doctor will be with you shortly."

"Is my nose broken, Nurse Ratched?"

The woman stiffened. "I don't know. The doctor will determine that." She left the door open.

Cecy watched the blue giraffes gallop along the wallpaper border. At the corner, two of them melded together as the edges of the pattern met. How sweet, she thought. Love among the pastel wild kingdom . . .

The door opened again, admitting a rotund figure with wire-rimmed glasses and a white lab coat. "Cecily Scatterton?"

"Yep."

"I hear we're a little out of it this afternoon, eh?"

"My nose is broken. Can you fix it?"

"Let me see." The doctor examined it, probing and prodding gently.

"Ow," Cecy complained.

"No, it's not broken. Just a little banged up. What happened?"

"I was waylaid by a shtack of roving catalogues."

"Ah." The doctor looked at her and shook his head. "All righty then. I tell my wife those things are dangerous, but I didn't realize the extent of the damage they could do."

He made a note on his clipboard. "Ms. Scatterton, I'm going to give you a prescription to ease the swelling and the pain in your nose." With a stern look, he continued. "I'm going to trust you not to take any of these pills for at least six hours. You have enough stuff in your system for the moment."

Cecy smiled sweetly at him.

"I'm serious."

She nodded.

"Keep your head elevated, and stick with the ice pack. Now, here's your paperwork. Go to the front desk, and they'll get you processed to go home."

"Thanks, Doctor."

Moments later, Cecy stood unsteadily at the checkout counter and passed her forms to the administrator across the expanse of blue laminate.

The woman typed busily for a few moments, and then made the pronouncement of doom. "Your insurance has expired, so it will be two hundred and ten dollars, please."

Cecy squawked. "Two hundred and ten dollars!"

"Yes, ma'am."

"But my nose wasn't even broken! He didn't do anything. He just poked it."

"That's the total, Ms. Scatterton."

"I can poke my own nose for free!"

The administrator sighed. "Cash or charge?"

Muttering furiously, Cecy dug into her purse and produced her wallet. She pushed a Visa card at the woman, and waited while she swiped the card through her machine.

"I'm sorry, but the card was declined. Do you have another one?"

Cecy pulled out her MasterCard, and drummed her fingernails nervously on the counter.

"Ms. Scatterton, this doesn't work either."

She flipped her Discover card at the woman, who kept her expression carefully blank and swiped this card. She keyed in the third set of numbers, waited, and then shook her head.

Cecy inched her American Express card toward her, and the woman bit her lip.

"We don't take American Express."

Calm, Cecy told herself. Stay calm. She slid out a Diners Club card, with pleading eyes.

The administrator shook her head apologetically.

Cecy yanked out the remainder of her plastic and held the cards up to the lady out of sheer desperation. "Macy's? Rich's? Neiman Marcus? Talbots? Sears? Texaco?"

The administrator looked down at her keyboard, and Cecy detected an embarrassment that she herself was beyond feeling at this point. Or so she thought.

"Look, is there something I can do in trade? Filing, or opening the mail?" She pleaded.

The woman closed her eyes. "I'm afraid not."

"Can you type?" an impossibly sexy male voice said from behind Cecy.

Her heart stopped again. Her liver requivered. And shame spontaneously combusted within her, flaming until she was sure she would be charred for life.

The voice belonged to Him.

She couldn't force herself to turn around. "T-type?" She managed.

"Yeah," he said, impatient. "Four-letter word meaning to utilize a keyboard."

"Yes, I can type."

"How fast?"

"Um, about forty-five words a minute." Cecy concentrated on not slurring her speech.

"Accurate?"

She nodded, still keeping her back to him.

"Are you free tomorrow, or do you have time during the evenings this week?"

She thought about rent and food. Again, she nodded.

"Do you have a criminal record, or do any illegal drugs?" he growled.

"No," Cecy said.

"Fine."

Silence ensued.

Curiosity got the better of her embarrass-ment, and Cecy turned toward him. He had commandeered her bill and was writing a check, with some difficulty, since his third finger was in a splint. She stared at him from behind the ice pack. "You're paying my bill."

"Yep." He kept writing.

"Why?"

"Because you can type."

Bewildered, she said nothing.

"I can't, for the next few weeks." He waggled the injured finger at her.

"But you don't know me."

"I wouldn't know a temp from a service, ei-ther. And they'd charge me more than you're go-ing to."

Cecy swallowed. "What am I charging you?"

The man ran his good hand over his jaw. "You're charging me five bucks an hour, until you're paid up."

"Five dollars an hour! That's slave wages."

"But I don't know you," he said, tossing her words back at her, "so I'm taking a risk by em-ploying you. You could walk out that door right now, and I'd never see you or my two hundred and ten again."

He had a point. "I haven't made money that bad since work-study in college. You'll have to pay me eight an hour."

"Nope. Six. You're really not in a position to bargain, you know."

Cecy's shoulders stiffened, but she knew he was right. "Six, then." She said it with as much dignity as she could muster.

The administrator was eyeing both of them with fascination.

"No refunds," she said, as she stamped the check and scribbled down the man's driver's license number and expiration date.

Cecy read the name on the check upside down. Her rescuer was one Chas Buchanan of Brookhaven Way. She swept her useless pile of credit cards off the blue counter and into her purse. "Can we please discuss the details outside?" She fished out her car keys.

His long strides got him to the door before her, and he opened it to let her go first. Cecy held her head high, ice pack and all, and swept past him toward her car, looking for the familiar bottle green hood. It wasn't in the row where she thought she'd left it.

She sighed, cursing her terrible sense of direction. This wasn't the first time she'd had trouble locating her car in a crowded parking lot. Putting a hand up to her eyes as a shade, she scanned the rows to the right and the left. It wasn't there, either.

"Lose your wheels?" He-Man asked sardonically, as he rocked back on his heels.

"No, I haven't, thank you." Cecy began walking through the lot.

"Why don't you get into my Jeep, and I'll drive you around until you see it."

She stopped and looked at him levelly. She knew nothing about this man. What if he was some kind of sick, twisted creep?

"No, thanks. No offense, but I don't know you." It was one thing to go to a public place of business and do some typing for him. It was quite another to risk being kidnapped—or worse. Cecy kept walking.

"Look, Cecily," he started.

She whirled. "How do you know my name?"

"Because it was on the doctor's form. The doctor will also have my name and address on file, not to mention my driver's license number. If you disappeared, the nurse back there, who was very interested in our conversation, could notify the cops with a description of me."

His argument was reasonable. Logical. And Cecy felt light-headed, dizzy. Water from the ice pack dripped down her chin and trickled along her neck. And her feet, in their high-heeled summer sandals, were beginning to hurt almost as much as her nose. "Fine. Where's your Jeep?"

Half an hour later, they had woven in and out of every row of cars in the hospital parking lot.

"It's not here," Cecy gulped, fighting a rising tide of panic.

"Do you know your license plate number?" He-Man asked her.

She shook her head. "Not by heart."

He picked up his cell phone and pushed the ON button.

"What are you doing?" Cecy asked quickly.

"Calling the police."

She grabbed the phone from him and turned it off. "No need to do that."

He stared at her. "Your car's been stolen," he said, as if she were a two-year-old. "You need to file a police report."

Cecy squirmed in the passenger seat. "It might not have been stolen, exactly. You see, I've missed a couple of payments."

He-Man looked stunned. "A couple?"

"Well, maybe three and a half."

His right eyelid began to twitch. "What do you mean by a half, for God's sake?"

Cecy fidgeted with the ice pack. "I mean that the last payment I sent them was only half what I owed. But I figured sending something was better than nothing."

"Let me get this straight," He-Man said slowly. "You haven't made a car payment since February? It's now the end of May. How is it that your car hasn't been repossessed until now?"

Cecy was silent.

"Isn't that a little odd?"

"I kind of went out a couple of times with the repo man," she admitted.

He choked. "You were sleeping with the repo man? Do you have any standards at all?"

"I never slept with him!" Cecily shouted. "I only went on a couple of dates. And who the hell do you think you are, lecturing me when I don't even know your name?"

He sat very still for a moment. "I'm sorry. You're right. I was out of line. I've just never met anyone quite like you before." He held out his hand. "I'm Chas Buchanan."

Cecy smoothed her hair and tucked it behind her ears, then readjusted her ice pack. "Well then," she said, in her normal soft Southern tones. "It's a pleasure to meet you, Chas." She clasped his hand briefly.

"Of course it is. I just paid your doctor's bill." Chas seemed grimly amused. "And if you think jiggling and giggling over a few margaritas is going to wipe out your debt to me, you're mistaken. I'm no sex-starved repo chump."

"No, you're a self-righteous jerk," Cecy muttered under her breath. Louder, she said, "I told you I would do your data entry, okay? Can we stop with the insulting assumptions?"

Chas nodded. "Okay."

"What kind of data entry is this? What do you do?"

"I'm a financial planner and investment consultant. I also do some basic accounting work. My assistant's gone on vacation for the next two weeks, and I need someone to fill in. You'll be typing letters and inputting records for me."

"Oh."

"Think you can manage that?" Chas cast a glance at her.

"Yes, of course."

"What kind of work do you do?"

"I'd just finished up with school when my

brother got sick. I moved to Atlanta and took care of him full-time until he died—there wasn't anyone else to do it." She plucked at her skirt.

Chas's expression became more sympathetic.

"There was some insurance money," Cecy went on. "It seemed like so much." She shut her mouth and didn't elaborate any further. She wasn't going to talk to a stranger about those long, awful months after Brock had died. The months during which she'd spent a lot of time staring at the wall, listlessly following the melodramas of daytime television—and shopping. Then an unexpected thirty-thousand-dollar medical bill of Brock's had jolted her out of the blues.

"So you don't have a job at the moment?" Chas asked.

She shook her head. "I guess you're my new temporary boss."

"All right. The first demand I'll make of you, then, is—"

"Request," Cecy cut in. "Maybe up North, or wherever you come from, you make demands, but you're in the South now, and you make requests. Especially of ladies."

"I beg your pardon, Miss Scarlett," Chas said drily. "The first request I'll make of you is that you give me directions to your home, since I'm apparently taking you there."

Cecy flushed. "Oh. Yes, I suppose you are. Get on 400, and exit at Abernathy."

Chas drove in silence for a while. So she

thought he was a rude Yankee, did she? Well, at least he wasn't on the verge of bankruptcy. Just what had he gotten himself into by trying to help her out and save himself some money in the process?

He tried to be a fair employer; Jamie got two weeks paid vacation. He just hadn't budgeted in the cost of a temp for the time she was gone. He'd resigned himself to staying late and doing her job himself until she got back. But that was out of the question now, since he'd slammed his damned finger in a door.

When he'd seen the little fluff ball in the emergency room producing her endless stream of useless plastic, the idea had hit him: They could help each other out. Chas told himself that his decision had nothing to do with the fact that she was awfully cute.

He cast a glance at her as he maneuvered onto the highway. Sometime in the last few minutes, Cecy's curly blond head had drooped onto her shoulder, and smoky brown lashes just brushed the edges of her small, proud cheekbones. Her tender pink mouth hung open like a child's, and the faintest, tiniest snore wafted in his direction.

Chas grinned. The little Georgia peach snored, did she? Ha. Wouldn't she be delighted to know that. He wondered what kind of painkillers she'd taken. Whatever they were, they sure had made her loopy. Understandable, given the circumstances. How had she injured her nose?

He exited on Abernathy before nudging her awake with an elbow. "Cecily? Pardon me for disturbing your beauty sleep, but I need to know where I'm going."

"Mmmm. Oh. Take your second left, and then the third right." She rubbed at her eyes. "Sorry I nodded off on you."

"No sweat. I imagine that it's polite, here in the South." Chas crossed three lanes of traffic smoothly, ignoring her glare, and turned into a residential neighborhood in Sandy Springs. The tall maple and oak trees dripped with sunlight and fresh leaves. Hydrangea bloomed everywhere, competing with graceful hostas, cheerful marigolds, and lush geraniums, begonias, impatiens. Atlanta in May was spectacular with color. He could see why his grandmother had never left.

Following Cecy's directions, Chas pulled up at the eighth building in her apartment complex, then handed her a business card. "Both my work and cell phone numbers are on that," he told her. "Will you give me yours?"

Cecy nodded and dug around in her handbag for a pen and a scrap of paper. Pressing it against her knee, she scribbled the number for him.

"Do you have a friend who'll give you a ride to my office?" Chas asked her.

Cecy blinked several times. "Absolutely. When do you want me there?"

"Eight o'clock."

She gulped. "No problem. Thanks for the ride."

Chas watched her walk to one of the blue-painted doors. She plucked an official-looking envelope off of it, fumbled with the lock, and disappeared. Cecily Scatterton, no matter how cute, was a walking mess. A mess he'd just hired—at least for thirty-five hours. He shook his head. Lord only knew what would come of it.

Cecy sank down on the love seat in her living room and put a hand to her head, which throbbed in three-quarter time. Her nose throbbed in double time, and together they created a horrible clashing symphony in pain. *Wagner*, she thought. *This is what he must have felt like when he composed—nothing else could have inspired him to create such noise.*

She smiled a little at her thoughts—Brock would have laughed, being a musician. God, she missed him. He'd liked Wagner. Memories of her brother's pale face swam before her, sharp-featured, always wearing that groove at the left corner of his mouth, where his smile began. It started slowly, at the corner with a twitch, and then widened, spreading into laughter and sparking his pale blue eyes.

Cecy wiped a tear from her swollen nose and sniffed gingerly. Barney padded in and wrapped himself around her legs, rubbing his head against them. She stroked him, glad that they had dinner for tonight. There was another cake of pâté for him, and crackers and cheese for her. But how was she going to pay for her prescription or some ibuprofen? She got up and went to her closet, hoping there was something else she could return. She couldn't go back to Neiman's . . . As she flipped through the items, going down the row of hangers, she realized how foolish her efforts were. None of the department stores had pharmacies.

As she turned away in frustration, something caught her eye. Electric blue and rubber, it stuck out from a box on the floor. Cecy fished it out from among the skirts and trousers, and brightened. A lucky break!

Ten minutes later she was arguing with the pharmacist at Eckerd Drugs around the corner. "This ThighMaster has done me no good at all. If anything, my thighs have become mistresses of their own destiny, and have developed a magnetic force which attracts chocolate bars from miles around."

The pharmacist coughed. "Do you have your receipt, miss?"

"Not precisely," Cecy told him with a charming smile. "But as you can see, the price sticker on the box has your store name on it, and I only bought it here a few weeks ago."

"Our store policy is that we give refunds with receipts only."

"Well, I don't quite know what I did with mine."

The pharmacist cleared his throat and began to reiterate his position when Cecy swayed and put a hand to her head. "Ohhhh," she moaned. "My head. I feel so dizzy."

He popped out from behind the counter and helped her to a chair. "Are you all right, miss? Can I get you some water?"

Cecy felt like the worst kind of dirtball. "That would be wonderful. Do you mind?"

"Not at all." He scurried away.

Cecy opened one eye and watched him, arranging herself in an even more pathetic position. Guilt nagged her, but this was an emergency.

When he returned with a full Dixie cup, she took it from him with a little gasp of thanks.

"Not at all, not at all. Is there anything else I can do?" The little man rubbed his hands together and fretted.

"Well," Cecy said, sighing, "if you would consider exchanging the ThighMaster for my prescription and perhaps some aspirin and Meow Mix, I'd be grateful. Would that be possible? That way you don't have to give me a refund, and we'll both be happy."

He caved immediately and offered to call a cab to take her home. "You shouldn't be driving, miss."

"Oh, no thank you. I do appreciate the thought, though. You've been very kind." Cecy accepted her white paper bag with a slightly trembling hand and left. In penance, she'd write a glowing letter about him to the drugstore management.

She managed to get back to her apartment and flopped on the couch to think. As she lay back, the envelope she'd thrown there crackled, and she pulled it out from under her. The folded letter inside was brutal and to the point.

"Dear Ms. Scatterton," she read.

"Due to your failure to remit payment for the lease of unit 814, Happy Hollow Apartments has already given you thirty days' notice to remove your personal belongings from said unit. We hereby remind you that your notice expires in four days . . ."

Cecy balled up the letter. Oh, dear God, what was she going to do now? She had an empty checking account, a bare pantry, no car, no more credit, and now no apartment. How had she done this? What had she been thinking?

After Brock had died, she'd allowed herself to slip into a haze of depression and apathy. It seemed so unfair that such a momentous event in her life had registered so little upon the rest of the world. Cecy had watched, disbelieving, as the mail was delivered the morning of his last breath. Traffic still piled up, drivers honking impatiently at each other and exchanging rude gestures. Telemarketers still called her, hawking this and that. *Stop!* she'd wanted to yell. *Stop, you don't understand. Have some respect and pay attention to what's happened. Brock is gone. He was my whole family.*

Of course, the world had ignored her. So *she'd* stopped, and with a vengeance. She'd dug her heels into the dirt, and stuck her head in the sand. Belatedly, Cecy realized where that left the rest of her: fanny in the breeze, just waiting to be kicked. She hoped against hope that the Big Foot in the Sky didn't wear combat boots.

From the sofa, she could see a corner of The Box lurking under the coffee table. Cecy reluctantly dragged it out and stared down at it for a long moment before lifting the lid. Inside were the stacks upon stacks of bills she'd been avoiding, the polite and then cajoling and then threatening letters that went along with them, and more bills and letters on top of those.

As she stared into it, the bills and letters became sharp, jagged teeth in the mouth of a rectangular, corrugated monster. Roaring at her, it prepared to engulf and digest her in one slashing bite. Cecy lurched backward with a squeak of alarm.

At least she'd paid Brock's hospital bill. And now she was making a new start: She'd gotten herself a job. For at least—she frowned, dividing two hundred and ten by six—thirty-five hours. A job was something to be proud of, even if it had been offered out of pity by a rude Yankee. She'd do it well, and list with a temp agency immediately for other jobs.

Miss Scarlett, indeed! Where did Chas Buchanan get off, calling her that? Cecy steamed as she fixed a saucer of pâté and chutney for Bar-

ney, and garnished it with a few Meow Mix kib-
bles. Then she turned the air conditioner down
to fifty-five degrees, started the gas fireplace,
and slowly fed the contents of The Box into the
flames.

There was nothing like a new start to make
you feel better.

2

"No." Chas Buchanan said it with absolute finality, shaking his head. "Absolutely not. I am not giving you an advance so that you can get your nails done."

Cecy's wide blue eyes met his limpidly.

Chas ignored their appeal. "First of all, you're already starting in arears. You owe *me* two hundred and ten dollars. Second of all, you're late, and third, you're . . ." His gaze raked her dripping body, drawn unwillingly to the clear outline of her breasts. He took a deep gulp of air. "Third, you're wet. The bathroom is over there. Find a towel."

"My friend couldn't give me a ride this morning, so I had to take the bus, and it started to pour while I was waiting at the stop."

"That," Chas said, "is not my problem. Neither are your nails, for the love of Christ. Your typing skills will not be impaired by chipped polish."

Cecy laughed lightly, trying to disguise her desperation. She *had* to get some money for food. "Well, of course not. But they need to be filled in the back."

"Filled?" Chas stared at her, uncomprehending.

"They're acrylic, you see. If you don't add more to the space where they grow, they can pop off. That's bad," Cecy confided, thinking quickly. "Because if a nail pops off, it could end up falling into the cracks between the keys on the computer." She widened her eyes dramatically. "The whole keyboard could jam, and then where would you be?"

Chas set his jaw and folded his arms. "I don't know, Cecily. Where would I be?"

"In a *terrible* situation. It could grind your whole day's business to a screeching halt."

"Cecily," Chas said in ominous tones.

"Yes?"

"How stupid do you think I am?"

"Oh, not at all."

"Then I suggest that you go and dry yourself off while I open this word-processing program for you."

"Okay." Cecy knew when she'd lost. With a small sigh, she trudged to the bathroom and wiped at herself with a wad of nonabsorbent brown paper towels. Her plan had failed miserably, and she looked like a hedgehog with the flu.

Cecy bent forward and shook her wet head, but it didn't help much to fluff her hair. She brightened when she saw a hot-air hand dryer. Punching the round steel button, she crouched underneath it so that it blew on her head. She didn't really give a damn about her nails—she'd rip the acrylic off this evening.

After emerging from under the dryer, she went to the sink to fix her face. A dab with another paper towel removed the mascara smeared under her left eye. She powdered her nose. She pulled at her pale blue silk blouse, unsticking it from her bosom, and buttoned her vest across it. If she could maintain a pulled-together exterior, surely her insides would follow suit.

When she left the bathroom, Chas was waiting for her, foot tapping impatiently in a polished-leather loafer. The movement tautened the muscles of his thigh, which affected her even from ten feet away and through utterly conservative khakis. As she walked toward him she wondered what kind of underwear he wore. A tiny purple banana-hammock, perhaps? Or pink-and-green-plaid boxers? Maybe those cartoon-studded ones. She recalled seeing some covered with neon household appliances. Did Chas cover his privates with runaway toasters and blenders?

"... asking you a question, Cecily," he was saying.

"What?" She blinked.

"For the third time, do you know how to use WordPerfect?"

"Sure," she said. "I wrote my thesis using that."

"Pardon me?"

"My thesis," she repeated. "I wrote it in WordPerfect."

Chas appeared to have difficulties understanding. "Thesis," he repeated. "As in master's? You?"

Cecy nodded.

"In what?"

"French literature."

"Ah." Chas stared at her, and began to laugh.

"What's so funny?" She glared at him.

"Miss Scarlett's done got herself some book learnin'," he gasped. "It just wasn't anywhere in the arena of finance—or common sense."

"I'll thank you to keep your opinions to yourself, Mr. Buchanan," she snapped, and swore at him in French.

"What did you say?"

"Something unspeakable."

"You just spoke it. What was the general idea?"

"I challenged the legitimacy of your birth and

the occupation of your mother, then cast aspersions upon your character in general."

"Why, thank you," Chas responded, grinning. "Anytime."

"May I ask you one question?"

She nodded.

"Why didn't you study something useful? Why frog tales?"

"Frog tales?" Cecy choked. "I studied it because I loved it."

"But did it net you a job?"

"There's more to life than making money, Buchanan." She deliberately dropped the mister. "I suppose you haven't figured that out, yet."

"Maybe, but it sure is hard to live life without any money, isn't it, Cecily? Frog tales and fancy cussing don't pay the bills."

Cecy ground her teeth. "Can we get to work, now?"

"Funny how you got struck by the Puritan ethic all of a sudden," Chas mocked.

She sat in the chair near the desk and picked up the forms lying on it. "These look pretty self-explanatory."

Chas nodded and pulled up a chair next to hers. "I'm glad you have that outlook, but let me go over a couple of things before you begin." As he talked, he inhaled the sweet fragrances of her body. Cecily's hair smelled like fresh peaches. Underlying that was the soap she'd cleansed her skin with, and a faint, flowery perfume.

Chas cursed himself for noticing, and hoped

that Jamie would return from the beach early. He finished his instructions curtly and retreated to his office as her fingers began to fly over the keyboard. Astonishing—she seemed to be on the brink of competence. Chas shook his head. Cecily Scatterton was a study in contradictions.

When lunchtime rolled around, he looked up from his client files and stretched. A burger would do the trick today. Chas got to his feet and strolled to the outer room, where Cecy was still typing busily. "How's it going, Miss Scarlett?"

"I'm not going to answer to that ridiculous name." She didn't even glance up at him.

"Looks like you're working hard." Chas watched as she came to the end of the form and hit the print command on the keyboard. "You are entitled to a lunch break, though. I'm going to pick up a burger. Do you want one?"

Cecy hesitated, and he would have sworn he heard her stomach grumble. "No," she said. "Thanks, but I'm on a diet."

Chas frowned, scanning her from head to toe. She was damned close to skinny already. Why the hell was she dieting? He shrugged. "Okay. Do you want a Coke?"

"That would be nice." Cecy reached into her purse and began to dig. "I have some change in here."

"Don't worry about it," Chas told her, waving his hand. "See you in a bit."

Cecy breathed a sigh of relief. She'd found a

dollar and twenty-seven cents in her couch this morning, but that was the sum total of her food budget. She couldn't afford the Coke, but she needed something to get her through the rest of the day. If she sipped the soft drink little by little, she could ride the crest of sugar and caffeine until it was time to go home.

She turned her attention back to work to distract herself from the rumbling in her stomach. The forms tracked Chas's recommendations for the investments of one T. Barry. His suggestions spread Mr. Barry's money over several different stocks, bonds, and funds, some US-based, some international. All of them had performed exceptionally well over the last couple of years, according to Chas's research. His plan also included Barry's insurance, a budget of monthly living expenses, and advice on how much money he should be saving from each paycheck.

Cecy bit her lip. My goodness, Chas wanted him to save a lot—four hundred dollars a month. But he'd also traced the development of the proposed savings over ten years, based on an average yearly return of twelve percent. Her eyes widened. Over ten years, the sum of money would grow to enormous proportions. And here, in the next column, he'd listed what it would do over twenty years.

Her mouth was still hanging open when Chas returned with a large bag which smelled like heaven, and set a tall lidded cup on her desk, along with a straw.

"Thanks," she said, and inhaled the aroma of french fries appreciatively.

"You sure you don't want any food?"

"No, really. You go ahead."

"Any problems with the work?"

Cecy shook her head. "Can I ask a question, though? Why do you count insurance as an investment? It always seems like a dead loss to me. I mean, you pay and pay and pay. You hardly ever get anything back, and if you do, you're diseased or dead. What's the point?"

Chas's mouth quivered. "Well, that's true of term life policies. But I have Barry set up for a whole life policy." At her blank look, he said, "The basic fact of insurance is that you're paying for protection against catastrophic loss. It's an investment you make to protect your other investments."

"Oh," Cecy said. "I've never learned about any of this."

"They don't teach you this stuff in Frog Lit, eh?"

"Stop calling it that."

The corners of his eyes crinkled, and he retreated to his office with the bag of food. Cecy tried not to sniff the air like a hound, and returned to typing.

Out of the corner of her eye, she watched as Chas inhaled a burger and a half, interspersed with forty-seven french fries. She couldn't help counting, or noticing that he left a few of them in the paper container, next to the remaining half sandwich.

A frown crossed his rugged face as he scanned his own computer screen, and he rubbed at his jaw. Pushing the food to the corner of his desk, he logged onto the Internet to research something.

Cecy eyed the half burger avidly, but forced herself to wait a few minutes. She felt like a cat burglar plotting to heist the Hope diamond. After enough time had gone by, she stood up, stretched, and picked up a note Chas had written by hand. She traipsed into his office with it. "Excuse me, but what is this word right here? I can't quite make it out."

He glanced at it. "Global," he translated. "Sorry, my handwriting can be tough to read."

"Global," Cecy repeated. "Thanks. Here, let me throw this out for you. You're finished?"

"What?" Chas barely looked up. "Oh, yeah. You don't have to do that."

"It's no problem at all." Cecy smiled and neatly snared the remaining food. She folded the paper around the burger and swept it back into the bag, along with the rest of the fries.

Chas continued to work, pecking away with his index fingers, as she exited and slipped back behind her desk. There she stowed the bag in her purse. Dinner was served. She could keep the dollar twenty-seven until tomorrow.

At five-thirty, Cecy began to straighten the

desk and put things back in their files. She yawned from afternoon fatigue and lack of food. The last thing she felt like doing was trudging the half mile to the bus stop, but the friend she'd spoken of to Chas was nonexistent. She knew no one in Atlanta except a couple of Brock's old friends, and she didn't want to bother them. Gathering her purse, she stood up and waggled her fingers to Chas in his office.

"Good night. I'm going to catch the five-forty-five bus home."

He looked up from a yellow pad and spun his silver pen through his fingers. "I'll take you home," he said. "It's still raining out there."

"It's okay. I don't want to trouble you."

"I said I'll take you home." Chas stood up and stretched his broad shoulders, rolling his head forward and back.

Cecy tried not to notice the way his white cotton shirt molded his chest and contrasted against the bronze of his skin. She looked instead at his hands, which dwarfed the silver pen between long, brown fingers. They were capable hands, with neat, squared nails. She imagined them swinging a hammer with ease, hurling a baseball, stroking and exploring a woman. She flushed and looked away.

"Ready?" Chas asked.

"Mmm hmmm."

He dug his keys out of his pocket, turned out the lights, and opened the door for her. Cecy breathed the clean, laundered scent of his shirt as she brushed past his arm, and underlying that, a faint whiff of expensive aftershave and musky skin. An odd electricity flickered through her stomach and left her feeling weak and warm.

She told herself not to be silly as she walked with him down the hallway of the building and out to the parking lot. Chas Buchanan might be heart-stoppingly male, and she might have a primitive cavewoman's craving for him, but that didn't matter. He also had a wide sarcastic streak and an obvious lack of respect for the situation she'd gotten herself into.

Cecy sidestepped the issue of whether she herself could respect it. She wasn't going to think about that right now. What she needed to focus on was keeping this job, and for longer than a week. It was her only hope of eating, of surviving.

So, she resolved, she was not going to pant over Chas Buchanan. She would keep her hormones in their hive, and they could make all the honey they wished as long as they didn't fly out of control and sting her stupid.

She let Chas open the door of the Jeep for her and settled back into the comfortable leather seat for the ride home.

Chas frowned. He could not for the life of him figure out why his car smelled of fast food. The usual scents of dusky leather and Armor All were overridden by the aroma of french fries. He checked in the backseat to see if he'd left a wrapper or bag there, but it was immaculate. He shrugged and shook his head. Maybe the smell had hung in the Jeep since lunch.

He listened to the radio as they drove, chuckling at an occasional wisecrack by the DJ and shaking his head over the traffic update. "Interstate 285 is a parking lot, folks. Accident still being cleared near the entrance ramp at Roswell Road . . ."

As he turned into Cecy's apartment complex, a speed bump reminded Chas that his bladder was uncomfortably full. "Do you mind if I come in and use your bathroom?"

"Oh, sure."

He followed Cecy to her apartment door, trying not to notice the way parts of her wiggled seductively when she walked. The last thing he needed was a bankrupt bimbo in his bed. His instincts were confirmed when she opened the door into his idea of hell.

Her place was infested with expensive knick-knacks, useless clutter, silk flowers, pillows, and candles. Things covered every available surface, and most of those which weren't technically available. Cecy's home looked like a department store stocked by speed freaks.

Chas closed his eyes and pinched the bridge of his nose between his fingers. Good God almighty.

"The bathroom's down that hall," Cecy told him. "Do you have a headache?"

"No, no," Chas assured her. Suffering from visual overload spiked by claustrophobia, he went to use the facilities.

When he returned, Cecy was lighting a bank of candles on top of her refrigerator with a dangerously low-burning match, and the ugliest cat he'd ever seen approached him boldly and began sniffing around his ankles. It was orange with unblinking yellow eyes, and its jaw was twisted comically to the left in a bizarre underbite. As if that weren't enough, his tail had been broken at some point in his life, and the tip hung at a sixty-degree angle to the rest.

"Your cat," Chas said succinctly, "looks like Edward G. Robinson on a bad day. Where's the cigar?"

Cecy's laugh rang out, and she looked toward them, match in hand. She looked like a small curvy Statue of Liberty in that position, Chas mused, until his eyes widened and he realized that Liberty's torch was ignited—in the form of her fingernails. "Jesus!" he uttered, and sprang forward to grab her roughly and plunge her hand into the sink.

Two of Cecy's long, pink, perfect nails were blackened and smoking under the tap water, and she quivered against his chest.

"Are you all right?" he demanded.

She nodded without making a sound.

"What the hell did you say these things are made of? Acrylic?"

Cecy nodded again.

"Don't they tell you how flammable that is?"

"The woman at the salon did ask me if I smoked," Cecy said in a small voice. "But I didn't think about anything like this happening."

Chas shook his head in disgust. "If I were you, I'd get rid of those things right away. They cost you money you don't have, they look ridiculous, and they endanger your life." He realized suddenly that Cecy was still in his arms, against his chest, and that at least one part of his body was enjoying having her there. *Down, boy!* he commanded mentally, and moved back.

"You think they look ridiculous?" Cecy's lip quivered. "They're supposed to look nice."

"Oh, damn." Chas sighed. "I didn't mean to insult you. But trust me, a man doesn't look too hard at a woman's fingernails."

"He doesn't? What does he look at, then?"

Chas narrowed his eyes, but her face was guileless. His gaze flickered down her body, stopping at her slim, sweet calves, moving up to that neat little waist, climbing higher to her breasts. He forced it higher yet, to her eyes. His voice was gruff as he replied. "He looks at, er . . . her other . . . qualities."

"What qualities?"

He stared at her helplessly. She seemed to be asking the question genuinely, and with an edge of urgency. There was a disturbing innocence about her, in spite of the elegant clothes and the artfully streaked hair. He was drawn to it, and didn't know why.

Without conscious thought, Chas backed her against the sink and took her mouth with his.

Cecy inhaled sharply and took in the taste of him—mint and man. His lips were hot, demanding, and thorough. His tongue explored the crevices of her mouth and teased her own. She opened to him, caught on a crest of desire that rushed through her body.

The kiss shook her, left her breathless. His hands raked through her hair and then along her jaw to cup her face for more. His chest flattened her breasts as he devoured her, and her knees went weak with pleasure. She'd never felt this kind of response to a man before—this electricity shooting through her, leaving heat in its wake.

Cecy shifted against him and became conscious again of the acrid smell of smoking acrylic. She snapped to awareness. What was she doing, wantonly pinned to the sink and grinding against her new boss? Had she lost her mind?

She pushed against his chest, and he released her abruptly, muttering an apology.

"This," she managed, "is a really bad idea."

"No kidding. I'm sorry—I didn't mean to do that. I'll leave." Chas turned on his heel and strode to the door. "We'll just pretend this never happened, and I'll see you tomorrow."

Cecy tucked her hair behind her ears and swallowed. When she ventured to raise her eyes again, she saw that Chas was frowning at something on the little table by the door. It was her purse, the flap open. Too late, she realized that the McDonald's emblem on the bag inside was just visible.

He stared at her, hard, and then opened the door. "Good night, Cecily," he said, and was gone.

Cecy leaned weakly against the counter, absently picking charred acrylic from her fingernails. Her lips felt bruised, her nervous system hummed, and her brain whirled.

"Eeeoooww," Barney mewled.

"Yeah, yeah, yeah," Cecy muttered at him. "What did you do today, besides spread hair on my furniture?" She made her way over to the little table and retrieved the squashed McDonald's bag. Trying not to think of Chas's shocked, frozen expression, she placed his half-gnawed burger on a pretty sandwich plate, lifted the top half of the bun, and pulled off the limp lettuce. Then she put the burger and fries in her microwave for forty-five seconds.

Meanwhile, she poured Barney a bowl of Meow Mix. "Nothing gourmet for either of us tonight, cutie."

Barney purred anyway and attacked the kibble with relish. His pointed little teeth foraged and crunched around the bowl.

Cecy took her steaming, sagging burger out of the microwave when it beeped. She hoisted it to her mouth and then slowly put it back onto her plate. Ugh. She had no appetite for it.

It's food. You've got to eat something today. Be glad you were able to get it. She forced herself to consume a few of the rubbery french fries. Okay, so Chas now suspected that she was reduced to picking through the garbage for her next meal. Why did that bother her so much? He already knew her charge cards were maxed out and her car had been repossessed. What did it matter that she moonlighted as a bag lady? After all, the remaining shreds of her dignity had gone up in flames with her nails this evening.

Chas drove on autopilot, stunned at his own behavior. Why had he kissed the bewitching little bimbo? He struck his forehead with the heel of his good hand. What in hell was wrong with him? He could still taste peaches and . . . what was it? Hydrangea. It drove him insane. He'd wanted to lick her all over, once he'd tasted that sweet little mouth. He'd wanted to bite and tease and invade. To spread her right there on the kitchen counter, like warm honey on toast.

He smacked himself in the forehead again. *Cut it out!* Lust was something he controlled easily—until today. Today he'd been unbelievably stupid, and was paying for it now, negotiating Highway 400 with a raging anaconda in his shorts.

He forced himself to think of the Dow, instead. The Nasdaq Composite for the day. That should be up a few more points. What was going on in Southeast Asia? He fumbled for the radio and turned the dial to a news station.

He maneuvered the Jeep two lanes to the right and exited on Paces Ferry Road. Going to see his grandmother's house would help get his mind back on track.

He slowed as he approached. The house rose gently out of a soft hollow, a treasure at the end of a vast expanse of soft peridot lawn. Azaleas and ornamental peach trees lined a long U-shaped drive that curved gracefully on either side from the street to the polished mahogany door nestled under the portico.

The house was of mellow cream limestone, lit by huge multipaned windows. Built in a gentle arc, it hugged a flower garden to its breast and echoed the shape of the driveway.

The homes along West Paces Ferry Road were fit companions for the Georgia governor's mansion, which they flanked. They radiated grace, gentility, and charm. They bespoke old traditions, old families, old money. Upon his divorce, Chas couldn't have afforded even a doghouse on Paces Ferry Road, but he'd been working hard ever since to change his circumstances.

Chas gazed at the house, resolved to have it back in the family no matter what the price. Grandmother would never have wanted strangers living in it, as they were today.

He could still see her out there, her white hair tucked under a straw hat, planting annuals along the border of natural stone. She knelt on an old cushion, her gloves discarded on the wooden bench because she liked the feel of the soil between her fingers.

"Shhhh, now Chas, don't tell anyone. We Southern women aren't s'posed to like gettin' in the dirt like a hog."

He'd grinned at her, a freckled eight-year-old. Turning the end of his nose up with a finger, he'd oinked.

"Very good!" She was delighted. "Hand me that flat of begonias, will you? Thank you, dear . . ."

Chas smiled at the memory. He missed her. It wasn't right that her house had been sold upon her death, but his parents hadn't been able to afford it on their own, and his uncle had been more interested in the cash it would bring.

Since Chas had moved to Atlanta nine years before, he had driven by the house three to four times a week, waiting fruitlessly to see a "For Sale" sign in the yard. The owner had laughed at him when he'd mustered the nerve one day to knock on the door with an unsolicited offer.

"That's a few hundred thousand below the market value, son. And frankly, we're not ready to retire yet."

Chas had pressed his business card into the man's hand, and told him to call when the time came. "I swear to you, sir, I'll have the money by then. Just give me the first option. Please."

"Sure, son. I'll give you a ring." The guy hadn't even tried to hide his amused skepticism.

Chas cracked his knuckles and continued to stare at the house. It would be his one day. *Help me out, Grandmother. Rattle some chains. Creak the floorboards. Just a little friendly haunting, okay?* He put the Jeep back in drive and pressed the gas pedal. Time to get home, catch the news, and rustle up something to eat.

His thoughts turned back to Cecily Scatterton and her open purse with his leftover burger in it. Surely she wasn't so hard-up that she had to swipe the remnants of his lunch? She lived in a decent apartment, after all. She had nice clothes. Chas drummed his fingers on the steering wheel. Maybe she was a kleptomaniac. Maybe that ugly cat of hers liked Big Macs. Who knew? She was one strange woman. And she had an even stranger effect on him.

He didn't need that. All he needed were her typing skills, and he wouldn't need those for long. Sturdy, dependable Jamie would return soon, and the helter-skelter bimbo could find another job.

3

Cecy gulped, horrified, as two burly men hoisted her navy-and-burgundy-striped sofa on the count of three. Desperation drove her to speech. "B-but...I've had it for six months, now. It's depreciated a lot. What good will it do you?"

The men exchanged looks and wrestled the couch out the door and onto their truck. She trailed after them.

"Can't we at least talk about this?"

They turned around, one wiping sweat from his brow, the other transferring sweat from his hands to his pants. "Ain't nothin' to talk about, lady. You didn't pay your installments."

They muscled past her into the apartment again and retrieved the matching love seat.

"But I've explained to you what happened, and I have a job now!"

"Tell that to Accounts Receivables," Sweaty Brow said.

"I did. They don't understand."

"Real sorry to hear that. Get the chair next," he told Sweaty Hands.

"Wait!" Cecy shrieked. "I haven't searched it for money yet." Depositing Barney on the ground, she ran after the man and got to the chair first. She lifted the seat cushion, scrabbling under it. Sweaty Hands contemplated her as if she were some particularly odd species at Zoo Atlanta, but she found hidden treasure.

"Seven quarters," she cried. "Three dimes, two nickels, and six pennies. What luck!"

"Can I take the chair now, ma'am?"

Cecy glowered at him. "Be my guest."

He hefted it out of her living room, shaking his head.

Cecy clutched her fistful of change and turned slowly on her heel. She took a deep breath of air and dropped the change into a bowl on the windowsill. She was going to have to make the best of this.

Restraining a sniffle, she called after the two men. "Don't forget the tables." She removed her crystal lamps from her marble-topped neoclassical end tables and dragged them toward the door. She unloaded a carved music box, a dish of glass candy, two bronze statuettes, and a silk flower arrangement from the matching coffee table. Gripping it by two legs, she hauled it along the carpet, moving backwards until she bumped into Sweaty Brow.

He grunted. "Pardon, ma'am. I'll take that."

"I'm sure you will. What else are you taking?"

He shifted uncomfortably and produced a list from his hip pocket. "Two crystal lamps," he read, "one area rug with woven urn motif, and a wrought-iron mirror. Sixty-four limited edition porcelain plates from the Salubrious Sellabrations Collection."

Cecy swallowed. "Fine," she said, squaring her shoulders. "I'll get the lamps for you." They could have them. She had candles, lots of them. And as for the mirror—she didn't particularly want to see her face these days, anyhow. It was an irresponsible face, not one to be proud of. A lone tear trickled down her nose and plopped onto her lower lip.

She'd surrounded herself with things, like a child hugging stuffed animals. She'd brought home all of these objects, trying to comfort herself and stockpile security. The security that had been taken from her along with Brock.

Now Cecy stared at the walls of her apartment and saw them through new eyes. They positively vibrated with nonsensical items. Had she been systematically trying to cover up any blank white space, so she wouldn't be alone?

She plucked the lamp cords out of their sockets and unscrewed the finials that held the shades. These she stacked on top of each other, wishing she could wear one to cover her face.

Sweaty Hands came back inside and heaved the verdigris mirror off its hook. He mummified it in bubble wrap and sealed it with tape, and Cecy's thoughts grew morbid.

If she persuaded him to leave a piece of the plastic behind, she could wrap it around her head. She wondered how long it would take to suffocate, then discarded that option. No doubt her face would turn blue and she'd be very unattractive at the funeral.

She could pop her upper body into the oven and turn on the gas. Cecy wrinkled her nose. But she hadn't cleaned the damn thing in so long that it would be disgusting. Besides, her utilities had been turned off this morning.

She couldn't jump off the roof, because she had a fear of heights. What was a down-on-her-luck girl supposed to do when she needed to put paid to her existence or her bills?

She banished all thoughts of suicide upon realizing that she had no money for her own burial. There would be no one to take care of Barney, either. She couldn't abandon him. Not to mention the fact that Chas Buchanan would be furious if she stiffed him the remaining hours of work she owed him.

That decided it. She didn't want Chas to be angry with her. A man who could kiss like that deserved to be paid back, didn't he? Maybe it was a lame purpose for choosing life, but for now, it would have to suffice.

The room, stripped of its furniture, had grown larger around Cecy. It was actually rather liberating. She took a deep breath and began to take down the plethora of limited edition plates from the left wall. Why did they call them that? The only thing that limited the edition was that the manufacturers wanted to make money on a new set and encourage collectors to buy it, too. You couldn't even eat off the silly things. Why had she paid hundreds of dollars for them?

Cecy stacked them in towers of ten, waiting for one of the furniture men to bring in more bubble wrap. There was now—unbelievably— an entire wall of white space in front of her. Look at that! It was so clean, so open. Soothing, even.

Sweaty Brow stumped in for her lamps while she stood in front of the wall, hands on her hips. "Look at all them holes to putty," he grunted.

The wall did look a little like a Peg-Board. But no matter—it wouldn't be her wall for much longer. She had to vacate the premises by the day after tomorrow. She took another deep breath of air and sucked in some attitude with it. She was glad that these nice men were there to confiscate her belongings, because they were ridding her of the problem of what to do with them. Cecy produced a brilliant smile and trotted out to the open truck.

"Is there anything else I can help you with?" she inquired.

The two men swung around to face her, sporting slack jaws and raised eyebrows. Slowly, they shook their heads.

"Then at least let me offer you some bottled water. You've been working awfully hard."

"Thanks," Sweaty Hands muttered uncertainly.

Cecy stepped back into the apartment. "That woman," she heard his companion hiss, "is crazy as a bedbug."

Chas tossed and turned in his bed, but he couldn't get the image out of his head. The carefully folded McDonald's bag in Cecy's purse haunted him, no matter how he tried to avoid it. He was positive he'd heard her stomach growl during the workday. And if a woman was on a diet, she didn't eat burgers and fries. His ex-wife had existed on lettuce and bell peppers all her life; he couldn't imagine her even sitting next to ground beef.

If Cecily Scatterton's charge cards were all maxed out, her car had been repossessed, and she had no other job, it stood to reason that she probably had no cash. While his mind boggled at the thought that the woman could wear silk and yet have no money for food, Chas decided to conduct an experiment on Monday—just for peace of mind. He couldn't have Cecily dying of starvation in his office. It would be just his luck for her to pass out at the computer with her nose firmly pressed to the DELETE key. . . .

Several hours later, Chas's eyes flew open. He lay in a state of extreme frustration. It took him a moment to realize that he'd been having a very unsatisfying experience making love to his pillow. He pulled a feather off his tongue and shifted his hips, swearing. The pillow had felt small and blond and curvy in the groggy underworld of sleep. It had possessed the face of an angel, with innocent, laughing blue eyes and soft nude lips.

Chas straightened the pillow angrily. What the hell was wrong with him? He was behaving like a callow adolescent, fantasizing about the most inappropriate woman imaginable. If he decided to hook himself up with another woman, she'd be a sensible brunette with an economics degree and an allergy to malls.

Though it was only five o'clock in the morning, he swung his legs out of bed and made his way to the coffeepot. Comforted by its familiar hiss and burble, he switched on the CNN financial news and monitored stocks, pursing his lips.

The Dow had gained sixty points yesterday, which was decent. Merck was up, Dell was down, the Asian market was going to absolute hell. Chas grinned. His friend and client Tom Barry was going to kiss his feet for getting him out of there.

He eyeballed a few more listings and then shut off the television set, reaching for the paper.

As he always did, Chas twitched out the coupon sections and leafed through them with a pair of old nail scissors.

He possessed a very manly-looking leather organizer that Jamie had given him for Christmas last year, and he carefully filed each coupon by product type so that they'd be easy to access on Triple Coupon Day. Chas calculated that he saved an average of twelve dollars on his grocery bill each week by going through this routine.

His average register total at Kroger was a hundred and eight dollars, which meant that clipping coupons produced a ten percent cost reduction, well worth the trouble. Over a month, he saved forty-eight dollars, and during a year, five hundred seventy-six, which could be invested at a return of about fifteen percent.

He sighed in satisfaction. Saving money was easy, when you put your mind to it. He put the nail scissors and the coupon organizer back into his kitchen desk drawer and closed it. Then Chas began his morning push-ups.

Lowering his body to the floor, he lifted his torso smoothly, finding his rhythm after the first couple of seconds. Energy began to surge through him, pumping with his blood and sweat and effort. Up and down, up and down, up and down. He felt lactic acid begin to build in his biceps, but pushed past it until he reached the count of fifty. Next he began the first of three sets of crunches, twenty per set, with a minute's rest between each.

Red blood cells rallied, he splashed some water on his face, and went to tackle his Saturday mowing. His present house was a modest three-bedroom contemporary like many of its style in Atlanta.

As he wheeled the lawn mower out of his garage, he cast a glance over the bushes. None of them needed trimming, and they were perfectly squared off at even heights. Chas started the mower's engine with a couple of smooth tugs and moved into the grass.

He began at the edge bordering the driveway, made a sharp right turn at the street, and another at the line of his neighbor's property. He completed his mown square with the side along the house, and then repeated himself, moving ever inward in a perfect pattern. He liked the methodical approach to cutting grass, just as he liked it when it came to saving and investing.

Chas's last chore for the day was to scrub and wax the Jeep, but he decided to take a break and run it through a nearby automatic car wash. Sitting in the air-conditioning and listening to a CD while a machine did the work sounded good.

He backed out of the driveway and wove along the residential streets until he came to Abernathy Road, where the car wash stood on a busy corner. He pulled in, got in line, and dug for fifty cents to feed into the slot.

The giant brushes whirred into place around the Jeep and began to spin, slinging soapy water into the windshield. Chas lowered his eyelids, leaned back, and listened to the Indigo Girls croon about the *Shaming of the Sun*. When the rinse cycle was finished, he saw the car-wash light flicker from red to green, and pressed his foot to the gas pedal to exit.

Then he saw her. Chas stamped on the brakes so hard that the Jeep wobbled like a jack-in-the-box.

Cecily Scatterton sat cheerfully outside the car wash at a battered card table. Taped to it was a piece of neon green poster board, which proclaimed she was selling "Treasures for the Home at Astounding Prices." Countless small crystal animals littered the table, and at least ten dried and silk flower arrangements sat beside it. In a semicircle around her, Cecy had arranged picture frames, glassware, embroidered napkins, and ceramics.

She wore a scoop-necked turquoise-cotton top that clung to her curves, and her hair was caught up in a disturbingly sexy ponytail. She'd set up on the small grassy median between the car wash and a fried-chicken shack, so that she could curve her lips prettily at drivers leaving either business.

Her enticing smile flash-froze as she recognized Chas in the dripping Jeep.

He stared at her, inched the vehicle toward her, and lowered the passenger-side window.

He could feel his eyebrows crawling up into his hair.

"Cecy?"

She caught her lower lip between her teeth, and a flush rose in her cheeks. "Chas, what a nice surprise. . . ."

"What in hell are you up to?"

"I'm having a housewares sale. Can I interest you in a crystal giraffe? Perfect as a birthday or Christmas gift for female clients." Her eyes appealed to his.

A crystal giraffe? Chas could think of nothing else as useless. "Er, no."

"Perhaps the tiger or the elephant is more your style."

"Cecy—"

"It's never too early to be thinking of the holidays, you know."

He vaguely remembered seeing these things cluttering up a display cabinet in her apartment. "I don't send bric-a-brac to clients—just cards."

"Oh. Well. Your mother would love a flower arrangement, don't you think? These were done by a professional florist." Cecy had a gleam of desperation in her eyes. It made Chas distinctly uneasy.

"My mother," he said, "died ten years ago. Cecy, this is insane, and probably illegal. Do you have a permit to do this? How did you get all this stuff out here, without a car? Are you actually selling anything?" *And don't you find this a little humiliating?*

Her eyes clouded. "I'm sorry about your mother."

"It's okay—it was a long time ago." He gazed at her, waiting for an answer.

"What? No, I don't have a permit, but the owner of the car wash said it was okay. He let me put some boxes in his office while I went back for the rest."

"Why? Do you know him?"

"No." She avoided his gaze. "He said that as long as I positioned the table so he could see my legs, I could stay out here all day."

"That's awfully nice of him," Chas said darkly. He frowned and peered into the car-wash office. A man with three chins and a steel grey crew cut stared back at him. He wore a T-shirt that stated proudly, "The Best Women are like Spaghetti: Hot n'Saucy."

Chas shuddered. "Cecy, let's get you packed up and out of here."

"But it's lunchtime—it's just starting to get busy over there at Bird in a Bucket. I could get some good sales."

Chas didn't know why it bothered him so much to see her hawking her personal belongings at what amounted to a kid's lemonade stand. But it did. It upset him "something fierce," as his grandmother would have said. "Cecy, get in the Jeep."

She stood up and put her hands on her hips. "No."

He climbed out and strode over to the table,

yanking off the sign she had taped to it. He dropped it to the ground.

"What are you doing? I have to sell this stuff. I need the money!"

"Have some pride," he snapped.

"I can't afford pride right now, Buchanan. Now put that back." She tugged at the sign, but Chas had his cross-trainer planted on it, and began tossing flower arrangements willy nilly into the nearest box, ignoring her.

She swatted at him, trying not to fixate on the long, muscular brown legs revealed by his shorts, or his fabulous backside. "Chas, you're making me angry. You have no right to do this."

"I'm just gathering up my purchases. And it doesn't say much for your customer service that you're refusing to help me."

"What? You can't buy this stuff. You don't want it."

He continued to scoop things into boxes.

"I'm not selling it to you!" Cecy hollered.

"You are."

"I'm not taking your charity. Get lost."

"I'm not offering charity. I'm offering cash." Though why, he couldn't fathom.

"No!"

Chas straightened. "I'd appreciate it if you didn't holler at me."

"And I'd appreciate it if you'd listen to me."

"I'm not in the mood." Chas scooped her up, opened the back hatch of the Jeep, and dumped her unceremoniously inside, where she lay sprawled, opening and closing her mouth like a fish. He took advantage of her shock and tossed the boxes and the card table in after her, effectively cutting off her exit. Then he walked calmly to the driver's side, got in, and started the engine.

When Cecy began to shriek at him, he turned the Indigo Girls up full blast, hit the auto-lock button, and pulled out into traffic. He hadn't gotten to the first light before she was crawling over the console and tumbling into the seat next to him head first.

"Chas!" she uttered.

"Yes?"

"You—you—"

"Try the French again," he told her kindly. "I won't understand it."

"*Merde!*" she screeched. "No, I want you to understand exactly what I have to say to you."

"I'm all ears." He turned down the music volume.

"You cannot dump people into your Jeep like sacks of potatoes and kidnap them. It's illegal."

"So is selling merchandise without a permit."

"That's not the point!"

"I was only drawing a reasonable parallel."

"What you're doing is dictatorial, interfering, and charitable, and I won't have it." Cecy banged the console with her fist for emphasis.

"May I ask you a question?" Chas interjected.

"What?"

"You were out there to sell the contents of

your boxes, correct? And you've done that. So what's your problem? I'll give you cash."

"I don't want your money."

"Well, I don't want your clutter, so call it even."

"I'm so confused!" Cecy wailed.

"Me too. Let's go to lunch. My treat." Chas had noticed that her face looked pinched.

"No."

"I know a great Thai place," he coaxed.

Cecy eyed Chas balefully over spring rolls and dipping sauce. He was the most stubborn man she'd ever met. How he could toss her into the Jeep like a bag of pine bark and then take her to lunch was beyond her. Why was she permitting it?

He flashed her a charming smile and bit into one of the appetizers. "Mmmmm. You've got to try this peanut sauce. It's incredible."

Her stomach rumbled like an old tractor, and she gave in, reaching for the food. She was permitting all of this because she was starving and on edge . . . and he had such gorgeous coal black eyes. Not to mention the fact that she'd like to trace that strong, stubborn jaw of his with her fingers and feel that mouth of his on her own again.

"That's quite a roar for such a tiny tummy," he teased. "You still dieting?"

Cecy shook her head, munching. As she wrapped her lips around the spring roll once again, she looked up to find his gaze riveted to her mouth. A pulse beat rapidly in his strong throat, and he swallowed, but his gaze was steady.

She felt suddenly embarassed, as if she were performing in a lurid video. With him watching her like that, was it worse to bite through the spring roll or shove the whole thing into her mouth? To her horror, she felt sauce dribbling down her chin.

Cecy decided on option number two, and pushed the rest of the roll into her mouth.

Chas's eyes widened and glazed.

She grabbed desperately for her napkin and blotted her chin. Her breathing had quickened, and heat suffused her face. She swallowed and groped for something—anything—to say. "That was very tasty," she managed, and then realized how it sounded.

"Was it, now," Chas murmured softly.

She could have cut her tongue out.

"I like to watch you eat." He pushed a bowl of soup toward her.

"Um . . ." She fidgeted with her spoon. "That's nice."

He smiled at her and moistened his lips with his tongue.

She felt breathless, needed to get away. "Excuse me. I've got to make a phone call." Cecy all but leaped from the table, and dug into the pocket of her shorts on the way to the pay phone. She squandered one of the precious quarters she'd found in the chair on a call to Time and Temperature, nodding and smiling when she noticed Chas's gaze on her.

"Thank you very much," she said to the recording. "I appreciate your dedication to your job."

The professionally cheerful male voice repeated that it was 1:27 P.M. and ninety-two degrees.

Cecy got her breathing under control. "Yeah, got that. No problem. Bye." Smoothing her hair, she fixed what she hoped was a serene expression on her face and walked back to the table.

"Everything okay?" Chas inquired.

She nodded. Her hormones had been buzzing out of their hive again, raging and humming through her body, but she was breathing normally now.

Chas settled back in his chair and rested his hands on the table. "Cecy," he said, "you told me about your brother. But where's the rest of your family? Could they help you out? You're obviously having some problems. Why not call them?"

"There is no 'them.' "

He waited for her to elaborate.

She sighed. "Brock and I were in foster care from early on. Several places. I was five, he was six. We never knew who our father was, and Mama—well, she couldn't take care of us. She had a lot of problems of her own."

Chas's mouth twisted, and he pressed his

hands flat against the tabletop. "What happened with your brother?"

"Brock developed leukemia. Not a whole lot they could do, after a while. I took care of him to the last day." She pushed the soup away. "Brock put me through college. He said I was the smart one, and he wanted to see the Eiffel Tower one day. I was going to get us there and translate for him." Cecy stopped and traced the pattern of the tablecloth with her index finger. "We never made it to Paris, though.

"I had a couple of credit cards," she continued. "I was going to put the trip on them—I didn't care how much it cost. But he was too sick, too weak to go." She fell silent.

Chas rubbed his hands over his face.

"So that's my sob story," she said brightly, as the waiter brought their entrées. "Mmmmm, smells delicious." She attacked her chicken and vegetable dish, eating five mouthfuls before she glanced up to find Chas gazing at her somberly, not touching his food.

"Eat," she urged him. "You've got to keep up your strength if you're going to keep tossing women around like Cro-Magnon Man. Protein, red meat. Swallow it whole and beat on your chest."

He shook his head at her, though a corner of his mouth twitched. He took a bite. "So what's the price on your clutter? We'll go by an ATM on the way home."

"I told you already that I don't want to sell it

to you." Cecy considered. "But since you've been so high-handed and stubborn, I think you deserve it. I'll sell the works to you for two hundred and fifty dollars."

Chas pursed his lips and narrowed his eyes. "Nope. The inventory you've got is worth at least three times that. You paid a pretty penny for those idiotic crystal animals."

She bristled. "They're not idiotic; they're collectibles. I'll bet a thousand dollars you have some kind of collection in your own house—probably guns," she scoffed.

"Flasks," Chas admitted. "Antique. But you're in no position to bet any amount of money. And at least you can drink out of a flask. A crystal animal just gathers dust."

"Fine. Then you can pay me four hundred and fifty dollars, since you respect them so much." She smirked. Chas wasn't *that* kind.

"Seven hundred and fifty," he said, firmly.

Her smile disappeared. "What? No, absolutely not. I won't take that kind of money from you."

"Seven hundred and fifty," he repeated.

"Five hundred. You're beginning to deserve this, so I'm going to stop letting my conscience bother me."

"Good. But mine's starting to bother me. Were you planning to pay taxes on what you sold out there? You'd owe a state sales tax, not to mention state and federal income taxes, darling. My conscience might start to demand that I report you to the proper authorities, and then where would you be?"

"This is blackmail," Cecy sputtered.

"You bet. Now, will you take the seven hundred and fifty?"

"Six hundred," she threw out.

"Seven twenty-five, and that's as low as I go."

"Seven hundred?"

"Done." Chas set his glass down like a gavel.

"You're a camel merchant in disguise, Mr. Buchanan."

His smile was big and white. "I know."

Cecy dug into her food again, relishing the spicy flavors in the sauce. She was actually beginning to feel full, a sensation she hadn't had for days. Why Chas was being so nice to her, she had no idea. She supposed he felt sorry for her, which hurt her pride. But as she'd told him, she couldn't afford the luxury of pride right now.

He'd called her "darling" just a few moments ago. Darling. It sounded wonderful, especially coming from his mouth in that deep sexy voice. Too bad he'd only used the term to punctuate his sarcasm.

"Are you finished?" He interrupted her thoughts. "If you scrape that plate any harder, the pattern will come off." He seemed amused, and it annoyed her in spite of his kindness.

"Yes, thank you. Aren't you going to eat that?"

"I'm not very hungry. Do you want to take it home in a doggie bag?"

"Wouldn't you eat it later yourself?"

He shook his head. "I hate leftovers." He pushed the plate away from him with emphasis.

Why didn't she believe him? Still, when the waiter returned with Chas's entree in a white Styrofoam box, she took it. Since she was going to be seven hundred dollars richer, though, she didn't bother with the sweetener and sugar packets on the table.

4

Cecy's fingers clicked away on Chas Buchanan's keyboard, while her mind clicked away on a solution to her upcoming homelessness.

She could go to a shelter. She could rig a tent in the woods somewhere. Or—her eyes fell on the green leather couch in Chas's reception area—she could begin working late. Very late. All night.

The more she turned the idea over in her mind, the more she liked it. It was a comfy sofa, with all its springs intact. Around the corner was a clean corporate bathroom to sponge off in, with a sink deep enough that she could wash her hair in it. And a desk complete with credenza to store a few personal belongings.

A few boxes could go into the basement of the office building, marked with Chas's name and suite number. Most likely, no one would bother them.

A set of keys gleamed at Cecy every time she opened the drawer to Jamie's desk. Not a doubt existed in her mind that one of them fit the office door. She'd try them when Chas went to lunch today.

She began to type faster as she thought about it. She could pull this off. There was only one obstacle to her plan, and he was four-legged with whiskers. What on earth was she going to do with Barney? Hmmmmm.

He usually slept all day. Cecy ran her eyes over the credenza next to the desk. It had a couple of holes in the back for electrical cords. No— that would be cruel. Barney would go nuts in there.

Could she keep him outside? No, he might wander off when he didn't see or smell her. Or worse yet, get run over in the parking lot.

There was only one thing to do. Barney was going to have to pretend illness, and need supervision until she came up with a better plan. Surely Chas couldn't refuse to let him stay in the office if he was injured?

That evening, she purchased some gauze, medical tape, and poster board from Eckerd with some of the cash Chas had given her. Out of the poster board, she cut a large circle, then poked a hole in the middle and cut another inside it. Cecy grimaced. Barney wasn't going to like the straits they were in any better than she did. It couldn't be helped, though.

Putting her purchases aside, she packed the remainder of her worldly possessions into some cardboard boxes she'd culled from the corner grocery, and called Jimmy, the maintenance man for her apartment complex.

"Jimmy? It's Cecy Scatterton in number eight-fourteen. How are you? No, my garbage disposal works fine. Yeah, I'm still dating that professional wrestler. The jealous one. Listen, Jimmy—I was wondering if you'd do me a big favor. I've got some boxes I need delivered to an office building tomorrow afternoon . . ."

"You seem to be under the impression that I'll allow you to put that cat in my car," said Chas, when he picked her up for work the next morning. "I have two words for you: leather seats."

"He's very ill," Cecy pleaded.

"He doesn't look ill. He looks spitting mad. What's that space-age thing around his neck?"

"It's a ruff," she explained. "It's to stop him from gnawing off his bandage." She showed him Barney's left back leg, which was wrapped in gauze and medical tape.

"Get in." Chas sighed. He couldn't resist those melting blue eyes, not when she looked at him like he was the only one who could save the planet from certain disaster. "What happened to him?"

"He got caught in the door."

"The cats I've known have had faster reflexes than that."

"He's getting older," Cecy said defensively.

Chas pulled onto the highway. "Where's the vet's office? I assume it's on the way."

"Well, you see, he's already been to the vet. And here's the situation—he needs to be under constant supervision. So I thought—"

"Oh, no you didn't!"

"Well, yes, I did. . . ."

Chas beat his head against the steering wheel. "You're not bringing an ugly, three-legged, broken-tailed hairball into my office."

"He's not ugly! He's adorable."

"He's probably hopping with fleas."

"Not a one."

"Did it ever occur to you that I might be allergic to cats?"

"Are you?"

"No. But one of my clients might be. Animals don't belong in the workplace, Cecy. For God's sake!"

"I'll keep him out of your way, I promise. You'll never even know he's around."

"I should make you open the door right now and drop him onto the highway."

"How can you even say such a thing?" Cecy stroked Barney's fur as he began to howl. "It's okay, baby. Shhhhhhh. I won't let the evil man hurt you."

Chas rolled his eyes in disgust, and Barney howled again.

"He doesn't like cars," Cecy announced.

"I'm devastated to hear that." Chas glanced in the rearview mirror and pulled ahead of a minivan loaded to the rafters with kids. They spied the kitty and began waving and pointing.

The benign mom driving them switched lanes and sped up next to the Jeep so that the children could see better. Cecy waved back at them with Barney's paw until he decided he'd had enough torment for one morning. He leaped up and over her shoulder, gripping fast to the leather headrest with his claws.

"Eeeeeoooowwww!" he complained, and flew into the backseat, using Chas's expensive briefcase as a landing pad.

Chas began to swear, choicely and at great volume.

"Hush," Cecy exclaimed. "Lots of children can read lips. Come here, Barney. Come here, boy." Unfastening her seat belt, she turned and bent over the console, trying to reach her wayward cat.

Chas was treated to a delicious expanse of bare calf and thigh as her skirt rode up, and he gulped as he glimpsed the outline of her panties under the flimsy fabric. He bit his tongue, hard, and wished for the first time in years that he had a gearshift to handle. He wouldn't mind accidentally brushing against that silky skin of hers.

The thought created a tent in his khaki trousers, and he grabbed for something to cover it before Cecy turned around. The only thing within reach was a Blues Traveler CD, which he propped against himself. He tried admirably to focus on the road in front of him, and resolved to get a copy of *101 Uses For a Dead Cat* before the day was out.

Eventually Cecy got her pernicious animal settled down and returned to a normal position. Chas breathed a sigh of relief and relaxed his murderous grip on the wheel. He switched lanes and slowed down a bit. Then came the words he least wanted to hear.

"I just love Blues Traveler!" Cecy exclaimed. She grabbed impulsively for the CD, and gasped. "Oh, *my*."

Chas winced, and set his jaw. He was speechless with humiliation. A pause ensued.

"I'm sorry." They said it simultaneously, in strangled tones.

Silence fell on them like a piano from five stories high.

"Traffic's just terrible this morning," Cecy squeaked an eon later, as he pulled into the parking lot of his building.

"Sure is."

"Clouds are rolling in over there," she continued, bravely. "Looks like more rain."

"Cecy." Chas could hear the edge in his own

voice. "Get that animal out of my Jeep." He flung open his door, slammed it, and strode inside without a backward glance.

Cecy stared at Barney helplessly. "Oops. I don't think he's too happy with us right now, kid."

Barney writhed and twisted, tumbling over himself to get out of his ruff. Finally, he gave up and just howled.

"I know. I feel a little like that myself. Come on, let's go inside." She hitched the cat up over her shoulder and locked the doors, approaching the entrance to Chas's suite with trepidation.

When she stepped in, she saw that he had closed his office door, treating her to a forbidding expanse of wood instead of his face. She deposited Barney on the floor next to her desk and slumped into her chair with her head in her hands. What did she expect? The man wasn't going to bring her coffee and donuts after she'd grabbed his most private part.

Shame washed over her, and a mad giggle began to spiral inside her. It burbled out of her throat and rose in pitch, metamorphosing into hysterical gasps. Cecy braced herself at the desk and laughed until tears ran down her face.

That's when the door opened. "I'm glad you find the whole situation amusing," Chas snapped.

She sobered immediately and mopped at her eyes. "It's not what you think," she began.

"For your information, I am not some kind of

pervert," Chas ground out. "But when a woman bends over my console and practically slithers out of her clothes, I can't help having a normal male reaction, damn it all!"

"I did not slither," Cecy stated, with dignity. "And I want you to know that I'm not embarassed about it. In fact, I'd be embarassed if I hadn't reacted."

"I'm sorry that I grabbed your—"

"It's completely natural," Chas broke in, his face reddening. "It doesn't mean anything at all, so don't think I'm going to jump your bones when you come to work."

"Oh, no—"

"Or that I'll behave unprofessionally toward you in any way. That one kiss—I was just worried about you when your nails caught on fire. You know that, don't you?"

Cecy found her gaze riveted to his lips. "Yes," she forced herself to say. "I know."

"Good. Well, that's settled then." He turned on his heel, then stopped, his back to her. "Just for future reference," he added, "it doesn't make a man feel too great when you laugh hysterically after touching his—er, him. It could make a guy feel inadequate."

"It was more than adequate," she said softly. "Quite impressive."

Chas's shoulders straightened and flexed. Then he retreated once again behind the door.

"I knew that," he muttered to himself. "I've been in plenty of locker rooms." What was it about Cecily Scatterton that put him in any doubt? The damned woman had him twisted every which way, like a pretzel.

He was a man who prided himself on saving over six hundred dollars a year, methodically, by clipping coupons. Yet he had given Cecy more than that for several boxes of junk he didn't want. And he'd done it in the blink of an eye. What was wrong with him? He never behaved on impulse. He was a planner. The bottom line was: Cecy Scatterton had a bad effect on him, and he needed to get her out of his office as soon as possible. There were only a few hours left of what she owed him, thank God. He would pay her to stay for the remaining few days until Jamie returned, and then kiss her good-bye— figuratively speaking, of course.

Chas shook his head to clear the cobwebs and reached down for his briefcase. Swinging it up to the desk, he began to unlock it and froze. A medley of punctures and angry scratches marred the smooth golden calfskin. He inhaled with such violence that his nostrils sucked closed. His right eyelid twitched several times. Chas made himself count to three before he exhaled again and sat down.

"I, Chas," he stated, "am not a serial killer. I do not butcher small animals for fun." He looked at his briefcase again, and remembered what he had paid for it. "I, Chas," he insisted, "am not a serial killer. I do not butcher small animals for fun." Barney's yowl reached his ears from the other side of the door, and he blocked out the image of what his leather seats must look like. "I, Chas, am not a serial killer," he growled. "I do not butcher small animals—or blondes—for fun. . . ."

5

"I won't be needing a ride home this evening," Cecy told Chas at the end of the workday. "But thank you." Jamie's keys weighed heavy in her skirt pocket.

"Have you taken up jogging in traffic? Or do you have big plans?" To her relief, Chas had calmed down enough to tease her again.

"I have a date," Cecy lied. "He's picking me up in the lobby. We'll swing by my apartment first and drop off Barney." She looked at Chas curiously. He was suddenly very still. His right eyelid twitched.

"An early dinner, isn't it?" Chas jingled his car keys. "But then, I guess that's perfect for a weeknight, when you want to turn in by nine. I'll bet you need a lot of sleep."

Cecy raised her brows. "No more than the average person. You're in bed by nine? That's pretty geriatric of you."

He flushed. "No, no. I'm usually up until at least midnight. I just think it's dangerous for a woman to be out past nine or ten. It's a scary world out there."

"Ah. Good thing I won't be alone."

"Yes, of course. Right. Well. Have fun on your hot date." Chas ran his fingers through his hair, ushered her out of the office, Barney in her arms, and locked the door behind them. He gazed at the cat with dislike but stalled in the corridor. "Would you like me to wait with you?"

"Oh, no," she said. "Don't bother. I'm sure he's on his way."

Chas shrugged and walked woodenly to the exit. "Fine. Good night, Cecy. Don't stay out too late—we have lots to do tomorrow."

The doors swung shut behind him, and Cecy admired the view as he stalked away. What had put him in such a mood? He couldn't possibly care if she had a date. But he looked a bit steamed as he made his way to the Jeep. Why was he opening the back door? He glanced down at the seat, and she winced. Barney's claws this morning hadn't been kind.

Chas pounded on the roof rack with his fist.

He stood shaking his head with his hands on his hips. At last he got in and drove away.

"Barney, buddy," Cecy murmured against her cat's fur, "I'm sorry I bandaged you up, but it was the only way. By the time we find a real place to live again, you'll be the only feline up for an Emmy award." She retrieved Jamie's keys from her pocket and opened the office door once again, kicking it closed behind her. She set Barney on the floor, crouched down next to him, and relieved him of the poster-board ruff. He set to work on the faux bandage himself, tearing at it with his teeth and eyeing her with resentment.

"D'you want help?" She reached toward him and was rewarded with a nip. "I guess not. It should come off easily, since I was careful not to get any of the tape on your fur."

The cat lashed his tail and pulled on the gauze until the tube slid off. Then he dropped one front paw on it and shredded it in vengeance.

"Feel better?" Cecy picked up the keys again. "I'll be right back. I'm going to get some of our things."

Cecy went out the north door—Chas always used the south—and saw with satisfaction that Jimmy had delivered her boxes, as promised. She had written in large black marker on them: BUCHANAN. TAX FORMS. DO NOT REMOVE. She searched for the one which she had marked with a star and heaved it into her arms, then trudged back to the office.

Once there, she caught her breath, slit the box open, and removed a pair of shorts and a T-shirt, along with Barney's double bowl and a can of Fe-Lion Feast. He forgot his irritation without a blink and began gobbling. Cecy stroked him fondly and then changed, ready to haul the remaining boxes to the basement.

An hour later she stood nude in the corporate bathroom, sponging down with a cool washcloth. She spritzed herself with eau de cologne, wrapped a towel around her body, and stuck wads of toilet paper between her toes. Then she hoisted herself up onto the long marble countertop, propped her foot on the faucet, and began to paint her toenails in a rich shade of plum.

Barney joined her on the other side of the counter, washing his face with his paw. That inspired her to do a basic facial afterward. Cecy hummed as she walked to the kitchenette and poured a pot of clean water into the coffeemaker, *sans* coffee. She switched it on and opened the minifridge, rustling around for the leftover sub Chas had given her. He'd claimed that he usually ate two for lunch, but wasn't very hungry today. While she found that a bit suspicious, she hadn't wanted to look a gift horse in the mouth.

Cecy unwrapped the sub and sniffed at it. Italian. Smelled pretty good. She lifted the top of the sandwich, plucked off the onions, and dropped them into the garbage. She drizzled some Taste of Tuscany viniagrette dressing over it, dropped the bread back on, and took a large bite.

As she munched, she looked around at Chas's boring office furnishings. The green leather couch was the only spot of color, other than a waxy-leafed plant in the corner.

She thought about it as she took the glass coffeepot into the bathroom, wrapped her hair in a towel-turban, and held her face over the steaming water. She'd taken a couple of basic design classes in college. Maybe she could liven up the place a little, as a surprise to Chas. Cecy chewed on her lip. Maybe he didn't like surprises, though. Maybe she should feel him up—er, out—a little before she did anything.

The steam warmed her face and opened her pores. She let it roll over her skin, which tingled with the heat. It felt wonderful. Once the water began to cool, she blotted her face with a towel and spritzed it with toner. She combed out her hair and donned a silk nightshirt. Grabbing a blanket, pillow, and her Walkman out of the packing box, she settled down on the leather couch and closed her eyes to relax to some soothing music.

Oops. She'd forgotten the travel alarm. Well, she'd get it in a moment. . . .

Chas frowned as the phone rang and rang. A recording came on the line and stated nasally

that the number he'd dialed was no longer in
service.

He hung up and dialed again—same message. It was Cecy's number, and he was dialing
it from his cell phone outside her apartment at
seven-thirty the next morning. She hadn't responded to his knocking.

Chas clicked the END button with an oath and
floored the accelerator, roaring out of the parking lot. She'd obviously spent the night with her
hot date. The woman had the morals of an alley
cat. And why should he care?

He cut viciously into traffic, blocking an old
lady from turning into the corner florist's. She
shook her finger at him, but he simply sped by
her. Damn and blast. Cecy hadn't even had the
decency to call him and let him know that he
didn't need to pick her up for work. He was
going to have to watch her saunter in, blowsy
and satiated, reeking of another man's aftershave.

Chas gritted his teeth and darted rudely in
front of a bakery truck. The driver shouted and
shot him an appropriate gesture, which he returned with gusto. He began tailgating a brand-
new, red convertible Corvette.

He saw red all right. Cecy appeared to him,
sporting a scarlet harlot's ensemble, moaning in
the arms of some faceless muscle man. In his
mind, the faceless guy then disappeared without so much as a "pouf." Cecy smiled wickedly

and crooked her finger at Chas, then began unfastening one of her garter straps.

Chas began to take fast gulps of air. "Cecy," he hissed at the slinky, lace-clad image in his head, "you just hook that garter strap right back up again. Don't you dare undo the other one! Stop it right now."

She pouted, smirked, and—moistening her lips—stuck her tongue out at him. Then she lifted her hair, twisting it into a knot on top of her head, and let it cascade down again.

Chas groaned, and wiped his brow. "You're not listening, you bad girl. Do you want a spanking?"

The apparition of Cecy nodded slyly. She shrugged her shoulders out of the straps of her crimson bra, and her fingers sought the front clasp.

Chas's pupils dilated, and his breath came in harsh rasps.

Cecy flicked the two shreds of lace apart, baring her breasts. She was magnif—

A horrible, grinding crash jolted Chas out of his daydream. Glass splintered and tinkled to the tarmac. Metal crumpled. His neck snapped forward, then back, feeling as though it had pulled free of his head. A man's voice screamed, "No, no, no, no, no! You stupid son of a bitch! No, no, no, no, no! You blundering bastard! You marauding asshole . . ."

It took Chas a moment to realize that the

words were meant for him, and that his Jeep had crumpled the man's brand-new sports car like a used tissue. The hood of his own vehicle was folded at an unlikely angle.

"God," he prayed, "please help me. The Devil has obviously sent Cecy Scatterton to ruin my life. There is something about Cecy that makes me crazy. Something about her makes me not myself. God, please restore peace, calm, and order to my life and make that woman disappear. Please—"

His prayers were rudely interrupted when his door flew open, and he found himself staring into the furious face and glazed eyes of the Corvette's owner.

"Aaaarrrrrgh!" the man roared.

"Yes, thank you, I'm fine," Chas replied, struggling to pull himself together. "Maybe a minor case of whiplash. And you?"

The man refused to be shamed. "I just drove that car off the lot three days ago, you imbecile! You jerk! What do you have to say for yourself?"

Chas passed a hand over his jaw.

"Well?" the man raved. "What do you have to say?"

"Er, my insurance company will buy you a new one."

"Damned right they will!"

"And they'll nonrenew me in a heartbeat."

"Damned right they will."

Chas sighed and pulled out his wallet. "Here's my license and insurance card."

"What the hell were you thinking, anyway?"

Chas screwed up his face. "You don't want to know."

Cecy opened one eye, focused it on the digital clock across the room, and leaped up screeching from the leather office couch. "Eight-fifteen! Dear heavens . . ." She tore the bedclothes off of it and stuffed them underneath. Chas would walk in any minute. In fact, he should be here. He normally got in before eight.

She belatedly remembered that she hadn't called and told him not to pick her up this morning. Oops. He wouldn't be happy when he got here.

Yanking a dress, undies, bra, and slip from the cardboard box, she pushed the box under her desk, then ran into the bathroom to jump into her clothes. She piled her hair onto her head with a clip—no time to wash it—and scrubbed her face and teeth with laser speed. Chas was never late. Where was he? Was he all right?

She applied lipstick, blusher, and powder, then swept everything into her towel. This she tossed into the credenza. Where was Barney? She had to make him look injured again, poor thing.

Cecy plucked him from a comfy sprawl on the windowsill and attached the ruff to his neck again, to his great and vocal disgust. Then she laid him in her lap and started in with the tape and gauze.

Barney wriggled, squirmed, howled, and hissed, but she finally achieved something like a bandage.

She was picking the cat hairs off her dress when she heard footsteps approaching the door. Oh, no! She couldn't be inside when Chas came in, since he didn't know she had Jamie's keys. Crouching, she crept underneath her desk next to the box.

The office door swung open abruptly and hit the wall with a crash. Baritone curses, some particularly vile, kept time with the angry steps. Barney dived behind a plant, and Cecy's brows rose. Chas was normally so calm and controlled. She ducked down further and peeked past the box. Sure enough, those were his highly polished calfskin loafers pacing the floor. The knife-sharp crease in the trousers had to be his, too.

She bit her lip as the loafers marched, Gestapo-style, to the edge of the carpet and then slid into a military turnabout to march back the other way. Another military reverse, and back they went. At last they stopped, only to walk to the plaster wall and kick it, hard.

Cecy's eyes widened. Chas sure was in a tear about something. The Human Abacus was officially pissed off. She wondered why, and who the unlucky recipient of all this pent-up frustration might be.

At the same time, her legs were starting to cramp, and her back and neck ached from holding her pretzel-like position. She decided to try telepathy.

Calm down, Chas. She mouthed the message, sending it silently to him. *It's okay.* She tried to waft soothing vibes his way.

Cecy was amazed that it seemed to work. Chas took a deep, steadying breath and let it out slowly. And another. Craning her head, she watched him walk slowly into his office and sit down. He rubbed his eyes and folded his head on his arms.

It's now or never. She had to make a break for it. Backing out from under the desk, she crawled silently for the door on her hands and knees. One one thousand, two one thousand, three one thousand, four. She scudded along bravely, and was almost to the door . . .

"Cecy!"

"Aaack!" Her heart bounced against her tonsils and then fell into her stomach.

"Cecy, what in the name of God are you doing?"

"I—uh—looking for my contact lens. It fell out as soon as I walked in."

"You're late."

"I know, so sorry—"

"You didn't bother to call and tell me that your lover gave you a ride."

"My *what*?"

"Lover." Chas spat the word out like sticky, black tobacco juice. "You know—the guy who makes your toes curl at night." His eyes roved across her body, angry and hungry.

Cecy froze, and then remembered she was in classic doggie position. She stood up, brushing carpet lint from her dress and legs.

Chas thought she was sleeping with an imaginary man. It was on the tip of her tongue to deny it, but she'd only have to make up another lie to cover how she'd gotten to the office this morning. Oh, Lord. How did she get herself into messes like these?

"I guess I forgot to call you. I do apologize."

"You were preoccupied," Chas said silkily. His tone of voice suggested that she was a few leagues lower than cockroach dung.

Anger bubbled in her. If she *had* spent the night with a fabulous toe-curling lover, it was her right. How dare Chas Buchanan speak to her like this? She put her hands on her hips and deliberately yawned. "Preoccupied . . . I suppose. I was certainly occupied until the small hours of the morning." She flashed him a wicked smile.

Chas stared at her stonily, but she saw the muscle working in his jaw. And there was that telltale twitch of his right eyelid.

Ha, she thought with satisfaction. *Gotcha*. She felt her bra strap slipping, and an evil imp within urged her to turn the thumbscrews. With a quick shake of her shoulders, she walked forward and leaned her hands on his desk. She fluttered her eyelashes this time as she faked another yawn.

Chas choked audibly as her red bra strap slipped down her arm from under her sleeveless summer dress.

Cecy smiled sweetly at him. "What can I do for you this morning, Chas?"

"Nothing," he growled. "Go away."

She widened her eyes. "You mean I can go home—back to bed?"

He stood and his hand shot out, caught the back of her neck, and brought her face within range of his. "Listen to me," he said, in a menacing tone of voice. "Today is not the day to tease me. You make any more sexual overtures toward me, and you're likely to be taken up on them. I don't care how big lover-boy is or what he benches. Do you understand?"

"Yes," Cecy breathed. "Oh, yes." Her hormones erupted from their hive in a mighty swarm. She crawled over the desk and almost onto Chas Buchanan's lap, sealing her lips to his.

Chas groaned and took her mouth, his tongue making hot advances inside, exploring and tasting her. One big hand cupped her face, the other her bottom. He dragged her to him, papers on the desk be damned.

Warm honey rushed through the core of her as she spread her thighs over his lap and kissed him back with fervor. God, she had never felt like this, never experienced such a perfect blending of energy. It didn't seem wanton to sit in his lap—Cecy felt she had been made to sit there.

Chas ran his fingers through her hair and devoured her mouth, his teeth nipping her lower lip, his tongue now plundering. He ran kisses down her jaw and to her throat, his hands moving possesively down her shoulders and at sweet last to cup her breasts. She moaned, and pressed against him.

His hands disappeared for a moment. The rasp of her zipper broke the silence, and her dress bagged about her. Chas pulled it down her arms and pushed it to her waist, his breathing labored. He stared for a long moment at her red-lace-covered bosom, and then unsnapped the front clasp in sudden frenzy.

"Ah," he breathed, at the sight of her bare breasts. "Oh, God." He buried his face between them, took them in his warm palms, and gently squeezed.

Cecy nearly collapsed when he pushed her breasts together and took the rosy tips into his mouth, laving them with his tongue, sucking and pulling, teasing and torturing. Tension swelled and built inside her, electric shocks zinging through her entire body. Chas's titanium erection rubbed her in just the right place, and suddenly she was rocketing, eyes closed, to another place altogether, and calling his name.

When she came to, he was staring at her through half-closed eyes, breathing like a freight train, his tongue caught between his teeth. She was still straddling his monster erection, and her eyes rounded. "I—I'm so sorry. That's never happened to me before."

A strange fleeting expression crossed his face. "I can't say that I've ever given a woman that much pleasure with so many of her clothes on." Then his face darkened. "And especially not when she's just spent the night with another man." He lifted her off of him and set her on her feet. "Get dressed, Cecy."

She stood, horrified, and pulled her dress up to cover herself. Chas thought she was an insatiable slut. "I didn't do anything last night—I didn't even have a date."

His gaze raked her face. "Save it," he said shortly. "Don't start with the lies now." He swiveled in his chair and removed a binder from the credenza, burying his face in it. He kept his back to her.

Flames of embarrassment singed her face and neck, and she wanted to die. She'd just lost total control of herself in front of the man, and he'd never even dropped his immaculately pressed khaki trousers. Now he was dismissing her, like a carhop who'd gotten his order wrong. She had disgusted him, turned him off, and now he thought she was lying to him. This was so bad she couldn't think of a word to say. Clutching her dress to her, she ran toward the bathroom.

Chas clenched his teeth and waited once again for his erection to subside. This was getting ridiculous. Men should have a deflation valve for situations like this. His balls had to be a nice shade of violet, but he was damned if he'd take another man's leftovers. Just the thought of Cecy with her lover last night made him physically ill. Unfortunately, it didn't make a dent in his desire for her.

He concentrated on what his insurance company would say when they heard about his stellar driving this morning, and the discomfort in his trousers subsided immediately.

Jamie was due back Friday, thank God. Sturdy, dependable Jamie, who never did anything flighty or unexpected.

6

"I'm getting married!" Jamie's voice repeated the words over the fuzzy connection. "We're going to live here, in Aruba!"

"Say what?" Chas heard his voice crack.

"I'm going to stay savagely tan all year round and teach scuba lessons . . . are you there?"

"Yeah." He clenched his jaw. "I'm here."

"Aren't you going to say 'Congratulations'?"

"Congratulations. So . . . you're not coming back at all?"

"No. Sorry to spring it on you like this. We just decided last night, on impulse."

Chas frowned. He disapproved of impulsive decisions. The only one he'd ever made was bringing Cecy into his office, and look where that had gotten him. "Well, Jamie—I wish you every happiness. I'll miss you. Keep in touch."

He hung up the phone and stared at it. This was rotten timing. Within the next month he had to meet with each of his clients to give them a yearly update, which required extensive preparation. He had to generate reports and graphs for each of them, showing their financial progress. He'd been counting on Jamie's skilled and efficient help. What now?

He'd have to train Cecy, starting today. He had no choice. Chas got up and stalked into the reception area, looking around for her. Where had she gone?

He saw no sign of her. He pulled a couple of tufts of cat hair off of the windowsill with disgust, and dropped them in the wastebasket. Come to think of it, he didn't see that ridiculous beast anywhere, either. The room was far too silent.

Chas pulled open the drawer where Cecy normally kept her purse. It was gone. He glanced at his watch. Ten-thirty was far too early for lunch. Had she been so mortified that she'd left?

He turned back toward his office and saw the note on the door.

"*Chas,*" he read with consternation, "*the thirty-five hours I owed you are up. I've actually worked forty-one, but you can consider the extra six an interest payment. Thanks for paying my bill when*

I needed help. Sorry about your leather seats—I hope the enclosed will cover repairs. Sincerely yours, Cecy Scatterton."

She'd left a hundred-dollar bill, part of the money he'd given her for the "clutter," in the envelope.

Chas crumpled the note, threw it toward the wastebasket, and cursed. He wasn't about to take money from a bankrupt woman, no matter what her cat had done to his car. And he needed her back in the office, now. Where was she? Cecy had nowhere to go but home.

He muttered invective all the way outside, and winced when he saw the Jeep. It shuddered and banged when he started it, creaking out of the parking lot at a snail's pace. Chas pinched his nose between his thumb and forefinger as another tenant of the building stopped walking to stare and shake his head. Chas pretended not to see him.

He drove carefully in the late-morning traffic, though he needn't have bothered—other drivers, after taking one look at his vehicle, gave him a wide berth. When he reached Cecy's apartment, he knocked politely but firmly on the door. No one answered.

He knocked again.

Silence.

"Cecy," he called. "I know you're in there." He stood with his hands in his pockets and waited for her to give up and open the door.

She didn't.

"Cecy!" He yelled. "Open this door. We need to talk."

He could only assume, after a couple of minutes, that either she wasn't here or she didn't agree. Chas was turning away when he spied an angular man hoofing a ladder across the parking lot. He pawed at a mop of shaggy hair that blew every which way in the breeze, and painter's tape clung to the right leg of his baggy pants.

"You lookin' fer Cecy?" He had a reedy voice.

"I am," Chas replied.

"She don't live here no more."

Chas stared at him. "What do you mean?"

"Moved out t'other day."

"Where did she go?"

"I ain't at liberty to say. An' anyways, I don't know," he added hastily, as Chas took a step toward him, fists curled loosely. "I hear she couldn't pay the rent, so out the door she went."

"Are you saying she's homeless?" Chas swallowed.

"All's I know is some guys come and took back her furniture one day, an' the next she was outta here."

"Good God. You're sure you don't know where she is?"

The man shrugged. "She's prob'ly shacked up with that wrestler boyfriend o' hers."

Wrestler? Chas fought off a mental picture of Cecy snuggled up with a Hulk Hogan type in a sequined muscle shirt. Did the guy hold her down for the count every night before bed?

"I see," he managed. "Thank you for your time."

"No problem, man." The lanky man walked off, trailing his painter's tape.

No problem? This was a *huge* problem. Cecy was in trouble, living with some sleazebag, and he, Chas, had money which belonged to her. He needed her assistance, and—hell—he was worried about her. He might as well admit it. How was he going to track her down?

Chas returned to the office, anxiety gnawing at him. What was she going to do? The thought hit him that he was responsible. He'd prayed for the powers-that-be to remove her from his life— it was his fault that she was living with Hulk Hogan or wandering around homeless with her wounded cat. How could he live with himself?

He fiddled about on his computer and reviewed a couple of portfolios with half an eye, the other focused on his watch. The second hand went round and round, dragging the minutes along in its wake. Would this cursed day never end?

He ordered two sandwiches for lunch delivery without thinking about it, and only realized when he paid for them that Cecy wasn't there to protest graciously, and then devour one of them when she thought he wouldn't notice.

Chas called her apartment complex and asked questions. When he replaced the handset of the phone, he rubbed his eyes. The manager at Happy Hollow Apartments had no knowlege of whom Cecily Scatterton might be dating or what his name might be. She had left no forwarding address. And even if the manager had possessed such information, she would not able to disclose it. So sorry.

Chas told himself to give up and call a temp service, but his conscience urged him to keep looking for Cecy. She needed the job, and she was already familiar with some of the basics of his files after working in his office for the week.

He wandered over to Jamie's old desk and scanned it for any helpful information. Nothing on the surface. He opened the top drawer. Inside were the usual pens, pencils, stamps, and paper clips. A few random slips of paper with names and numbers scrawled on them. "Haircut, 6:00 p.m., with Pam," he read on one. A telephone number followed. Chas leaped on the clue, shoving the paper into his pocket. He also found a card with the name and address of a beauty salon. The telephone numbers were identical. Bingo! He had a lead, and if he had to follow it beyond hell and into Daisy Darling's Day Spa then so be it.

The walls closed in upon him, and the silence shrieked until he couldn't stand it anymore. Chas shut off the computer, grabbed his keys, and locked up the office two hours early. He headed toward the Day Spa.

* * *

Cecy yawned and crossed her ankles on the makeshift chaise. She'd constructed it with a pillow, a quilt, and the cardboard boxes that held the rest of her belongings. It was dark down here in the storage room, but she had to wait it out until Chas was gone. She didn't know the building's security code, as Jamie undoubtedly did.

She'd done a good day's work before coming back here. She'd filed with three different temp agencies, using her old professors as references and giving Chas's office number as an after-five residence phone.

Cecy peered at her watch. Another fifteen minutes, and it should be safe to go up to the office suite. She doubted he'd work past five-thirty.

She felt like a mole, lurking in this dark underground storage room. A single sixty-watt bulb illuminated the space and cast shadows on old furniture and odds and ends. Extra desks, chairs, and printer stands stood against one wall. Two long, low windows showcased the businesslike feet and ankles of those who entered and exited the building. A few daring weeds poked out of the cracks of the walkway, risking annihilation by the landscaping service but craving sun.

Cecy sympathized with them. She'd been stuck in the basement for an hour now. If she was forced to stay for another hour, she'd bypass mole status and begin to slither.

Barney, blessedly free of his ruff and bandage, was digging furiously at something in the far corner. Cecy tucked her feet close beneath her and hugged herself. She hoped fervently that he hadn't found a mouse—or anything else with more legs than she had. The unsettling thought encouraged her to glance at her watch again. Five-twenty-eight. Chas had to be gone by now. She peered carefully around her for critters and, seeing none, jumped off the box. She'd come back for Barney when the coast was clear.

Cecy took the stairs to the second floor, opened the heavy metal fire door, and took a peek. No one about. She eased the door closed behind her and strolled casually to Chas's suite. The lights were off—excellent.

She used Jamie's keys to unlock the door. Shutting it behind her and flipping on the light switch, she leaned against it and surveyed her new home. The air smelled faintly of after-shave—Chas's aftershave. It was a spicy, musky scent that conjured visions of Glenlivet—drunk neat, and big comfy wing chairs in front of a fire.

Cecy's lips curved. His aftershave smelled just a tiny bit stuffy, like Chas himself. Damn, but she'd love to strip those knife-creased khakis off of him and toss them up on the ceiling fan. She blinked. That was very unlikely to happen, given the mortifying scene between them this morning. She'd probably never see him again.

She sighed and walked to his desk, rolling out his chair. She plopped into it and imagined him sitting there, rubbing at his chin reflectively. She placed her hands on the keyboard of his computer, where his own had been that day, and pressed down on the buttons restlessly. A flash of green caught her eye. She turned her head to see the hundred-dollar bill she'd left him in payment for the damaged seats. The brand-new bill had been crumpled savagely into a ball, indicating that he hadn't taken her departure well. Great, so now he was not only disgusted with her, but angry.

Chas kept his credenza across from the desk against the far wall. Hanging next to his framed college and graduate school degrees was a large antique mahogany abacus with heavy brass disks. How characteristic of him. Cecy gazed at the abacus, wondering about its history. It could have been a merchandising prop in a Ralph Lauren display.

No other pictures or ornaments hung on the simple white walls. She had the urge again to liven up the place, paint a mural across one wall, even if it were something as heinous as a fox-hunting scene or a polo match.

A silver-framed picture on a small table caught her eye, and she moved toward it to pick it up. An older couple smiled out at her with a warmth and directness not often captured on camera. The man squeezed the woman's shoulders with obvious affection, and she brushed his cheek with the backs of her gently curved fingers. Her hair was pulled back loosely, but one strand of white hair had escaped and hung, girlish, in front of her ear. Deep laugh lines radiated in half sunbursts around her blue eyes and were echoed on either side of her mouth. Cecy thought she'd probably been a lot of fun.

She turned the photograph over curiously and opened the back of the frame. It was none of her business, but she wanted to know who these people were, what role they played in Chas Buchanan's life. On the back of the photo he'd scrawled, "Grandmother and Grandfather Chastain, 1982."

Not Gram and Gramps. Not Nana and Papa. Grandmother and Grandfather. Terribly formal. She closed the frame and turned it over to scrutinize the photo again. The couple stood in front of a large graceful Southern house. A mansion— there was no other word for it.

A second perusal of the couple told her more about them. Grandfather's suit and white shirt were immaculate. The camera disclosed no upstart wrinkles, and the Windsor knot in his tie was impeccable. Any breeze on that day hadn't dared displace a hair of Grandfather Chastain's head.

Grandmother, on the other hand, was subtly mussed. The telltale lock of hair hung over an open collar, revealing a necklace with the clasp turned toward the front. The hand that curled against her husband's cheek wore a lovely ring, but slightly chipped nail polish. Cecy liked her all the better for it.

She replaced the photograph and looked down at her own hands, which still sported acrylic nails, though she'd cut down the burnt ones. She plopped down on the green leather couch and began to chip away at them. Why did Chas have a picture of his grandparents in his office, but no other family members? He'd mentioned that he'd lost his mother ten years ago. What had happened to her? Where was his father? Did he have any brothers or sisters? Had he ever been married?

There was a reserve about Chas that dissuaded questions like these—as if he wore a mental Burberry overcoat. It was so conservative and tightly woven that it repelled curiosity droplets.

Cecy succeeded in cracking off part of the acrylic on her middle nail, and the chip went flying over the end of the couch. She crawled after it and discovered a cache of financial magazines under the end table. She flipped through them. *Forbes, Business Week, Money,* and others stared her in the face. She grimaced, and then hit gold. Lurking under them was a Victoria's Secret catalogue. She brightened and snatched it. What was Chas doing with a Victoria's Secret catalogue in his office? She turned it over and saw that it was addressed to Maria S. Buchanan. Was Chas married?

The thought horrified her. Had she crawled, half-naked and panting, into the lap of a married man? Her stomach gave a lurch, and she felt ill.

Her mind raced. He wore no wedding ring, had no pictures of a smiling wife and children on his desk. Surely that was something he would have mentioned during the week she'd worked in his office. No. Chas was definitely not married. He had to be divorced.

She wondered what Maria S. Buchanan looked like. Tendrils of a sensation uncomfortably close to jealousy snaked through her chest. She opened the glossy pages, ignoring the feeling. Cecy chewed her lip and peered with mild resentment at a model with shiny dark hair. Her breasts burst like ripe pomegranates out of a tiny spandex tube top. Her white teeth gleamed behind prehensile lips, and her sleepy eyes suggested that the viewer could obtain her, with the top, for a clearance price and free shipping.

The model opposite her had been greased and squeezed into a sausage casing that doubled as a pair of jeans. She was draped over a chair, ready to be mounted from behind.

Cecy turned another couple of pages and discovered that Maria Buchanan's desires had encompassed midnight blue silk pajamas and a full coverage coffee-colored bra and panty set. Both items were circled with a ballpoint pen. She frowned, unable to find anything direly wrong with the woman's taste.

She just preferred the little camisole and tap

shorts covered with pancakes, bacon, and eggs. A shame the catalogue was over four years old. She was surprised it hadn't been thrown out long ago.

She put it back, yawned, and stretched. Time to retrieve Barney from the basement and search out dinner for them both.

7

Daisy Darling's Day Spa was perched on a small hill, like a good-time girl on a barstool. Pink clapboard siding failed to disguise the fact that the old house had seen better days. Chas made his way up an undulating stone walkway to a magenta front door—the color of a streetwalker's lips.

He ran his finger around his collar, swallowed, and opened the portal of Daisy Darling's. He might have been beamed to another planet.

What he noticed first was the overpowering smell. A mad scientist had mixed up a scent to singe the eyebrows off a man: chemical fumes and perfumes, ammonia and gardenia.

The eye-popping visuals assaulted him next.

In one corner of the pink shack, a gum-snapping female in a daisy-dotted smock presided over an alien reading a magazine. The smocked woman had covered the Martian's head with shimmery foil and pulled sections of hair through holes in it. These she was painting with sticky, foul-smelling goop.

In the opposite corner, another daisy-clad technician was rolling her victim's locks around rubber rods and securing them with metal pincers. The victim's face was outlined with cotton wool, which served, Chas supposed, to soak up the acrid liquid the technician then sprayed on her head.

Right in front of him sat two women on opposite sides of a small table. One of them was attacking the other's fingers with a drill. Yes, by God, it was a minidrill, the same brand as Chas had in his own garage. Dust and nail particles flew into the air and settled on the clothing of both women. What was wrong with a good old-fashioned nail file? At another table, a frizzy-haired harpy glued long, curving, plastic nails onto her customer's hamlike hands.

The woman occupying the last corner lay tipped back in a vinyl chaise longue. In her early forties, she shrieked and blinked tears from her eyes as her daisy-clad torturer ripped a gauze strip from her upper lip. "Dad gum it, Lorna! I swear you like to hurt me . . ."

Overriding the visuals hummed eight different conversations at once.

". . . tole him I'd slap him upside the head if he didn' 'pologize to her that minute . . ."

". . . the most gorgeous wedding gown you've ever seen . . ."

". . . why does she marry these loser men? I don't understand it . . ."

". . . could have died when I found out what we owed in taxes. . . ."

". . . cutest little girls—twins, you know. . . ."

Chas shifted his weight from foot to foot, standing like a deer in the headlights.

A raven-tressed woman in purple approached him with a smile bigger than the ceramic yellow flower which adorned her lapel. "Can I help you, handsome? I'm Daisy. You looking to try out our new tanning bed?"

The thought of basting himself like a turkey in a fluorescent coffin had never appealed to Chas. "No, I—"

She plucked his hand from his side, examining it. "A manicure, then? We're running a special today."

He pulled his hand back. *Hell no.* Chas shook his head and opened his mouth again.

"A gift certificate! For your wife's birthday."

"No. I'm really just here because I'm looking for someone."

"You're a private investigator. Oooh, how thrilling. Do tell—you can trust us. Are you tracking a desperate criminal?"

"Um, no. I'm looking for a woman named Cecily Scatterton. I believe Pam cuts her hair?"

Daisy clapped her hands. "A romance! Girls, it's a love story. You saw her across a crowded room," she intoned, her voice deep with drama. "There was something in the way she moved— you knew she was The One. You swore from that moment that you'd carry her, dressed all in white, across your threshold one day, for life."

Chas recoiled. Marry Cecy? God, no. He'd rather be eaten alive by wild animals. Disembowled by savages. Boiled in oil. He was saved from having to answer when one of the technicians came forward. "I'm Pam. You said you're looking for Cecy Scatterton?"

He nodded. "She gets her hair cut here, doesn't she?"

"She does. I saw her just last week. Sweet girl." Pam eyed him curiously.

"I need to talk with her about a job, and her phone's been disconnected. Do you know of any friends, or a boyfriend she might be staying with?"

The technician shook her curly red head. "Cecy used to complain that she didn't know anyone in Atlanta. She never got out to meet anyone, taking care of her sick brother all the time. No social life."

Chas frowned. "She never mentioned a boyfriend who was a wrestler?"

"No. Where'd you hear that?"

"Some maintenance man at her apartment complex told me."

Pam laughed. "Super-skinny, dorky, and named Jimmy?"

"I don't know what his name was, but the rest fits."

"It's Jimmy. He kept asking Cecy for dates. She made up a phony boyfriend so she wouldn't have to hurt his feelings. She hates to make anyone feel bad."

So Hulk Hogan wasn't holding her down for the count at night. Chas sighed in relief.

"She's really a sweet girl. I know she was having money problems, because she bounced her last check to us. But when we called her, she came in with half what she owed in cash and offered to be our shampoo girl for a day, or clean the salon to work off the rest. We let her do the shampoos. Gave us all a nice little break between clients. You get real tired, standing on your feet all day."

Chas nodded politely. "I imagine you do. If you see Cecy, will you tell her that Chas Buchanan wants to offer her a job? Here's my card."

Pam took it from him and dropped it into her apron pocket.

Daisy sauntered toward them again from the back. "Well, sweetie, good luck with your lady love. Sure we can't interest you in a manicure or massage?"

He shook his head. "Thanks anyway."

"Sure, sugar."

Before the magenta door swung closed behind him, Chas heard her say, "What a shame. He's got a real nice ass."

"Daisy, you're terrible," Pam's voice exclaimed.

At the end of the day, Chas was forced to sit back on his nice ass and admit defeat. He had no idea where to find Cecy. The only options left were to hire a private investigator or to put an ad in the paper and hope she would see it. He cursed himself for an illogical idiot.

He had prayed to get this woman out of his life for the sake of his sanity, and now he was jumping through hoops to bring her back. What the devil was wrong with him? He didn't want to worry about her. Besides, she was fine.

While he was glad that Hulk Hogan didn't exist, there was the more recent lover, the one with whom Cecy had spent the other night. Women like Cecy would always find a man to solve their problems, just as Maria, his former wife, had. Chas repeated his personal motto since the divorce: Love is a second mortgage at an interest rate you can't afford. Not that he was in love with Cecy—not remotely. He was only sexually attracted.

Chas shoved away the image of her working off her debt to Pam by shampooing customers at the salon. It was an image which didn't fit with his deliberately uncharitable view.

He drove the Jeep toward Buckhead, toward Grandmother's house. Maybe he'd find some peace there. He cruised listlessly down West Paces Ferry Road, going well under the speed limit. His crumpled hood began to rattle and screech every time he sped up. He didn't even register the "For Sale" sign at first, but as he got closer it swam into focus, along with a prominent realtor's name and phone number.

The day had come, at last: After five years of driving by twice a week, his childhood haven was within reach. He lunged for his cell phone. He needed to reach out and touch that Realtor immediately.

Cecy returned from the basement with her cat draped over her shoulder and his food bag open under her arm. He hung his paws down and traveled with his head in the bag, munching.

"What do you think I am, a drive-through?" Cecy chided him. She carried a portable CD player in her left hand, some music discs and a can in her right. Spaghetti-Os had been a favorite of hers and Brock's as children, and since they were on special in the grocery store, she'd bought a family-sized can.

She set the boom box down on the floor and deposited Barney and the bag beside it. Her cat simply stuck his head back into the Meow Mix and kept chowing. She shook her head at him and put on some music, dancing to it as she walked to the kitchenette. Chas was gourmet enough to own a manual can opener and a microwave.

She fiddled with her acrylic nails again as the Spaghetti-Os began to bubble. Construction workers were lucky they could use a sledge-hammer to remove old concrete. She had to employ her teeth instead, and her real nails underneath were so soft that it hurt to pull the broken acrylic chips off. The normal route to natural nail freedom was to pay a technician to dissolve the cement in foul-smelling acetone, but Cecy didn't have the money to spare.

The microwave chirped, and she removed her evening meal, wishing that Chas had a television in his office. Though the music was nice, it left her mind too free to wander. The first bite of Spaghetti-Os burned her tongue, so she set the spoon back in the bowl and began to pick at her false nails again. One had peeled up partway, and she applied as much pressure as she could, grimacing at the pain. She was rewarded when half of it pulled free.

One final jab bent her natural nail double and sent the acrylic one flying. It landed in the hot Spaghetti-Os and sank without a trace.

Cecy stared at the bowl in disbelief. No way she was wasting the food when she had so little money to spare. She was going to have to pan for a fingernail. Cecy dug around with the spoon, but came up empty. Had the acrylic, glue, and polish melted? Would they all have a chemical reaction and explode? Her brain flashed a picture of Chas walking into his exploded office and finding pieces of her, gilded with Spaghetti-Os, stuck to the charred walls.

She watched the bowl, looking for telltale bubbles, green steam, or smoke. Nothing happened. Okay. So maybe it wouldn't cause a firestorm. But was it all right to eat? Her stomach growled. She hadn't had anything all day. Cautiously, she poked at the stuff with her spoon again. Should she call the Poison Control Center?

It seemed the only thing to do. She located a telephone book and dialed the number.

"Poison Center."

"Yes, hello." Cecy struggled with wording. "I've . . . managed to submerge an acrylic fingernail in my dinner."

Silence. Then, "Go on."

"I was wondering if it's still possible for me to eat it without suffering any, um, ill effects."

"You want to eat this food?"

"Yes."

Silence. "Have you found the fingernail, ma'am?"

"No. It's vanished. I think it might have melted."

"And the entrée in question, ma'am? What is it?"

"Microwaved Spaghetti-Os. Would any type of chemical reaction have taken place?"

"Did you drop the fingernail in the Spaghetti-Os before or after you microwaved them?"

"After."

"That's probably a good thing."

Cecy could hear the man clicking busily on the keys of a computer.

"Acrylic nail filler," he said at last, "contains butyl acetates, which can have narcotic and highly irritating effects."

"Highly irritating to what?"

"Most likely your stomach, ma'am," the voice said dryly. "However, it's doubtful that such a small quantity would do you much harm."

Cecy digested this. "Do you think the fingernail has melted?"

"It's probable that acrylic melts at some temperature, but I can't tell you if Spaghetti-Os' boiling point would do it."

"I see. Thank you very much for the information."

"You're welcome."

In the background, before he hung up, Cecy heard him yell, "Hey, Irv, wait 'til you hear this one!"

She replaced the telephone handset and walked back to the bowl, frowning at it. Butyl acetates. They didn't sound healthy. Narcotic and highly irritating? Her stomach growled again, but she couldn't bring herself to eat the stuff. Gingerly, she carried the bowl into the kitchenette.

It seemed like a horrific waste to pour an entire family-sized portion down the disposal. Maybe she could steel herself to eat it tomorrow.

She found some plastic wrap and put it in the refrigerator. What else was in there?

Cecy pulled out a bottle of Thousand Island dressing, some sliced pickles, and a container of rice left over from Chinese takeout. Hmmmm. What could she do with these? She poked around some more and uncovered some cashews in a bag in the door. The final treasure was a package of sliced provolone cheese.

She piled it all on the counter and stared at it for a moment, then got a plate out of the cabinet over the sink. She slapped two round pieces of the cheese onto the plate, spread them with dressing, and sprinkled rice on top. Then she added a layer of pickles and cashews to each, rolled them tortilla style, and secured them with toothpicks she found in a drawer. *Voilà!*

And would you care for a beverage this evening, madam? Cecy liked the idea. She set her plate on the coffee table in front of the green leather sofa and pirouetted into Chas's inner sanctum. He kept a silver tray, glasses, and a decanter there. She hesitated, feeling a little guilty. Would he mind if she raided his liquor? Surely he wouldn't begrudge one drink. She'd had a hard day of pounding the pavement at temp agencies. Her feet hurt. And she'd put in a few extra hours for him.

She pulled the stopper from the decanter and sniffed it. Bourbon. Not her favorite, but she sloshed a little into a heavy crystal highball glass anyway.

A tentative sip caused her nose to wrinkle. She set it down on the coffee table with her food and went back to peer into the fridge. Orange soda? Why not.

Cecy carried a handful of ice and the orange soda back to the couch and mixed her drink, settling down with a contented sigh. The flavor was a bit peculiar, but better than the straight alcohol. She was brilliant. She'd invented a whole new cuisine.

Midnight found Cecy reading a murder mystery by flashlight, though Barney was making it difficult. It was impossible to hold the light completely still for a long time, and Barney found the wobbling beam of light irresistible. He'd nearly given her a coronary when he jumped on the book just as the bad guy was offing a minor character.

She'd shrieked, the innocent man had died instantly, and a startled Barney was unable to catch the flying beam of light. Just like the antagonist, however, her cat was relentless in his pursuit. He leaped onto the coffee table after the circle of light, sending her bourbon a l'orange flying.

"Barney, stop it!" she scolded. He flourished his tail and jerked it skyward a couple of times—the feline version of shooting her the bird. Then he pounced again.

Cecy sighed. She'd been pretty mean to him for the last couple days, wrapping him in bandages and forcing him into a ruff. She owed him some fun. She retrieved the flashlight and sent the beam bouncing along the carpet.

Barney made salacious little clacking noises with his teeth and stalked the light with gusto. She laughed as he leaped full length upon it, somersaulting when it moved just out of reach. He shook his head, as if to question his motor skills, when he still came up empty-pawed.

With a feral growl, he launched himself at the beam as she sent it across the room and shimmying up Chas's coatrack. The heavy polished wood teetered, toppled, and crashed into a window. After a brief spat, Barney emerged victorious in his struggle with the Buchanan London Fog.

He panted, casting his eyes about for the light, while Cecy giggled helplessly on the sofa. She sent the beam dancing up the wall and onto the ceiling. His teeth clacked involuntarily, and he performed the instinctive feline butt-wiggle in preparation for takeoff. Houston had no problem, so Barney flew up the wall, breaking the sound barrier, and hung ten.

Cecy shifted the beam onto the ceiling, and Bat Cat dug into the wallpaper with his back claws before vaulting back and up. The force of his body dislodged a rectangular ceiling tile, which crashed to the floor with him.

"Oh, sweetie, are you okay?" Cecy rushed toward him, but he took cover behind the waxy-leafed plant, disgruntled. She shined the light up on the ceiling to see what damage he'd done. Some insulation and wires were hanging out of the hole. Oh, dear. She hoped she could fix it before Chas came in tomorrow.

Chas paced bare-chested through his house, unable to sleep. Images of Cecy haunted his head. He pictured her stumbling along dark alleys, clasping Barney to her, terrified. He saw her slip in a puddle, lose her balance, fall forward onto her knees.

Then his cynicism took over. He saw her sprawling on black-satin sheets, scantily clad, yawning in her lover's den of iniquity. She pursed her lips to kiss a man with a hairy back. Ugghh. Chas blacked out that picture.

Where was Cecy? He told himself that both she and Barney would land on their feet.

He yanked a sheet of notations off his kitchen counter and forced himself to focus on it. It covered the various options for interest rates, loan origination fees, and points to be paid on his grandmother's house. The owners were asking a fortune for it, and even with all he'd saved, Chas would be on a strict budget if the deal went through.

He wanted to enter the numbers into a spreadsheet program and play with the different options, but he'd left his laptop at the office in his hurry to get out of there.

Chas groaned. He saw two options. He could lie flat on his back in bed and count the bumps in the textured ceiling until morning, or he could drive to the office and retrieve his laptop. Counting ceiling bumps didn't excite him.

He pulled a T-shirt from his dresser and shrugged into it, jamming his feet into loafers at the same time.

The night air was cool as he drove, and the moon full. It cast silvery light over the budding tree branches and neatly pruned bushes in his neighborhood. Everyone else who lived there seemed asleep, the only lights those of street-lamps and porches.

He rattled and sputtered along in the Jeep, hoping the noise wouldn't drive people from their beds in a panic. He needed to get the damned thing into the body shop. It was beyond embarrassing.

The office parking lot was as dark as an abandoned graveyard. Chas made a mental note to mention it to the leasing company. They needed to install spotlighting, at the least. Yawning, he climbed out of the driver's seat, creaked the door shut, and walled to the building entrance. He unlocked the first set of glass doors and keyed his entry code in at the second. The silence was broken only by his own breathing.

He strolled down the hallway to his office, unconcerned with the darkness until he heard rock music—from behind his door. What the hell? Was he being ripped off?

His heartbeat quickened, and his muscles tightened. Teeth clenched, Chas stole closer, back against the wall, chin jutting forward. It occurred to him that he should call the police, but outrage drove him onward. He worked goddamn hard for his money, and any thieving bastard who thought to relieve him of it had another thought coming. His fingers itched to close around the jerk's throat.

As he stuck his head around the door, he saw the beam of a flashlight bouncing around the ceiling tiles. Uh-huh. The burglar didn't want to turn on any overhead lighting and call attention to himself. But what kind of thief burgled to 10,000 Maniacs? The flashlight beam bounced along in time.

The guy was obviously on drugs, and there was something warped about stealing to the lyrics of "More Than This."

He slowly pushed the door open and crept inside. The flashlight beam vanished, the music cut off, and Chas heard a sharp intake of breath. He froze, trying to place where in the room it had come from.

A dark shape ran in the direction of his inner office and disappeared. Chas lunged after it.

He hurtled through the doorway and knew a moment's smug satisfaction that he had the guy cornered. His glee was bashed out of him by something sharp-edged and heavy that rattled. His last realization, before he lost consciousness, was that he'd been assassinated with his own antique abacus.

8

Cecy dropped the abacus. Her heart slammed against her rib cage and left her shaking; her teeth chattered like squirrels on amphetamines.

The big, undoubtedly male form swayed and then toppled to the floor with a resounding thud. She had brained the burglar, but for how long? She'd seen too many movies in which the dead villain rose more often than a sixteen-year-old's man-root.

Should she tie him up before calling the police? Perhaps. Then it hit her. She couldn't possibly call the police, because they would call Chas Buchanan, and she'd have to explain to him what she was doing in his office after midnight. The cops might even arrest her and take her away for trespassing on his property. What was she going to *do*?

She forced herself to calm down. The first order of business was to flip on the light and inspect her burglar. Cecy picked her way around his dark form and found the light switch. She paused.

What in heaven would she do if she'd killed the man? She could justify a thief losing his hand for taking what was not his, but she couldn't justify him losing his life.

Could she argue self-defense? He had been chasing her. Cecy chewed her lip. This could all be decided once she'd turned on the light and discovered whether or not he was breathing. She curved her index finger under the switch, flipped it up—and illuminated her worst nightmare.

Surely those long, rangy legs, that tight butt, those sculptural shoulders didn't belong to . . . Chas Buchanan. No, this had to be some kind of cosmic joke. A bad one at her expense.

She ran to him and skidded onto her knees, grabbing his wrist to check it for a pulse. Two fingers—she'd seen it in the movies, they always used two fingers on the inner wrist. Cecy felt nothing, but her own hands were shaking so badly she couldn't be sure. She rolled him over with difficulty and tried his throat. Same problem. She laid her head on his chest and listened, frantic for a heartbeat. There it was—faint and slow, but blessedly there. She burst into tears.

OhGod—OhGod—OhGod what did she do now? Was he concussed? In a coma? She still didn't think he was breathing. *Eighth grade health class. The ABC's of STD's. Tourniquets. CPR. Annie, Annie, are you okay*?

Cecy gulped down a sob, wiped her face with the back of her hand, and gripped Chas by the nose. She pulled his head back so that his chiseled mouth came open. He was one hot man, even dead.

She fastened her lips to his and blew into his kisser, hard, three times. She released her death grip on his nose. Clasping her hands together, she pressed down on his sternum. *One, two, three.*

Nothing happened. Cecy repeated the process once, and then again. Silence.

With a wail, she grabbed his nose for the fourth time, and bent her head.

His eyelashes fluttered. "Owww," Chas complained. "By doze. What have you done to by doze?"

She emitted an hysterical laugh, and kissed him full on the lips without thought. "Just wait 'til you move your head."

Chas squinted at the overhead lights. "Good Christ," he managed. "Off." He threw an arm over his eyes.

"Oh God," Cecy sobbed, "I'm so glad you're alive." She sank down on her haunches and let the tears flow.

"Makes one of us," Chas muttered.

"Waaahhhh," Cecy responded brokenly. "Uh-heh-heh-heh. Waaaahhh . . ."

"You sound like a donkey in labor."

"Waaaahhh! Uh-heh-heh-heh. Hic. Do not!"

"What the hell are you doing here?"

"Uh-heh-heh-heh. Waaaahhh . . ."

"Did you assault me with my abacus?"

"I'm soooo-hic-sorry. Thought you were a burglar."

"I thought *you* were a burglar."

"Will you ever forgive me? Uh-heh-heh-heh . . ."

"If you'll stop making that god-awful noise, I'll think about it." The tone of his voice was gentler than the words themselves.

Cecy sniffled. "I'm just so relieved."

Chas put a hand up to his head and explored gingerly with his fingers. They came away bloody.

She gasped when she saw them. "What have I done to you?" She bent over him and parted the sticky hair around the wound. Blood oozed below him into the creamy expanse of carpet.

"Ummph. Cecy?" Chas's voice was muffled.

A moist warmth against her left breast made her aware that it was stuffed into his mouth. She shifted position hastily, but not before her nipple peaked and hardened. She was shocked at herself.

She'd spent the last ten minutes trying to pump the life force back into this man, and now she was deriving sick pleasure from blocking his air passage with her flesh? What was wrong with her?

"S-sorry." She jumped up and ran toward the bathroom for a wet cloth. "I'll be right back."

Chas had hauled himself to a reclining position by the time she returned, his head and shoulders propped against the green leather couch. One arm shaded his eyes from the light; the other lay listlessly by his side. The amount of blood on the carpet was alarming.

Cecy ran to him and knelt, blotting gently at his wound with the edge of a wet towel. Chas groaned.

"Leave me alone," he begged.

"We've got to see how badly you're hurt, and the only way I can do that is to clean up the area. You're probably concussed. I'm going to take you to the emergency center."

"I'm not driving anywhere with you!"

"Hey, we met there, remember? It'll be romantic," Cecy teased.

Her only answer was an anguished moan.

She tugged at the arm he'd laid over his eyes. "Come on. Move your arm away so I can look at your head."

He allowed her, squinting once again at the light.

She dabbed and explored, clucking at the rising goose egg and lacerations she found. The next time she glanced at his face, his eyes were fixated on the hollow between her breasts.

She was suddenly conscious of the fact that

she wore the strappy, thigh-skimming nightie in Passionate Peach. It featured a plunging neckline to which Barney had displayed utter indifference.

Chas Buchanan, however, made the transition from concussed victim to hound dog with ease. His lashes blinked a few times, and she watched a telltale eyebrow rise. His tongue prowled around dry lips and flicked out to moisten them. Ooooh, Mama.

Cecy's hormones began to stir again, buzzing around her honeypot. How could she covet the tongue of a brain-damaged man? She had a hunch that tongue knew Sanskrit, and Chinese, and probably Russian—all the languages of love. She only hoped that like a chicken with its head cut off, Chas retained his motor skills.

She shook herself out of her fantasy, which caused parts of her to jiggle.

His other eyebrow rose.

She forced her concentration back to his wounds and finished with the towel. "You have a very large lump, and it's rising fast."

"That's true," said Chas.

"How do you know? You can't even see it."

"Trust me," he muttered.

"Oh, Chas, how can I ever make this up to you?"

"Er. Now that you mention it . . ."

"Yes? Is there something I can do? Anything!"

"I have another lump—which is swelling to epic proportions."

"I'll get you a bag of ice."

"No," said Chas, grasping her arm. "You most definitely will not. This particular lump needs heat treatment, not cold."

Cecy's brows rose slowly. "I see."

"I was wondering if you'd kiss it and make it better."

"Mmmmmmmm."

"You did promise me anything that was in your power."

"I'm beginning to think that maybe you're not as hard up as I thought you were."

Chas pulled her to him and rolled with her so that he lay atop her curves, caging her with an arm on either side. "I'm very hard up," he murmured, moving against her.

Cecy's breath caught.

He bent his head and stole it from her.

There was nothing stuffy about Buchanan's kiss. It electrified her, plugging her into some sexual socket that lit her like a woman-shaped bulb. As he licked and drove into her mouth, she was barely aware that she should not be taking advantage of an injured man. He probably didn't know what he was doing.

Correction—he *did* know what he was doing. He was an expert, biting and sucking on her lower lip, teasing and flicking with that tongue of his. He settled his hard, hot bulk over her and her legs spread like a fever. His big hands captured her breasts and pushed them together. He nuzzled between them, and she could feel the shadowy bristle of his cheeks and chin through the fabric of her nightie.

He caught both her nipples, nightie and all, between his teeth, and she whimpered as his lips closed around them and he suckled her.

Whether it was the sensation or the sight of him devouring her curves, she didn't know, but she almost passed out from sheer desire.

Chas caught the straps of her nightie in his fingers and pulled the silk down to her waist. Then he reduced her to jelly—hungry jelly with nubbins of need, and a hot, wet ache that arched and rotated under him without her consent.

His erection rubbed at the center of her as he ran his tongue in a quick figure eight around her nipples. She began to rocket off into sexual outer space, but he caught her and dragged her back.

"No," he commanded. "Not yet."

Her eyes struggled open in something close to anguish.

He kissed her mouth, quick and hard, then jerked the hem of her nightie up over her hips. He grasped the lace edge of her panties in his teeth and tugged them down, his hands a hot caress over her buttocks. One quick scrape against her thighs and the panties were history. Nothing stood in his way. Her entire body quivered with need and wonder.

Chas's eyes were heavy-lidded, his hair wild. The dark shadow of bristle on his face outlawed rules or shame. Large, firm hands took her knees in opposite directions and spread her into an intimate feast.

He devastated her.

Lips, tongue, teeth—they were everywhere. He nipped the inner flesh of one thigh, then plunged his tongue into hidden recesses. His lips kissed her secret ones. He sucked and pulled at her until she bucked and twisted, clawing his shoulders, unrecognizable sounds coming from her throat. She tried to press her thighs together, but the strength of his hands held them apart. She reveled in the sexual helplessness.

He tongued circles around the most sensitive part of her, and with a wild cry, she disintegrated into a million fragments of light, her trembling uncontrollable. Chas licked her gently until the last wondrous spasm had racked her body.

Cecy opened her eyes through a haze of aftershocks to find him shirtless and shoeless, his head still nestled within her thighs. "My God," she whispered.

"No, just a concussed mortal. But I appreciate the praise." He grinned at her.

"What a . . . what a . . ." Cecy struggled for words. "You're such a gentleman."

"This Yankee likes it down South."

"Shut up and take off your pants."

"I thought you'd never ask." Chas rolled away from her and peeled off his jeans, freeing the raging Buchanan erection. He was beautiful—and he'd been commando. The mystery of his underwear remained unsolved.

Cecy eyed him, now fully alert. "Where do you store that thing when it's not in use?"

He chuckled, advancing upon her. "Top left drawer of my desk."

"It has to be a clip-on."

"Nope."

"You need three-legged pants."

"I need you." He dropped to his knees beside her, and she took in the breadth of his chest, the masculine definition of his biceps and forearms. He had the legs of a Greek god.

Cecy reached out to touch the bounty between them. He was satin-smooth, hard as forged steel. Heavy. Thick.

He groaned, and had her on her back again within seconds, probing her entrance, slick with desire.

He's too big, Cecy thought frantically.

Chas slid his hands under her bottom, bracing her as he eased inside slowly, inexorably.

Images flashed through her mind. Carousel horses, sliding up and down their poles. Cake icing, squeezed out of a fat tube. The hot oiled pistons of an engine.

He wasn't too big. She ceased to see anything but abstract flashes of sensation.

"In" made her tremble with delight, exult in the fullness. "Out" had her clawing at his back in a primal frenzy.

"In" was riding a slick rocket to destinations unknown. "Out" was the loss of all gravity.

"In" was the discovery of another galaxy. "Out" told her there was no way back to her own.

That was the end of thought. She was conscious of nothing other than lips, teeth, and tongue. Tangling arms and legs. Hot, wet suction and throbbing. That monster oiled piston sliding into her most intimate depths. An urgent need within her greeted his every thrust, pulled it, milked it for sensation. A balloon of wild, spiraling energy expanded and stretched within her. His rhythm intensified . . . and the balloon of desire burst. She climaxed, falling into blindness, spinning into a vortex that was Chas Buchanan.

He gave one last mighty thrust and groaned his own release. Cecy clamped her legs around him until he stopped shuddering within her, feeling deliciously impaled. He was still gripping her bottom as if he'd never let go. His eyes remained closed, and a sexy trickle of perspiration ran across his face. Cecy wiped it off with the back of her hand. That was when she noticed that an alarming trickle of blood still oozed from his head.

9

Chas shut his eyes as his Jeep, propelled by the Killer Bimbo, careened around another corner. His skull was splitting like a cantaloupe under a sledgehammer, and his eyes seemed to be permanently crossed, although he wasn't sure if that was due to the abacus or to the most incredible sex he'd ever had in his life. It felt like his brains had been mixed into batter and squeezed out through his dick.

His eyes popped open. Bad metaphor. God forbid the cake mix should rise in Cecy's little oven.

She was hunkered down over the steering wheel, her small hands clutching it in a death grip, her foot in a high-heeled mule slamming the pedal to the metal. She vibrated with anxiety. He could see it from the teeth that skewered her lower lip, to her quivering breasts, to her bouncing left knee, which tautened that long, delicious expanse of inner thigh.

She took quick, shallow breaths, and focused on the road with painful intensity. For the first time, she didn't look fashionable. She was still sexy as hell, with her hair rumpled and mussed, but her outfit was downright goofy. She'd stuffed the bottom of the nightie into a short skirt, thrown a ratty cardigan over the top of it, and grabbed two mismatched shoes.

He knew he didn't look like a *GQ* ad either—barefoot, T-shirt on inside out, and blood encrusting his hair.

The Jeep rattled, squeaked, and shook. He was sure it would fall apart around their ears and tumble them to skid ass first along the double yellow lines. He had to get the damned thing into a body shop. Right after he replaced his head with a new one.

This head was a lemon. Not only had it been bashed in, but it had allowed a cat onto his leather upholstery and manufactured the fantasy that had caused him to wreck the Jeep.

He was careful and methodical. He did not get into situations like this. He did not become overwhelmed with lust for women who displayed alarming tendencies toward violence and shopping.

What man in his right mind would hump a

woman who'd just attempted to murder him? Worse, he'd humped her without precautions—like a drunken teenager hopping onto his prom date.

But there she'd been, lurking in his office in that illegal shred of silk, dangling her luscious breasts over his parched lips. He'd never had so much sympathy for Tantalus.

His brow furrowed. What the hell had she been doing in his office, after midnight, with a flashlight? And how had she gotten in?

He opened his mouth to ask her just as they squealed into the parking lot of the minor emergency center. Cecy sped into the semicircular drive and lodged the Jeep's right-front tire over the curb. She stomped on the parking brake, ejected herself out of the driver's side, and ran around to open his door. All solicitude, she took his arm and helped him out. His teeth snapped shut as his head thundered. He reeled with her to the entrance.

The same administrator goggled at them from behind the expanse of blue laminate. She wore wire-rimmed glasses and a pencil behind her ear.

"He needs his head examined," Cecy told her in urgent tones.

"Don't we all," the woman muttered. "Fill out these forms." She pushed a clipboard at them.

"We're not filling out any forms." Cecy's tones were impatient. "We were both here just a few days ago. Can't you look it up in the computer? His name is Chas Buchanan. He needs to see a doctor immediately."

Chas gave his best imitation of a grin. He felt like he was suspended over the whole scene, peering at them through some fluffy clouds.

Far below, the woman behind the counter rolled her eyes. "Everyone here wants to see the doctor immediately. You're going to have to wait with the rest."

Cecy swiveled her head and looked at the other people in the waiting room. He did, too. A teenager with a swollen ankle, a thirtysomething woman with a rash on her forearms, and an old codger with a nosebleed stared back at them. Nobody was hyperventilating, screaming, or seemed on the verge of sudden death.

"Look," Cecy said, her voice dangerously even, "this man has lost a lot of blood and suffered a blow to the head with a heavy instrument. I want him to see a doctor now."

"And in order to do that, you need to fill out these forms." The woman pushed the clipboard back at her and eyed her snottily. Her gaze took in the rumpled nightie shoved into the skirt, and the ratty cardigan. She sniffed.

Chas watched from what seemed like a long way away. He leaned weakly against the wall and wondered vaguely about prosthetic skulls while Cecy's shoulders snapped back and her jaw jutted out. She leaned over the counter and snatched the pencil from behind the administrator's ear. She thumped each lens of her glasses with it a couple of times. "Hel-lo! Are you human, or a droid placed here by an HMO? We're not filling out forms. I don't need your attitude regarding my clothes. I do not want to be told you don't take American Express. Got it? Now press that little intercom button and get the doctor out here, before—"

Chas slid down the wall and lost consciousness.

Cecy stared once again at the blue giraffes on the wallpaper border. They galloped along with the same inane expressions, reached the corner, and started 'round for another lap.

For the umpteenth time, she wondered if she'd caused Chas permanent brain damage. She'd allowed—no, encouraged—the man to make love to her in his weakened state. But he'd seemed robust and enthusiastic enough for the task. It had even been something of a turn-on that he could rise from the dead and drill her for oil. It implied either phenomenal machismo on his part or irresistible charms on her part—or both.

Great. So he'd been thinking with his dick, and she'd been blinded by ego. Lust had then flattened both of them like a steamroller and left them for the two-dimensional idiots that they were.

The door opened and a doctor interrupted her self-recriminations.

"Mrs. Buchanan?"

"Ms. Scatterton," Cecy corrected.

"I thought you were next of kin."

She blinked rapidly. "I'm his fiancée."

The doctor's brow cleared.

"How is he?"

"He's conscious again, but we'd like to take him to a hospital for some tests."

She swallowed. "What kind of tests?"

"An MRI, for one."

"Oh, my God."

The doctor looked at her from under bushy brows. "There's no need for you to panic. He's probably just fine, but we'd like to take every precaution. He'll be transported by ambulance. You can ride with him, if you'd like."

Cecy nodded.

"Can you tell me what hit him? The abrasions are a bit unusual."

She hung her head. "An abacus."

"Excuse me?"

"He was hit with an antique abacus. A big one."

"Will you be needing a copy of my medical report to file charges?"

She stared at him, dread a knot in her stomach. "Charges," she repeated stupidly.

"Against the person who hit him."

Horror filled her. Would Chas want to file against her? For trespassing, assault and battery? She felt her face drain of blood. "N-n-no. No copy is necessary." She struggled with what she had to ask him, though. "Uh, Doctor."

"Yes?"

Cecy pulled her cardigan close around her and hesitated.

"You have a question for me?"

She gulped. "Yes. Um. Could Chas's condition be w-w-worsened by, um, physical activity after the um, assault?"

"What kind of physical activity? Jogging?"

"Er, no." Cecy stared down at her toes in their mismatched mules.

The doctor waited, his foot beginning to tap. "Ms. Scatterton?"

"S-s-sex," she whispered.

"Beg pardon?"

"Sex," she said, louder. She winced at the expression on the doctor's face.

"Ahhh." He pursed his lips. "Was it particularly . . . acrobatic?"

Was it her imagination, or was he checking out her legs? "Well, we didn't use the rapelling harness or the bob-cat this time," she said acidly.

"Wise of you." He furrowed his brows and thought about it. "No, I can't say that engaging in intercourse would have had a deleterious effect upon Mr. Buchanan. It might even have helped pump more oxygen to his brain. Well, then, Ms. Scatterton, here's the paperwork."

"Paperwork?"

The doctor handed her the bill. "You can go through that door there, and Doris will get you all taken care of."

Cecy's stomach flipped in foreboding.

* * *

Doris did indeed take care of her. She had rubbed the eraser smudges off of her glasses, but her attitude hadn't benefited from the polishing. If anything, it was worse.

Cecy cleared her throat, and Doris skewered her with a steely gaze. This was gonna be ugly. She mentally girded her loins.

Doris took advantage of her silence to pass her a business card. "You may pick up your vehicle at this address tomorrow. Be prepared to pay the charges in cash."

"*Excuse* me?"

"You cannot leave your transportation illegally parked and blocking the entrance to an emergency center."

"*Minor* emergency center. It's not like it was wedged into the door of the trauma room at Grady."

The woman shrugged.

Cecy fought with her outrage and lost. "Couldn't you have made an announcement over the intercom? I would have moved it."

"I was just doing my job." But there was a gleam of satisfaction in the narrow eyes behind the glasses.

"Of course you were." Cecy remembered the stack of paperwork clutched in her fingers. How was she going to pay this horrid bill? The stash of cash Chas had given her for her knickknacks was back in his office. Not to mention that it was dwindling fast. Not that Doris would care.

She placed the stack on the blue laminate counter and folded her arms. "This," she said, waving at it airily, "is Mr. Buchanan's bill."

Doris drew her lips into a feral smile. "Will that be cash or charge?"

"I said it's Mr. *Buchanan's* bill." Dammit, she didn't know if he had his wallet with him or not. She hadn't thought about it on their mad rush to the center.

"And you are Mr. Buchanan's 'fiancée,' so I assume you'll be taking care of it, or he won't be going anywhere in this ambulance for any tests."

"Can't you send him a statement?"

"Payment is due at the time service is rendered." Doris pointed to a plastic sign. "I'm sure he'll pay you back, especially—" the woman looked her up and down—"if you do some typing for him." Her tone of voice said clearly that Cecy would do the typing naked, on her back.

Cecy fantasized briefly about plucking the woman's head bald and then glueing the individual hairs to her face. Then she blew out her breath and rolled her eyes. "Just a minute. I'll go and see if Chas has his wallet."

She stomped back through the corridors until she found the room he was in. He was stretched out on a padded examination table, looking dazed and absurdly vulnerable with his backwards T-shirt rucked up slightly over his stomach. His large feet dangled over the end of the table. He had nicely shaped toes, she thought, and then blasted herself. She didn't need his toes, she needed his wallet.

"Hi, honey," she crooned, for the attendant nurse's benefit.

Chas blinked at her. "Hi?"

She kissed him on the lips and watched his eyes brighten and focus on her breasts.

"Mmmmmm."

"None of that, now, darling. I need that big, bulging tool of yours"—the nurse's eyes widened—"your wallet."

Chas looked vague. "Don't know where it is."

"Listen, sweetie." She rolled first one hip up and then the other, patting his rear pockets. "I need to pay your bill at the front desk, or they won't let you take any more tests."

"Don' want any more," he mumbled.

"Yes, you do. And you get to take a fun ambulance ride, with all the flashing lights." She kept frisking him for money.

"Bite me," said her faux fiancé.

She had one more pocket to go. "With relish, dear, as soon as we pay your bill." Ah ha! A small folded wad in his left front jeans pocket. She dug two fingers in for it, only to have his hand clamp down on hers.

She looked into his eyes.

He stared with suspicion into hers.

"Trust me," she whispered.

His right eyelid twitched. Then, eyes narrowed, he released her hand.

She withdrew a wad of bills and a gold card, clamped into a monogrammed money clip.

Doris looked a bit disappointed, but brightened when she saw the name on the card. "You can't use this," she said. "You're not authorized."

"Look, lady." Cecy sighed. "I was rude to you, and I'm sorry. I really am. I was just worried about him. So can we end this? He's back there in a room, and you know it. If you want him to make an 'x' on the signature line, he can probably do it."

Doris huffed, but processed the card.

Cecy watched with relief as it was accepted. "Thank you."

Cecy prowled back and forth in front of the entrance to Lord & Taylor the next morning. She was a starving panther in front of a shrink-wrapped side of beef.

It was just her luck there was a mall opposite the damned hospital, and that she happened to have a gold card burning a hole in her pocket. The fact that it wasn't her gold card was beside the point. All that meant to her in the heat of the moment was that the credit limit wasn't maxed out.

The hospital had kept Chas overnight for observation and was running more tests on him. She saw no point in staying in his room staring at his empty bed, so after eating breakfast in the cafeteria, she'd walked across the street.

"I'll just look," she promised herself. "And

it'll be good exercise. Lots of people walk around the malls just for exercise."

Her palms itched, and she salivated as she gazed at the outfit in the window. The dressy suit winked back at her, promising eternal beauty, glamour, and power to the lucky woman whose body it graced.

Here, chicky chicky chicky, it beckoned. *Feel like just another female ant, slaving away in the cosmic anthill? Are you dissatisfied and blue? Wondering if your life will ever be in control? Have I got the perfect upper for you! This suit, darlin', has magical powers. Put on the jacket, and your life will change. Wrest the helm of your destiny away from fate. Square your own shoulders inside these padded delights.*

And check out this skirt, baby. Beneath it, your hips will be forever tiny, plastic and perfect. See the mannequin? She got the cure. You can, too. You will strut your stuff right to the top of the world. And have we got a special for you. Ten percent off! Yeah, you heard me right. Only for you, only today.

Cecy's damp palm wrapped around the door handle and pulled. The air-conditioning vacuumed her inside, and her mismatched mules clicked down onto the yellow brick road of retail heaven. She was in Oz, all right, except that the Munchkins had been replaced by towering anorexic plastic bimbi, all in outfits to die for.

Though her wardrobe (stuffed into the multiple boxes in Chas's office basement) was bursting at the seams, she saw immediately that it wouldn't do, being hopelessly out of style.

After throwing out all her straight-legged pants for flared ones just months ago, she saw that now they either had to have huge unflattering pockets in the dreaded thigh area or they had to be cropped at the knee. Nobody seemed to care that this length immediately turned a woman's calves into monstrous mooing cows.

And her skirts! Dear heavens, they were much too short. The current style seemed borrowed from around 1910—hemlines brushed the ankles.

Cecy was also perspicacious enough to see, all on her own, that she did not possess the right colors in her wardrobe. She'd have to purchase something in that rather violent shade of orange. Funny how she hadn't liked the obnoxious green from the year before either, but she'd gotten used to it eventually. It had made her skin look like sautéed liver, until she'd shopped for the right cosmetics.

It was exhausting, keeping up with fashion. But she was up to the challenge, because it had been so much worse wearing the cheap, ill-fitting, sometimes stained hand-me-downs from the older children at Mama Sue's home. Mama Sue had always kept their clothes scrupulously laundered, but there was no denying that Cecy had wanted, just once, to go out and shop for new clothes. Brock hadn't cared so much.

She wandered down the aisles, gazing at racks right and left. She traveled the miles between the swimwear section to resort wear to Better Dresses as the yellow brick road took her ever deeper into Oz. She found herself in the Jungle of Accessories—belts, scarves, hats—which led to the Castle of Cosmetics and Jewelry, which was surrounded by a deep, impenetrable Moat of Shoes. What was a woman to do?

She slung several expensive handbags over each of her shoulders, turning this way and that in the mirrors. They all looked like a million bucks. They also reminded her that she had no money or available credit to carry in them.

Cecy moved on to belts. Snakeskin, polished-calf, mock-croc and microfiber. Gold buckles, silver buckles, bronze buckles. Woven, knotted, and pieced. Machine stamped and hand-painted. So many selections. She tried them on, and then realized that they wouldn't fit once she began eating normally again. She sighed and turned away.

She loved hats and scarves, and enjoyed playing dress-up with those for a while. She donned a black straw hat with dramatic netting and pursed her lips into a mirror. Hey, with a slather of red lipstick she could fit right in on *Dynasty* reruns. She exchanged the black hat for a white one, which made her feel like Ingrid Bergman in *Casablanca*.

The green velvet with the feather was another story. *Why, fiddle-dee-dee, Rhett!* She put it back in a hurry. Chas was already calling her Miss Scarlett.

It was true that she had plans for the curtains from her old apartment—but she was making palazzo pants from them, not a dress. She would be sure to point that out to him, if the subject ever arose.

Cecy hurried on to the Ladies' Shoe Salon. Her mouth began to water as she approached the size six rack. Her heart rate rose, and her knees weakened as she spotted it: a zebra-striped orgasm with a retro heel. Tiny rhinestones dotted it like tears of joy.

"Oooooohhhh," she moaned. It was the ultimate sandal de slink n' slither for an evening on the town.

"You like?" The salesman was on her in a flash.

"*Je l'aime,*" she breathed.

He placed it in her hand and she worshiped it reverently. Such design! Such craftsmanship! Such a price tag! She shuddered delicately.

The salesman slid the shoe out of her grasp, and she followed it, a dog after filet mignon, to a chair. She extended her foot, and he eased it on. He was a master of his art, and clasped his hands to his breast, so enchanted was he by her five toes in the sliver of Italian leather. "Spectacular!" he proclaimed. "Would you like to try on the other?"

Cecy smoothed her fingers over the slim plastic rectangle in her pocket. In braille, the raised lettering said, "Buy the shoes." In English, however, she knew it read "Chas Buchanan," with an expiration date that would be printed on her headstone if she used the card.

She looked up and caught the salesman checking out her odd ensemble. She pulled the edges of the ratty cardigan closer around her to hide her nightie, suddenly jolted out of consumer mania and conscious of her shabby appearance. The mismatched shoes were bad enough; now she also wondered, in the overperfumed atmosphere, if she reeked of sex. It was a horrible thought, and she watched the man's nose for telltale wrinkles. None were forthcoming. He must either hunger for the commission on the shoes or have a classic case of Atlanta allergies.

Nevertheless, the spell was broken, and Cecy now wanted nothing more than a cab back to Chas's office, where she could sponge off in the rest room. She'd come back later, and then they could go pick up the Jeep at the tow yard. She wasn't looking forward to telling him about that, and committing fraud with his credit card wouldn't raise her in his esteem either.

She sighed and slid her foot out of the sandal. "Will you hold them, please?" She couldn't bear for them to be put back out immediately.

"Of course."

Freshly sponge-bathed, her hair in a towel, Cecy felt like a new woman. Standing nude in the bathroom, she examined the note she'd found taped to Buchanan's office front door.

"Chas," said a masculine scrawl, "where the hell are you? Came by to kidnap you for nine holes of golf. Call me." It was signed Tom Barry.

So Thomas Barry was a friend as well as a client. She wondered if she should call him, to let him know Chas was a bit under the weather. She went into his office to flip through the Rolodex. Dropping her towel onto his cushioned leather chair to protect it, she located the number and began to dial. She'd say she was a friend.

As the ringing began, the front door swung open and a big Southern voice boomed out, "Buchanan, you dog, where've you been hidin'?"

Cecy dropped the phone with a clatter, whirled the chair around, and scrunched down as far as she could behind its high back. She hugged her naked knees to her chest and prayed.

God laughed.

Quick footsteps approached, and the chair spun around. She found herself looking up several feet, into amazed brown eyes.

"Tom Barry," the man drawled. "And your name?"

10

"None," Cecy squeaked. She kept her breasts pressed to her knees with one hand and pulled the towel up over her nether parts with the other.

Tom Barry scanned her mortified flesh. "If there's one thing I'm sure of, it's that you ain't no nun. Where in the dickens is Buchanan?"

"B-bathroom," she improvised, panic-stricken. If Chas found out she was living here, he'd kick her out on the street. She'd planned to explain her presence last night by saying she'd left a jacket. Hopefully he'd still be too befuddled to think about the key.

"Is that so?" Barry's eyes narrowed. "Why's he taking so long?"

Her mind raced. "The, uh, edible panties got stuck in his molars."

Tom choked.

She blinked her baby blues at him.

He reddened, backed away a few steps, and looked around the room.

The ceiling tile still lay on the rug, near the orange-soda stain Barney had left when he'd knocked her drink over last night. The window that had taken the beating from the coatrack sported a spider's web of cracks.

"Place looks like a war zone. What happened?"

"Oh, nothing. Nothing at all." Cecy said it in her most reassuring tones.

"Well, y'all are obviously occupied. I'll catch him later."

She nodded, ever so polite. "Would you like Chas to call you?"

"Yeah. But not nekkid."

"Have a nice afternoon."

"Do yourselves a favor, and lock the dang door before you start up again." With this sage advice, Barry left as abruptly as he'd come.

Cecy breathed a sigh of relief but began to worry again immediately. How close a friend was this Barry? Close enough that he would rib Chas about his sex life?

A quick knock on the door produced Tom's head and shoulders for the second time. "Miss? Would you also tell him that the contract looks fine, and my firm's getting everything in order for the closing on the Paces Ferry House. Thanks."

Contract? Closing? Tom Barry must be a real-estate attorney. Was Chas buying a house? Cecy wondered what it looked like as she changed into leggings and an oversize shirt. Then she called a cab and went to wait for it out front.

The Buchanan homestead would include a lawn jockey and a brass door knocker. A highly chlorinated swimming pool. Perfectly rounded shrubs with carefully calculated diameters. And a Terminix man in uniform who would stand guard over the place like a South American guerrilla, blasting renegade mosquitoes with an AK-47.

She had it all worked out in her mind as the cab dropped her at the hospital. When she got to Chas's room, she discovered she'd left out the doghouse.

"Nice of you to return," the patient growled.

"Oh, dear, have you been waiting long?"

"I've certainly had time to think. Cecy, you wouldn't by any chance have taken up residence in my—"

"How's your head?" She interrupted.

"What? It hurts."

"Did they do an MRI?"

"Yes. Lots of fun."

"And the results?"

"I'm fine. Thank you for asking. Now, about your living situation—"

"Goodness, I forgot the cab was waiting. We've got to go! Where's checkout?"

"What cab? Where's my Jeep?"

"It's safe," Cecy assured him.

"Cecy. What. Happened. To. My. Jeep."

She cleared her throat. "It took a little side trip when I wasn't watching."

"Please don't tell me it's at the bottom of the Chattahoochee River."

"No, no. Nothing like that."

Chas closed his eyes. "It went sky-diving off Stone Mountain?"

"Of course not!"

Those coal black eyes flickered. "You slammed it into the Coca-Cola plant and the carbonation ate off all the paint."

"Chas! Would I do a thing like that?"

His eyes bored into her. "Yes." The word was emphatic.

He had a nerve! "Your Jeep is fine. It's just in the SUV slammer, and we've got to go get it out."

"SUV slammer?"

"Not my fault!" Cecy injected her expression with all the appeal she could muster. "The psycho woman at the minor emergency center had it towed, for the most transparent excuse."

"Let me guess. You left it blocking the entrance."

"Well, yes, but she didn't like me to begin with . . ."

Chas swung his legs over the hospital bed

and stood up, his hand to his brow. "I don't want to hear it. Let's go."

Doghouses, Cecy discovered, were portable. She rode in one all afternoon, while a tight-lipped Chas bailed his vehicle out of Jeep jail, then drove her back in total silence to his office.

Once there, he strode around the place, his jaw working. He pointed at the window, and waited for her to explain.

"I'm so sorry," she babbled. "Barney and I were playing with a flashlight, and he knocked the coatrack into the window. I'll type as many hours as it takes to pay for it."

His face expressionless, Chas tilted his head back to look at the missing ceiling panel. He raised his brows.

"Well, that was Barney, too. But see, nothing's broken. I'll help you stuff the insulation in and we'll put it right back in place. I would have done it before, but we were rushing to the emergency room . . ."

He swung around and glared at the orange-soda stain on the cream carpet. He sniffed the air. "Why does it smell like bourbon in here?"

"I tried and tried to get that out of the carpet, but dish soap just didn't do the trick. Bourbon? Well, I had a little splash of it, and didn't like the taste. Not wanting to waste it, I mixed a little—"

Chas collapsed on the green leather couch. "Please deny that you poured orange soda into my Maker's Mark."

She chewed her lip and couldn't quite meet his eyes.

"Sacrilege!" he roared.

Cecy blinked.

"Mother of God, how could you? Were you born in a barn? Raised in pig offal?"

Mama Sue would be outraged. But then, Mama Sue had never kept a drop of alcohol in the house, much less Maker's Mark.

"Orange soda! You dared to blaspheme the Holy Water of the South with orange soda!"

How was she to know? Holy Water of the South, indeed. The man was a raving lunatic. "Chas, it's only bourbon. And it's not like I poured the soda into the whole bottle. Just one glass."

He whirled and stared at her. "Only bourbon? It's the finest aged Kentucky whiskey! The all-empowering ingredient of the Mint Julep! The Kentucky Derby couldn't go on without it. Therefore, the Triple Crown wouldn't exist. Without the Triple Crown, what would become of American horse racing? And then the whole British Empire would lose respect for us—"

Cecy threw up both hands. "I had no idea. You have my most abject apologies. How can I make this up to you?"

"Don't ever do it again."

"Understood. Can I make an observation, though?"

Chas waved her on.

"For a Yankee, and a Damned Yankee at that, you sure do seem to be adopting the ways of the South."

"What's the difference between a Yankee and a Damned Yankee?"

"Well, you must have learned *that*," Cecy said, her tone scathing.

"Nope. Enlighten me."

"A Yankee is a visitor from up North. A Damned Yankee is a Northerner who stays."

His face split into a grin, in spite of himself. "That's pretty good." He ran his gaze over her body. "Cecy, do you know what I'll have to do to you if you ever putrify my bourbon again?"

She shook her head. A hormone or two emerged out of her hive and gave a warning buzz.

His eyes darkened as they roved.

"Well?"

"I'll strip you buck naked and beat you."

A couple more hormones zipped through her stomach, doing a roll and then a free fall. "Is that so? With what?"

Chas mused. "How would I beat thee? Let me count the ways . . ." He pursed his lips.

She wanted to tug on the bottom one with her teeth. She moved closer. "With a feather?" She put a hand on his knee.

"No. Something more substantial than that."

"A pillow?" She touched the other knee.

"Something harder."

"Would this fit the bill?" Cecy tugged on the bulge that had appeared in the crotch of his jeans.

"Yeah. It just might." Chas closed his eyes as she massaged it.

"Mmmmmmm."

His eyes flew open again. "Are you living in my office, you perverted woman?"

She raised her eyes to his, and unzipped his jeans. She knelt between his legs and held him in her hands, squeezing gently. "Do you mind?"

He looked heavenward. "Not at all," he gasped.

She bent her lips to him.

"Ahhhhhh."

"Can I just stay for a few days?"

"Long as you—ohhhhh! Want."

"Now *that's* Southern hospitality."

Chas now knew that the MRI had irradiated his brain—what was left of it. He'd turned his office into a Holiday Inn for a gorgeous hussy. As if that weren't bad enough, he liked her. Not that he wanted to like her, but he couldn't help it. Something about Cecy was just . . . well, charming. She did the most horrendous, stupendous things, but apologized for them so prettily. He found himself unable to hold on to a good mad. It was really starting to piss him off.

But what could he say, when she did something incredible? Like just now, for example. His big head might hurt, but his little head felt like heaven. And after promising not to park illegally anywhere, she'd gone to get his pills at the pharmacy.

Chas rubbed lazily at his chest and ambled to the kitchenette refrigerator, where he spied nothing but a bunch of condiments and a bowl of what looked like Spaghetti-Os. Excellent. He withdrew it, removed the plastic wrap, and popped it in the microwave for a couple of minutes. Not the most gourmet of meals, but he was starving.

When a "ding" signaled that the food was heated, he took the bowl back to the green leather couch and sprawled there with a finance magazine. He spooned Spaghetti-Os into his mouth and read an article about emerging-market funds.

He was about three-quarters done with the bowl and the article when he encountered a *very* foreign object in his mouth. He ran his tongue around it, trying to discern what it was, and finally spat it into his hand. His right eye twitched something fierce as he realized what he held. His stomach gurgled unpleasantly, and he sprinted for the bathroom.

When Chas had finished hurling Spaghetti-Os, he stumbled back to the couch.

Cecy stood in front of it, aghast, gazing down at the bowl on the coffee table. "I brought your pills," she ventured.

He refused to look at her.

"I was going to pan for the fingernail. I never dreamed you'd get to the bowl first!"

Silence.

"I called the Poison Control Center. You won't die or anything. Even if you were a rat, it would only make you mildly ill. There aren't enough butyl acetates in one acrylic nail to hurt you."

"Relief leaves me speechless." Had he really decided he liked her? Well, decisions could be reversed. It was a man's prerogative, and he intended to exercise it—right after he killed her.

It took a while for him to get over that one. During the next several days, Cecy came to his home every morning and evening to sponge his head and change the dressing on it.

He suspected that she'd slept in his house the first night, possibly on the doctor's orders, but he never pushed the issue. She never served him anything out of a can, and watched patiently as he inspected the first couple of meals she brought him.

He knew she was doing her very best to make things up to him. To her credit, she had turned down her first temping opportunities to stay and help him with the presentation work for his clients. They'd arranged that she would pay for the window at a rate of twenty dollars a week. He forgave her the towing charges, and the blood- and orange-soda stains came out with some strong carpet cleaner.

When Chas returned to the office, they had a talk and set some ground rules—and he meant to abide by them. Sex in the office was a bad idea. Everyone knew that, even if they occasionally fantasized about it anyway. Office affairs hardly ever led anywhere good—and even when they resulted in marriage, one person usually had to give up the job.

Not that in his wildest dreams he'd ever marry Cecy. She might be able to suck a golf ball through a garden hose, but she certainly wasn't West Paces Ferry material. He wasn't a snob or anything, he told himself. She just wouldn't be comfortable in that type of environment, Frog Lit or no.

Why not? an insistent little voice kept asking him. He waved it away.

Did Maria make you happy? She had all the social graces you could possibly have asked for. And in private, the temper of a Tasmanian devil. Maria smashed things deliberately.

Cecy, at least, destroyed by accident. She also stayed around to clean up her messes. The problem was, he couldn't allow her to go on living in his office.

He also couldn't kick her out onto the street. And even though she was now earning an income, she'd trashed her credit so thoroughly that an apartment was an impossibility.

Over the next two weeks, Chas turned the problem over and over in his head. He had to do something about Cecy.

The morning of the closing on Grandmother's house, Chas woke early and dressed with care. He fought off a case of nerves, which was ridiculous, since he knew all the documentation and financing was in order. Tom Barry had assured him of that, although his friend had been acting really weird lately.

"Hey, buddy! How's your little nun?" he'd asked on the phone one day.

"My what?"

"She tie you up with her rosary beads?"

"Huh?"

"I'll bet you're enjoying a huge assortment of her habits."

"Tom, have you been drinking?"

"Dimples, a wimple, and nothin' else. You dog, you—I never knew you had these Catholic schoolboy fantasies. You come across as so cussed uptight."

Chas had hung up the receiver in consternation. What the hell had gotten into Tom?

At the closing, Barry greeted him with a slap on the back and a broad grin. Once they'd settled at the table, he threw a small white-plastic box at him.

Chas held up the package of dental floss. His puzzled expression was reflected in the highly polished surface of the title company's boardroom table. "What's this?"

The sellers, their broker, and the mortgage lender looked just as confused.

"Do I have a wayward spinach leaf between my teeth?" Chas knew he didn't.

"Let's just say it's a party favor."

"Party favor . . ."

"Useful on occasion for removing traces of the party which might be stuck in your molars."

"Tom, can I talk to you privately for a moment?" His friend must be *bathing* in the Holy Water of the South. He was submerged in it, and blowing bubbles.

Barry followed him outside the boardroom, and Chas shut the door. He couldn't smell any alcohol on Tom, and his eyes weren't bloodshot, but he sure as hell wasn't making any sense.

"Tom, what is all this about nuns and wimples and party favors? What's gotten into you? Why are you throwing dental floss at me in the middle of a freaking closing?"

"What's gotten into *me*? Oh, that's rich, Yankee boy." Barry guffawed. "The question is, where did you find this religious experience of yours? Is she for hire? How much do you have to put in her offering plate?"

Chas knit his brows.

"Does she charge extra to worship St. Peter?"

"Tom. Stop with the innuendo for a minute and tell me what the fuck you're talking about."

"Oh, please, Buchanan. I walked into your office just a couple weeks back, and I saw her plain as day, buck nekkid in your cushy office chair! Cheeky little thing says she's a nun, and that you're in the can fishing the edible undies outta your molars!"

Blood began to pound in Chas's temples. "She *didn't*."

"I'm tellin' ya, buddy, she did. What possessed you to go there in the middle of your office hours, I don't know. And with the door unlocked, too."

Chas clenched his hands into fists.

"Honestly, bud. You can tell me. Are you seeing a shrink? Is this part of some radical touch therapy for stodginess?"

"I am not stodgy!"

"Well, you were until real damn recently. She's a hot little number, too. I wouldn't mind takin' her for a spin—"

Chas's hands unfisted enough to go for Tom Barry's throat. He pinned him against the polished rosewood doors of the boardroom and glared at him. "Shut up! Just shut the hell up."

Tom's face had reddened and puffed up like a blowfish before Chas backed off. He pushed his friend aside, shook out his sleeves, and stalked back into the closing.

Barry rubbed at his neck. What was up Buchanan's butt? He had no idea, but one thing was for sure. He had it bad for this little "nun."

11

Cecy argued with her new landlord during the entire drive to West Paces Ferry.

"I did not sit naked at your desk!"

"A towel is not considered an article of clothing."

"I had just finished washing up. How was I supposed to know Tom Barry would come barging in?"

"Cecy, people do come to my office between nine and five. I'm an accountant. Couldn't you have locked the door?"

"I didn't think of it. All I wanted was to be clean. And I never told Barry I was a nun—where does that come from?"

"I have no idea. But I can't have my clients

thinking that I'm carrying on with a hooker in my office!"

"A hooker! You said he thought I was a nun."

"Get real, Cecy."

"You just *said*—"

"He thought you were a naughty nun. A rental. A toy. Get it? No one would ever mistake you for a nun."

"What's that supposed to mean?"

"Er . . ."

"You're saying I'm trashy!"

"I never said that."

"It's obviously what you think."

"Not at all." Chas racked his brain for a way out. "Why do we have to be caught up in the age-old binary opposition of virgin and whore?"

Cecy shot him a contemptuous look. "Don't patronize me, Bean Counter. You haven't read enough postmodern philosophy to parry a single thrust in that duel."

Outraged, he opened his mouth, then shut it again. Damn it, she was right.

"A pathetic attempt to distract me from your insult. Next you were going to tell me that I fit somewhere in between the image of virgin and whore."

Chas didn't like being second-guessed. "But it's true!"

Cecy folded her arms.

"I was also going to tell you that you're beautiful and sexy."

"Hmmmph."

"But since you read my mind so well, you already know what I'm going to say in advance, and therefore I don't need to say it. Being so book-smart and all, I'm sure you think my compliments are calculating and cheesy."

Cecy cast him a look from under her lashes. "Perhaps. But I'll need to hear more before I can decide whether they're complete cheese or not. Bring 'em on."

Just like a woman.

"Your eyes," he intoned. "Your eyes are twin sapphires crowned by a halo of spun gold."

Cecy made gagging noises.

He grinned and continued. "Your lips are ruby cushions upon which pearls of wisdom glimmer . . ."

She hooted.

"Your ears—they are delicate creamy shells—"

"Stop!"

"—the perfect size for a man to grip—"

"Oh!"

"And the top of your head is firm and flat enough to balance a good martini—"

Smack. But she was laughing so hard, it was difficult to aim. "Buchanan, you asshole!"

He widened his eyes. "What? You're every man's dream."

"Be serious."

"Okay. You're so lovely that you can't sleep in my office any longer. The other tenants will complain of power surges stemming from your radiance."

"Oh, please."

"That's why I'm giving you a room in my house—just until you get back on your feet again."

Cecy sobered. "I'd much rather stay in the office."

"I'm sorry, but I'm just not comfortable with that any longer. I've told you why."

"Well, I don't feel comfortable staying in your house. I feel like a mooch."

"What's the difference between sleeping in my office and sleeping in my house?"

"You're not in the office at night."

"So this is a personal insult to me."

"No; don't take it that way. I'd just rather be a vagrant than a mooch."

"You are the damnedest woman."

"Now *that* I'll take as a compliment."

Cecy clutched Barney to her breast with one hand, gripped a canvas holdall with the other, and stared around the entrance hall in awe. Striped silk in pale cherry and sage adorned the walls above intricate carved wainscoting. A graceful staircase poured in a sculptured wave from the second story. Rich mahogany floors gleamed under a tasteful chandelier. Nothing in the foyer was overwhelming or grandiose, yet it was stunning in its beauty and warmth.

She hadn't known quite what to expect from Grandmother Chastain's Paces Ferry house. The address had intimidated her, and the governor's mansion down the road had added to her tension. The last thing she'd anticipated was a feeling of welcome.

Chas had hung a painting of his grandparents near the door, and she discerned some of the same qualities she'd seen in the photograph. Though they were formally posed, Grandmother's expression betrayed a hint of mischief and humor. Her husband looked . . . patient.

Barney began to wriggle. She knew he wanted to go exploring, but she needed to confine him in her quarters with a litter box for a while, so that he'd get used to the new living situation without defiling it. Chas would never allow them to stay if Barney didn't behave himself.

As Cecy waited for Chas to bring in another load of his things and show her to her room, she glanced up at the portrait once more. The lovely old lady seemed to wink at her. She must have imagined it.

She held open the door for her landlord as his tall, muscular frame approached, holding a heavy, burled-walnut chest as if it weighed nothing. She followed him into the formal dining room, where he set it down. There were windows everywhere, and the multitude of small glass panes played with the light, reflecting it, bouncing it, catching a shimmer here and a sparkle there. The place was suffused with light, and Cecy felt it wash over her like a new dawn.

Chas stood with his hands resting casually on his hips, his expression inscrutable. She thought she saw a hint of both joy and regret, and wondered about his memories of this house. At any rate, she'd been wrong about the lawn jockey and the Terminix man, not to mention the geometrically pruned bushes. The back gardens were an overgrown mess, though the beds in front were carefully tended for the neighbors.

He beckoned her to follow him, and they ascended the staircase. Cecy ran her hand along the rich, smooth, polished wood of the banister as they went up, and tried not to stare at his buns. To divert her attention, she contemplated how much fun it would be to slide down the banister. She'd always wanted to do that, but she'd never lived in a house in which the darn thing wasn't attached to the wall.

"Did you grow up here, Chas?"

He shook his head. "No, but I visited often. My grandparents were wonderful—especially Grandmother. She led my grandfather a merry chase."

"What do you mean by that?"

"Grand was . . . the life of an ongoing party. She never took anything very seriously." He chuckled. "She was impulsive and impatient, and had an absolutely filthy sense of humor in an age when women were supposed to faint dead away if they heard a curse." Chas shook his head.

"She showed up at her coming-out ball in a pair of purple harem pants and a bolero jacket. That was the end of her entrée into polite society."

Cecy giggled.

"By all accounts, my great-grandmother had a fit of the vapors, marched her out by the ear, and despaired of ever finding a suitable husband for her after that. But Grandfather had loved her since they were children, and he married her in spite of her wild streak. Or because of it."

"What's your favorite memory of her?"

Chas ruminated, a sweet smile tugging the corner of his sexy mouth. He ushered her into a large, airy bedroom with an adjoining sitting room and bath. Cecy looked around, delighted with the arched floor-to-ceiling windows and the filmy blue draperies, and deposited the wriggling Barney into the bathroom, shutting the door on him.

A mahogany sleigh bed dominated one end of the room, and Chas had covered it haphazardly with some mismatched sheets, an old quilt, and a couple of pillows without cases. It was an ensemble obviously thrown together by a bachelor without a clue, but it tugged at her heart that he'd even bothered. The thought of him puttering around, trying to make her feel the least bit welcome, made her swallow hard. She knew he didn't really want her there.

He propped himself against the wall. "My favorite memory of Grand," he began slowly, "goes all the way back to a Christmas when I was ten. She'd broken her foot somehow, and she terrorized the whole household from a wheelchair. Called my father Young Stiff-Rump and forced him to play croquet with her on the front lawn. Embarrassed the hell out of my mother by telling off-color jokes in front of her Garden Club friends. Kept tossing the dog's toys into the ornamental pond and laughing when he dived in to retrieve them. Then she wrapped him in the good bath sheets and brought him inside so he wouldn't catch his death of cold. That dog lay on a pile of velvet cushions in front of the fire all night, farting up a storm from the leftover Yorkshire pudding she fed him."

Cecy burst into laughter.

"My grandfather hid behind his paper and would occasionally fan the bad air away with the paper and poke at the logs, hoping the dog would back off when they sparked. No such luck.

"That Christmas, Grand decided that she was going to cook us a dinner from her wheelchair that we'd never forget. She accomplished her goal, but not exactly the way she had in mind. She'd had a glass or so of champagne, I think, and she went zooming in, wearing red Chinese silk pajamas, to the housekeeper's domain. We heard a lot of squabbling—I'm not sure exactly what was said—but next thing we knew, Hildy slammed out of the house in her apron, the turkey giblets in one hand and an egg beater in the other.

"Grand burned a goose, oversalted the brussels sprouts, collapsed the soufflé, and forgot to bake the rolls. We had oatmeal for dinner."

Chas's eyes brimmed over with laughter.

"What happened to Hildy?" Cecy wanted to know.

"Grand had to give her a whole pound of French truffles and a fur stole to get her back."

"You're kidding."

He shook his head. "She was worth it. An extraordinary cook. She'd been with Grand forever, too. Long enough that she wouldn't take any guff."

Cecy went to the huge window, parted the filmy drapes, and looked outside instead of at Chas. Their backgrounds were so different. He spoke casually about a housekeeper, and croquet on the front lawn. His grandmother's coming-out party.

She knew someone who'd come out—of the closet. She'd never played croquet in her life. And to her, paid help meant the fifty-cent-per-week allowance she'd gotten for washing the dishes in Mama Sue's home.

She resolved to clean up the tangled jungle of weeds in the back while she was here. It was a way to pay back Chas for his forced hospitality.

She heard his footsteps recede to the door behind her.

"I'm going to go and get another load," he said.

She turned. "Okay. I'll be down in a minute." She walked to the bed, sat down, and ran her hands over the faded quilt. It looked handmade, and Cecy wondered if Grand had made it.

She examined one patchwork square and found that it portrayed two poodles in the act of love. She giggled. Another square showcased kissing monkeys. She found belly-dancing elephants, singing moose, and pigs playing hopscotch. Grand had definitely made this quilt. Sleeping under it would be almost like meeting her.

At the end of the hot June day, Cecy stepped into her private shower, a luxury she'd desperately missed. She left the tap on cold and let the rivulets of water rinse away all the sweat and grime of helping Chas move. She lathered up with deodorant soap twice, shivering in delight at being frozen instead of wilted and sweaty. This sure beat sponging off in the sink at Chas's office.

Once every hair on her body was standing up in protest and she was covered in goose bumps, she turned off the tap and toweled dry. She stepped into blue short pajamas and slipped between the sheets of her bed. God, it felt good. She let her tired limbs sink into the mattress.

Cecy turned her nose into the pillowcase and rooted for comfort. Its fresh, laundered scent made her think of Mama Sue and the bunk beds she and Brock had shared in her home. She wondered how Mama Sue was doing these days. Busy with a new crop of foster children, she was sure, though her age would be making things more difficult. She hadn't seen her since Brock's funeral. It had been sweet of Mama Sue to come.

Cecy and Brock had always understood, growing up, that though Mama Sue was loving, they were only two of many children. Cecy was ashamed to admit that she'd sometimes dreamed that all the others would disappear so that she and her brother would be special and have her all to themselves, like a real mother. At least her teachers had paid lots of attention to her, though, since she'd made good grades.

She yawned and shifted her toes under Barney's weight. He made a disgruntled noise, got up and circled, then settled his bulk evenly over her feet again. Cecy let him stay there. Liking his warmth, she'd learned to sleep without moving much.

Her thoughts drifted to Chas, who'd sweated his guts out all day. Surely if he had the money to purchase this enormous house on one of the most prestigious streets in Atlanta, he could have hired movers? It didn't make much sense to her, but she supposed that accountants must always be pinching their pennies. She hadn't minded, because she'd gotten to watch his deliciously bare, tan torso ripple with muscle while they'd lugged everything in. Maybe saving money wasn't so bad after all, if it encouraged nudity, provided exercise, and burned calories.

Cecy ran her hands over the patches in Grand's quilt, smiling sleepily in the dark, and let her eyes drift closed again. She was dimly conscious of tumbling backwards into the dark tunnel of oblivion.

She dreamed that Grand, wearing her purple harem pants, took her hand and led her to the top of the smooth mahogany banister. Together they slid down like children, flailing their arms and legs. They jumped off at the bottom, and in typical dream fashion it made sense that they landed in the middle of the back garden. This garden wasn't a tangle of weeds, however—it was a lovely riot of color contained by old stone walls and a flagstone path that meandered through trees and around bushes. The path circled around a small pond and led to a tiny gazebo. The garden was dotted with amusing stone statuary. Gargoyles squatted here and there, with pointed ears, evil grins, and spread wings.

Grand sat her down in the gazebo, propped her bare feet up on a railing, and looked at her seriously. "I'm relying on you, Cecy dear, not to let Chas turn into Young Stiff-Rump. His father is the most stolid man, and my daughter always paid far too much heed to convention."

Cecy thought of Chas naked, and didn't find

him stolid at all. But she couldn't say such a thing to his grandmother!

Grand seemed to understand anyway. "Not in the bedroom." She waved her hand dismissively.

Cecy's cheeks caught fire.

"I mean on a daily basis. The boy used to have a sense of fun and adventure, before Stiff-Rump began to feed him algebraic formulas along with his Cheerios. Then he married the Bride by Mattel, soul not included."

"I'm not the person—"

"Yes, you are. You're here, aren't you? Now run along dear, and remember what I said. You do have a purpose in life, even if you haven't come across it yet. You're here for a reason." Grand wiggled her fingers at her, and began to fade before Cecy's eyes.

"But wait—"

Grand had dissolved, leaving only the filmy harem pants, which still behaved as if they had legs in them. They swung the invisible legs down to the floor, then they too vanished.

Cecy blinked, and opened her eyes to darkness and the sound of Barney purring on the end of the bed. The dream had been so real. She could have sworn she'd been able to smell the rich earth of the garden, feel a light breeze on her face, and see the delicate textures of flower petals and leaves. Grand hadn't seemed like a vision, she'd seemed like a person.

As she shifted under the covers, she heard a faint trill of laughter. Barney jerked his head and pricked up his ears, as if he heard it, too. Then he resumed purring and walked up the length of her body for a chin and head scratch.

The rest of the night passed peacefully, dawning into a beautiful Saturday morning. But Cecy couldn't get the dream out of her head. It was hooked on instant replay.

She and Barney padded downstairs and into the kitchen, where Chas, bless him, had started a pot of coffee. He sat at the butcher-block island reading the *Journal-Constitution*, already showered and dressed. Clean blue jeans molded to his thighs, a knit shirt hugged his chest, and he wore the cowboy boots she'd tripped over the day they met. His short hair was still damp from the shower, and he'd shaved.

Cecy felt like a slacker in her short robe, bare feet, and uncombed hair. Even Barney squinted suspiciously at Chas.

"Good morning," she said. "It is Saturday, isn't it?"

"Morning." He gave her a quick once-over and shifted on his stool. "Yes, it's Saturday."

She looked at the clock he'd hung the day before. "Is that the right time? Seven-fifteen?"

He nodded.

She stared at him.

"I'm going in to the office today. Lots of work to do."

"Oh. Don't you want to relax, after killing yourself all of yesterday?"

"No."

His answer was simple and unsatisfying— just like a man. Ah, well. She looked around at the precisely placed furniture and the neat stacks of boxes. Perhaps Grand was right about Chas, and he was in danger of becoming Young Stiff-Rump, Jr.

"Did you sleep well? Would you like some coffee?" He was playing the polite host.

"Yes, thank you, and yes, please." She sounded equally stilted. "I'll get it." She saw that he didn't have any and advanced on the coffeepot. She poured his first, then got herself a mug. Why was this all so awkward? They'd been naked and sexually intimate. She'd been bathing and bandaging his head twice a day. She'd gotten him meals. They'd moved into this place together. . . .

Ah. That was it. He didn't want her to get comfortable here. Well, that was the last thing she was going to do. She'd work her fingers off around the house in lieu of rent—and Chas would actually be sorry when she left.

He obviously didn't want to sleep with her again. He'd made that clear days ago, with his, "It's a bad idea in the office" speech. Well, men were pigs, and they were known to move on to other items on the menu after an initial taste test. So she wasn't special. So what—she'd been that route before. All her life.

Cecy drank her coffee in silence and fed Barney. Chas finished the sports section, wiggled three fingers at her, and left. She wiggled her fingers back at him with a fake smile and blew a raspberry at the closing door. *Have a nice day, Young Stiff-Rump.*

12

Chas glared at his computer screen. Instead of seeing the spreadsheet, however, he saw Cecy's legs. Long and shapely, they taunted him. He'd memorized every lovely curve, every muscle and nuance of those gamine gams. He wanted to devour them, like Henry VIII with a turkey drumstick.

He hit the up arrow on his screen, hoping that he could start from the top again. Yeah, he could. At the top of those legs had shimmered the hem of a brief, silky robe. And under the fabric, she'd worn no panties. He could tell when she turned and bent into the refrigerator to retrieve the milk for her coffee. The blue silk had pulled—agonizingly—up to expose the creamy globes of her bottom, and Chas had almost had a heart attack and died right then and there. Now that was dignity: he'd have fallen facefirst onto the sports page and entered rigor mortis with a hard-on.

He'd gotten up so early and come to work because he'd been in danger of going hump in the night. She'd been right around the corner from his bedroom, spread out like a banquet on the old sleigh bed. But he'd sworn off sex with her. He was not going to take advantage of her when she needed shelter—she'd had a hard enough life.

Unfortunately, he remembered her breasts in minute detail, too. Chas ran his tongue around his lips as he mentally caressed the womanly curves. Her breasts were so sensitive. The tiniest flick with his tongue sent her nipples burgeoning, and she made throaty little sounds that drove him crazy.

He wouldn't even allow himself to think of the passion and sweetness at her core. *Stop it, Buchanan! Spreadsheet, not spread legs.*

He heard himself lecturing to her a few days back, in a voice that gave pomposity a new meaning. "Sex in the office is unconscionable." Had he really said that? Well, what about sex in the living room? The sunroom? The dining room, bathroom, pantry, foyer and toolshed? Hell, why not every hallway, the patio, and the front steps, too? The roof?

He wanted her, and he wanted her now. Any

and every which way. He sprang from his desk chair at the thought of her lips closing around him. How could she torture him when she wasn't even present? It had been bad enough at breakfast, when he'd sounded like a butler in starched Jockey shorts. "Did you sleep well?" *While I was thinking about having my way with you a hundred times?* "Would you like some coffee?" *I'll be your slave if you'll just let me see you naked again.*

She'd looked at him as if he'd just back-handed her across the mouth.

Chas scrubbed his hands over his face. What was a man supposed to do? Cecy had gotten under his skin, and he wanted to get on top of hers.

Numbers, man. Think numbers. Dividends and variables. The market. A ticker tape appeared in his head, running across his eyes. But damn it! There she was.

Like a James Bond vixen, she walked along the ticker tape to 007 theme music, clad in high heels and very little else. She turned her head slyly and sent him a come-hither glance. Then she swung to face him, legs spread. Her arms shot straight out in front of her, and once he'd torn his eyes away from her ripe cleavage, he saw that she held a can of whipped cream.

He needed to get out of there. Tom Barry was always up for a round of golf. Since working wasn't working, he'd go have some fun, damn it. Cecy was ruining his day.

He dialed Barry's number. "Hey, man, it's Buchanan."

"Well, if it ain't Mr. Chas-tity himself."

"You're such a barrel of laughs. I'm going to get a tee time. You interested?"

"Always. Get back to me within the hour."

"Will do."

Cecy unpacked a few of her boxes and put most of her clothes away in the old dresser in a corner of her new bedroom. That done, she spread clean litter in a pan for Barney and installed his feline privy in the cabinet under the bathroom sink, where it would be out of the way but still accessible.

Her cat strolled to one of the full-length windows and sprawled on the hardwood floor in front of it to take in the view. Cecy suspected that he was counting the birds in his new kingdom. His lips stretched almost to his ears, indicating his satisfaction with the numbers.

She left him to it, and threw on some old jeans and a T-shirt, suitable attire for a full-fledged garden attack. Then she made her way down the stairs and out the back door, where she stood on the old brick patio, hands on her hips. Where to start?

Old branches and rotten leaves covered most of the areas not overgrown by weeds. She walked to the detached four-car garage and found, among the moving cartons, a couple of garbage cans, work gloves, a rake, and a hoe.

Cecy pulled a rubber band from her pocket and scraped her hair into it before donning the oversize cotton gloves. Then she hauled her equipment to the yard and dived in. She piled sticks and branches in a heap on the edge of the brick patio and began systematically to fill the cans with leaves and weeds.

The morning got steadily warmer as she worked, and perspiration trickled down her face and soaked her shirt. The humidity was a tangible thing, thick and cloying in her throat and nostrils, but the good, clean scents of the garden made up for it.

She cleared enough debris to uncover what was left of a flagstone path—just like the one she'd seen in the dream. It was so eerie that she stopped for a moment and stared around her.

No, silly, there's no gazebo. You're imagining things. But the low stone walls were there, once she cleared farther back into the garden. The skin on Cecy's neck prickled, despite the heat. She half expected Grand to swing out from the trees on a vine, purple harem pants and all.

She wiped her face with the back of a glove and slicked loose strands of hair off her forehead with her damp wrist. *You do have a purpose in life, even if you haven't come across it, yet. You're here for a reason ...* Not for the first time, Cecy wondered exactly why she'd been put on the earth. Why was she alive, and Brock dead? Why hadn't their mother been stable enough to keep them? Why did God give children to women who were unfit to be mothers, while so many who longed to give birth were denied them?

The brief snatches of Sunday school she'd attended had taught that the Heavenly Father knew best. She found this unsatisfying in the extreme. If the Heavenly Father knew best, he should at least be required to share the reasoning behind his decisions. The Christian public had a right to know.

But God didn't seem to operate in a democracy or be bound by constitutional amendments, and why was that? Cecy raked leaves and pulled weeds ferociously. Each leaf was an unanswered question, each weed a prickle of frustration. How could she trust in God when she didn't understand what made God tick?

Why (*yank*) had he taken Brock away from her, when Brock was her only security, the only person in the world who made her feel special and connected, worthwhile and loved?

God wasn't going to pay her bills, or get her back on her feet. She had to do it herself. Cecy heaved another armload of uprooted weeds into one of the garbage cans, and leaned over it to mash them down.

" 'Self-Reliance,' " she muttered. She'd read the essay in high school, and still remembered it. Ralph Waldo Emerson. Or was it Thoreau? Cecy decided that every Southern woman should read it, especially girls with big diamond rings and no career aspirations.

If God was there to guide her, then he truly

did work in mysterious ways, as Mama Sue had often reminded her. She remembered a long-ago conversation with her foster mother. Mama Sue had been kneading dough on the old cutting board in her blue kitchen.

"Why doesn't God have a face?" Cecy had asked.

Squeeze, roll, thunk. "God has many faces, sweetie."

"Why can't he just pick one?"

"You ask too many questions."

"If you answered them, I wouldn't ask any more."

Sigh. "There's little questions, and then there's big questions." Mama Sue squished the dough down with her hands and then took a rolling pin to it, flattening it into a ragged-edged disc. "We all answer the big ones in our own way," she said. "That's the hardest lesson to learn, especially because we often don't realize we're learning it."

"You always talk in riddles," Cecy complained.

Mama Sue looked over at her, and her eyes held such understanding, that Cecy'd wanted to cry. She turned back to her dough and cut it into a neat circle around the edge of an overturned pie plate.

"Can I ask one more question?"

"Sure," said Mama Sue.

"Have you met God?"

Mama Sue hesitated. "Yes, I've met God. But,

honey, it's not like you sit down for a sandwich and a cola with God. I don't know how to explain it to you."

"Why don't I know God is there?" Cecy asked. "Lots of other people seem to know it."

"You know," Mama Sue said. "Somewhere deep inside, you know."

An hour later, her blueberry pie had come out of the oven, golden-crusted, steaming, and fragrant. Cecy had stared at it longingly; she still felt half-baked.

At the thought of food, Cecy stripped off her gloves and put a hand to her forehead. She'd been working in the heat far too long, and hadn't eaten anything. She also needed water.

As she walked toward the house, a soft voice said, "Thank you for clearing my garden." She whirled at the sound.

Nobody, absolutely no one, was around. Cecy felt an odd tingle go down her spine. She'd imagined the voice. She knew it.

She made her way to the faucet, turned it on, and held the hose over her head. The cold water washed away dirt and grime, sweat and uncertainty. It felt marvelous. She could feel the water, taste it in her mouth, smell the faint rusty undertones. She wasn't a lunatic—but she probably *did* have a touch of heatstroke. She turned off the hose and hauled the cans of weeds and leaves back toward the garage. Something, however, made her turn around again and look back toward the garden. "You're welcome," she whispered.

Chas walked the back nine with Tom Barry, who flirted with the beer girl and insisted on buying a round.

"Tom, it's too hot out here to drink alcohol."

"Would you yank the putter out of your ass?" He handed Chas a long-neck and turned back to the girl. "Thank you, darlin'. Keep the change." He patted her arm, gave her nineteen-year-old thighs an appreciative once-over, and turned back to the game.

"I'm getting tired of all these comments about how uptight I am."

"Tired enough to do something about it? You haven't been the same since the divorce, and that was five years ago, man."

Chas popped the top on the beer and stared down at it for a moment. Then he drank deeply. It was cold and foamy going down, and tasted damn good. He'd eat his towel before admitting that to Tom, though. "The usual carbonated piss."

Barry grunted. "Yeah? Well, you sure took a good long swallow." He lined up his shot, and swung through hard and fast.

Chas grinned as the ball zipped along the ground. "Burning some worms today, aren't we?"

His friend flipped him off. "So about the other

day—the closing. I was just razzin' you. Didn't mean to get into any sensitive territory."

Chas shrugged, ignoring the unspoken questions. He took his shot. "Not a problem."

"So who is she?"

Tom just had to be a pain in the ass, didn't he? "Her name is Cecily Scatterton."

"And?"

"And she's not for hire, as you seem to think. At least not that way. She's doing some work for me."

"What kind of work involves nudity?"

"Believe it or not, she'd just taken a bath in my sink."

"Say what?"

"I wasn't even there—I was at the hospital, enjoying an MRI. She'd taken up residence in my office, and whacked me over the head one night when she thought I was a burglar."

"You were letting this chick live in your office?"

"She didn't exactly ask my permission. That's not Cecy's style."

Barry absorbed all of this, and shook his head. "Where'd you meet her?"

"She went flying over my boots in the emergency center one day. It was fitting, really. She is a walking emergency. She couldn't pay her bill, so I agreed to pay it for her if she'd fill in while Jamie was on vacation. Next thing I know she's in my office dressed to kill, but starving and homeless."

"So . . . is she still living in the office?"

"Not exactly," Chas muttered. He lined up his own shot and swung through.

Barry chuckled as the ball lodged somewhere in a thicket of trees. "I may be decapitating worms, but you're huntin' squirrel." They walked on. "What d'you mean, 'not exactly'? She's not—you're not! Tell me she ain't livin' on Paces Ferry with you."

Chas ran a finger around his collar and tilted his head to crack his neck.

Barry whistled. "Son of a bitch. Are you crazy? Next she'll be suing your ass for palimony."

"It's only until she earns enough money to get back on her feet," Chas snapped. "And she's not like that."

Tom scratched at his jaw. "Now where have I heard that phrase before?" He adopted a false hearty tone. "Gee, Chas, Maria sure seems aw-fully eager for you to plunk down the dough for the Cherokee Town and Country Club." His voice changed to mimic a chump's. 'No, no, Tom—she's not like that.' "

Chas shot *him* the bird this time. "So Maria was a social-climbing bitch. That doesn't make Cecy one. She's like a kid. She's had it really rough, and I'm giving her a small break. I'm sure as hell not going to marry her—so get off my back."

"All right. Just be careful."

Chas sucked in a breath. "Look, Tom—you tell me to loosen up in one sentence and to tense up in the next. Make up your mind." He tossed back another swallow of beer.

Barry shook his head. "I just don't want to see you get used again. You've worked too damn hard for that house."

"Point taken. Now, I'm going to go get my ball out of the Black Forest."

"Good thing you suck as bad as I do, today. Otherwise, this would be embarrassing."

Chas pulled his rental car into the big garage and got out. He saw the trash cans piled high with yard rubbish, and his gaze widened as he looked at the backyard. Good Christ—two-thirds of the weeds were gone, and he couldn't see a single dead leaf. The stone pathways were visible again. Had Cecy done this? No, the sheer amount of physical labor involved was too great for one woman.

It was starting to look as it had in Grand's day, though the gazebo had obviously been torn down at some point, and the ornamental pond seemed to have been filled in. He remembered the games of horseshoe he and his brother had played, sometimes with Grand. Grandfather had a bad back, so he hadn't joined in.

They'd played Whiffle ball and badminton, too. As the older brother, he'd always trounced Hal, but Grand had given him a run for his money.

He stood back and looked at the old house. She was still a beauty, and had been well maintained by the previous owners. He wanted to restore the interior colors, and the floors would have to be sanded and refinished. He also wanted to replant and refurbish the back garden. He gazed around it again. He couldn't quite believe that Cecy had done this. It was so at odds with her fluffy, blow-dried appearance. But if not Cecy, then who? He headed for the house.

He found her sprawled on a towel near an air-conditioning vent in the formal living room, where the only TV in the house was set up. An old spaghetti jar full of ice water sat next to her, and a black-and-white movie played on the classics channel. She was oblivious to it—fast asleep.

Her hair drooped around her smudged little face, and dried mud and leaves decorated her T-shirt. Her long legs were clad in filthy jeans. She sported several scratches and bug bites on her arms. Her slightly parted lips were dry. Not a trace of makeup adorned her face, and Chas found her more beautiful than he'd ever seen her.

She stirred and rubbed one grimy hand over her nose, then turned her head to find a more comfortable position. He saw that she'd used an old pair of his cotton work gloves as a pillow, and his mouth twisted. Cecy had indeed been the surprise gardener. She'd done all that work by herself, in the hot sun, and had worn herself out.

If she continued sleeping in that position, she'd wake with a sore back and cramped neck. Chas knelt beside her and worked one arm under her knees, the other under her shoulders. He picked her up without much effort, then started up the staircase to her bedroom.

She curled into him with a murmur. Chas looked down at her golden head and swallowed. Had she exhausted herself like this out of a sense of obligation to him? He hoped not.

He laid her down on top of the quilt Grand had made him as a child and smoothed the stray hairs out of her face. He touched a finger to her lips—they were so dry. He looked around until he saw some salve on the dresser top, which he retrieved and opened. Gently he rubbed some of the balm across her parted lips, and when her tongue licked them slowly, felt a tightening in his groin. He cursed himself for a pervert and left the room.

Lusting after her was going to do neither of them any good. He should be helping her find a way out of debt, not helping her get naked. What was wrong with him? He'd seen bodies as good as hers before; he'd dated women as pretty. So what was this obsession with Cecily Scatterton?

Maria had been better-looking in the classic sense, but he'd tired of sex with her soon after their wedding. She was so thin it had been like humping a wishbone. She'd let out a tiny sigh anytime he made a grab for her, and had a habit of asking for things right as he drove home the last stroke. It was a touch transparent and demoralizing.

Chas made his way down the stairs and into the kitchen, where he skulked about looking for food. Since they'd just moved in the day before, his choices were limited to canned soup or canned tuna. He wrinkled his nose, then scooped his keys off the tiled counter and headed out to EatZi's, which served the most delicious gourmet takeout he could think of.

Cecy dreamed she was a potato, lying under the rich earth of the garden. She could feel the dirt all over her skin, and she enjoyed the serene darkness. She had no arms or legs, no debts to pay, and no disturbing thoughts about a lean, broad-shouldered man with a great ass and a reluctantly soft heart.

Yes, it was good to be a tuber, except that it was a tiny bit boring, and she was hungry. Her stomach growled, and she smelled the aroma of chicken parmesan. How was that, when tubers didn't have stomachs, or noses? Or lips . . . yet somehow a morsel of steaming, tomato-sauce-and-cheese-covered chicken had gotten into her mouth. She savored the different flavors—basil, a hint of lemon, a bouillon base to the sauce, perhaps?

Cecy opened her eyes to low lamplight and Chas, sitting beside her on the bed. His dark hair gleamed where the light touched it, and his eyes reflected affectionate amusement. His long, lean fingers wrapped around the fork he waved in front of her mouth.

"Do we have to play choo-choo or airplane? Or are you going to be a good girl and eat?"

She opened her mouth obediently, watching the muscles in his forearm tauten under the tan skin and light sprinkling of hair. He was so close she could smell him. Soap and faint, musky aftershave and man. The scent of the laundry detergent in his shirt. He was so clean. She took the bite of food, and chewed self-consciously.

She was filthy. She remembered hauling herself inside, getting the ice water, and sinking to the floor in front of the air-conditioning. She had no idea how she'd come to be on top of the quilt in her disgusting state. She was one tuber that needed a good scrubbing.

Chas fed her another bite, and said, in that deep voice of his, "I've run a warm bath for you. I figured after all the work you did, you might like one when you woke up."

Cecy swallowed. He was feeding her like a baby and had run a bath for her. A hot mistiness pricked at the back of her eyes.

When the next bite came at her, she grasped the fork. "You don't have to do that. I can eat by myself."

His fingers brushed hers as he relinquished it. "Okay. So what possessed you to clear the entire garden?"

"I didn't do the whole thing. I pooped out."

"Damn near. That was a job for a team of landscapers."

She shrugged. "I had the time. It looked so forlorn."

"My grandmother would have been appalled at the state it was in. She'd thank you."

Cecy resisted saying that Grand *had* thanked her. She didn't think he'd understand.

"Anyway, I'm overwhelmed. You didn't have to do it—you don't owe me anything."

"I just wanted to, okay?"

"Okay. I brought you a salt tablet. I don't want you to get sick."

"I'm a pretty healthy beastie."

"Yeah—I've seen you up close and personal." He ran a finger down her arm and looked into her eyes, leaning forward.

She thought for a moment that he'd kiss her, and held her breath in anticipation. But to her disappointment, he pulled back. He transferred the takeout container from his lap to hers, and she felt the warmth spread across her belly.

Chas got up and swiped his hand over his hair. "Well. You know where the towels are."

"Yeah."

He walked to the door.

"Chas?"

"Hmmm?"

"Thank you," she whispered.

He nodded.

As she ate, she heard his heavy tread moving down the stairs, and the television being tuned to a sports channel. Barney came out from under the bed and sniffed the appetizing aromas. She gave him a couple of tidbits, using the clear plastic lid as his plate.

When they were done, she swung her legs off the bed and walked to the bathroom, peeling off clothes as she went. The water temperature was perfect—not too warm, not too cold. She sank into the bath gratefully, and then noticed the brand-new bottles of scented bath gel and lotion Chas had set on the side of the tub. She unscrewed the top of the gel, inhaled the wonderful fragrance, and burst into tears. No one had ever bought such things for her.

13

Chas shifted on the sofa downstairs and adjusted himself for the third time. Watch the
game, he told himself. The Yankees had been
pounding the bejesus out of the Red Sox, until
this, the last inning. Now the Red Sox, backs to
the wall, were evening the score.

He should have been riveted, but he'd never
wanted so badly to be forty gallons of bathwater. By now, the steaming water was enveloping
Cecy's soft skin. From those plump little plum-
painted toes to the silky hollows in back of her
knees, on up those lovely firm thighs . . .

Chas had been the proud owner of a submarine bath toy as a boy. Now he imagined being

inside it, diving for the bottom of Cecy's tub, and—well, collecting intelligence.

His periscope extended itself, and he took hold of it. In his mind he toured every inch of Cecy's body from a fabulous new perspective. Her glorious calves swelled toward the windows of his sub, and he took stock of the small intriguing mole on the right one. A couple of silky blond hairs she'd missed with her razor swayed in the water and hypnotized him.

He passed under her calves with reluctance, but brightened at the expanse of thigh that awaited him. Long, creamy highways to heaven, they were. A dimple here and there proved only that she was all beguiling flesh, and not cold plastic Barbie Doll. He would love to swirl his tongue into those dimples.

His submarine chugged on, and he extended the periscope to peer up and over the water. *Caramba!* Cecy's breasts were phenomenal from this angle. In proportion to him they were gigantic, and they swelled in tantalizing curves far above him. He wanted desperately to rappel up her soft belly and straddle one of those cherry nipples, dangling his legs down the slope.

The air in his submarine was getting uncomfortably close. He took a deep breath and refocused under the water. Hot damn—he was approaching the Arc de Triomphe, the portal to Cecy's wild sweetness. It was shy, nesting behind a tangle of golden brown, and guarded by two sets of sensual plump lips.

Chas pressed all ten fingers to the window of his yellow submarine, and then his nose. He couldn't go outside the glass without drowning, but a gasping, waterlogged death might be worth it if he could part the portals of carnal heaven and ease his way inside.

He raged within the confined sub, desperate to escape and play with the nub that teased him from between the folds of her most intimate crevice. Coy, it pouted at him, begging to be charmed out of the sulks and filled with longing and joy.

He wanted to see Cecy arch under the water, legs trembling, and jerk with spasms of pleasure. He wanted to taste her signature peach flavor mingled with the flowered bath oil, hear the little sounds of her flesh rubbing against the porcelain of the tub. He wanted to look up through the water and see her eyes fly wide, then go blind. She was a darling.

Warmth spread through his abdomen, tingling down to his balls. Chas planted himself firmly at her entrance and drove home between her thighs. God, she felt good. Something about Cecy pulled at him, hot and wet and primal. He groaned and pulsed within her, fast and furious, while she urged him on in pants and whimpers. Pressure coiled tight within him, and suddenly released.

Chas shouted out loud, and he knew it had nothing to do with the platoon of sweaty guys on the television screen. He opened his eyes cautiously. Players hurtled into one another, chasing the ball like so many sperm after an egg.

He was disgusted to find that at age thirty-five, he still needed to jerk off.

What was it about the woman upstairs in his grandmother's tub? She was threatening his sanity, his way of life. He'd just spent a fortune on gourmet takeout food and bath scents, both unnecessary luxuries. He was regressing to age thirteen, relieving his fantasies on the couch. And he was getting hard again, damn it all! He could hear her walking upstairs, and she was undoubtedly naked. Chas groaned.

The only way to ease his pain was to get Cecy financially stable and out of his house. Then he wouldn't be able to smell her perfume, watch the sexy way her hair fell into her eyes, and know what she tasted like.

That meant sitting down with her this very night and talking turkey. Just how much debt was she in? What would it take to get her out of it? Full-time employment and no rent should help quite a lot, but he had a bad feeling about those credit cards of hers.

Half an hour later, as Chas faced Cecy across the kitchen table, he knew his hunch was correct. She sat and chewed on that delectable bottom lip of hers, her forehead wrinkled in worry and her damp hair tucked behind her ears.

"A thirty-thousand-dollar bill?" He asked her,

incredulous. "Why wasn't this covered by your brother's health insurance?"

"I don't know."

"And you paid it anyway?"

She nodded. "The Accounts Payable people were really nasty. They said I owed the money, and that was that. I had twenty-nine thousand left from the insurance, and I sold some things to raise the other part. The bill was thirty thousand, two hundred and forty-seven dollars and fifty-nine cents." Her face was pale, her eyes solemn.

He wasn't surprised that she had no problem recalling the exact figure of the bill even months later. It was ugly. Chas ran his hands through his hair. "And that left you with nothing to live on but credit."

"That's right. I had shopped some when I was depressed, thinking I had the money to pay off the cards. When the hospital bill came, I didn't know what to do. But I wasn't going to let Brock's bill sit out there. I wanted his name cleared."

"Did you look at the statement carefully, to make sure it was correct?"

"I added all the numbers, and that was the correct total."

"Are you sure you weren't overcharged for any procedures?"

"I'm not sure of anything. I'm not a nurse—I don't know what these things cost."

"If you still have a copy of that bill, I'd like to take a look at it."

"I—well, I burned it when I was having a bad day."

Chas pinched the bridge of his nose between thumb and forefinger. The woman didn't even keep records. God almighty. "Okay. What I suggest you do is request a copy from the hospital. Then I also need a copy of your brother's insurance policy. Do you have that?"

"Um. I think so. It might be in one of the boxes I kept of his things."

"Good. Now how much did you say you owed on your cards?"

When she told him, the hairs on the back of his neck rose. He put down his pen and stared at her. "I see. You're definitely going to need a debt-consolidation loan."

And just who was going to give her an employer reference for that? Chas warred bitterly with his emotions. He couldn't possibly give her such a reference without being sure she would stay long-term in the job. And if she stayed long-term, he was going to be sexually tortured long-term, whether he got her out of his house within a couple months or not.

You got yourself into this, buddy. Now see it through.

"I've heard of those. Is that a better way to handle it?"

"Yeah. Instead of paying between eighteen and twenty-two percent interest on your charge cards, and paying it multiple times to different companies, you'll be paying more like twelve to fifteen percent interest on one payment, depending on what I can find for you. I'll make some calls."

Cecy stared down at the scarred old wooden table and fingered a curving mark. He watched her lashes blink rapidly. "Thanks," she said. "Why are you doing all this for me?"

It was a question he couldn't answer. He knew that the official reason was because he wanted her out of his life.

Another one lurked in the back of his mind, however, and he didn't want to examine it too closely. He gazed down at her curly blond head. The strands weren't all one shade. He saw streaks of golden brown, and butter, and honey. It flashed through his mind that some of them were probably man-made, but her downy pale scalp was just visible beneath the artfully streaked hair, and it flashed vulnerability at him. So did the small ears, which poked through the tousled mass.

Cecy had been cut loose in the world with a pretty raw deal. She might be uneducated about money, but it wasn't as if she'd ever had any to manage before. Perhaps she'd never even had a piggy bank in her foster home.

"I—don't worry about it," he said aloud. "It's what I do for a living."

"This is a wonderful old table," she said, changing the subject.

"That? Oh, yeah. It's been around for a while. Hal and I used to race our Match-Box cars on it. We hollowed out a loaf of Hildy's fresh bread once, to use it as a tunnel. She was furious!"

Cecy laughed. "What did you do with the insides?"

He raised a brow at her. "We made dough pellets and threw them at each other, of course."

"Of course."

He watched her lips curve delightfully. She was dangerous. Though he needed to pinch every penny possible to reduce his whopping mortgage, she made him think about impromptu beach getaways, intimate dinners, and daiquiris. Had she ever been on a really wonderful vacation? Despite her fashionable appearance, had she ever owned a really nice piece of jewelry?

Perish the thought, you bonehead. You provided those things for Maria, and she used them to snare herself a neurosurgeon.

Chas got up and poured himself two fingers of Maker's Mark over ice.

"So who's Hal?" Cecy asked.

Chas shook the ice in his drink. "Hal's my brother," he responded, taking a gulp. The bourbon burned down his throat and restored his equanimity.

"Older or younger?"

"Younger, by two years."

"Where does he live?"

"In New York State, where we grew up. He

works with my father in the family furniture business."

"Are you close?"

"Reasonably so—we just don't see each other a whole lot. I moved to Atlanta when I met my ex-wife. I stayed after we went our separate ways because I'd established a good business here. I didn't want to rebuild everything up North."

"What happened with—" Cecy stopped. "Never mind."

"You want to know what happened with my ex."

She looked uncomfortable. "No, that's okay."

"It's no big deal. She used me to get into the right country club, where she could rub shoulders with the right people. There she met the right neurosurgeon, and she's been right at home with him ever since." He supposed there was an edge to his voice, but the words were already out.

"Do you miss her?"

"Not at all. My ego still has a few scars, however. Not to mention my bank account. Country-club dues aren't cheap, and neither are divorces."

They sat for a moment in silence.

Cecy got herself a glass of ice water. "The day I was trying to sell the clutter—remember?" Her voice was tentative. "That day, you told me your mother had died ten years ago."

Chas looked down into his bourbon again,

and swirled the ice. "Yeah. She developed breast cancer, and it was too advanced by the time they caught it. So, even though I haven't known you for very long, I'm going to give you a piece of advice: Go to your gynecologist for regular checkups, and have mammograms done. It may not be fun, but it might save your life. I get so angry when I realize that my mother would still be alive if not for her squeamishness about going to the damned doctor."

Cecy put her hand on his arm. "I'm sorry."

He stared down at her fingers, which burned through his sleeve hotter than the Maker's Mark had down his throat. "Yeah, well. It happens."

The Maker's Mark swirled through his stomach, and he wished she would put her hands back on him—all over him. He closed his eyes for a moment, annoyed at himself. What was he, a goat? Yep. He was a bourbon-swilling goat with horns and cloven hooves. Why not? He'd been a Lilliputian in a yellow submarine, earlier. Good God—he wasn't sure *who* he was, these days. And it was all Cecily Scatterton's fault.

Cecy rinsed her mouth that night and ran her tongue over the smooth surfaces of the teeth she'd just brushed. Unbidden came the thought of Chas doing the same thing: covering her mouth with his own, exploring every nuance and crevice inside her. She closed her eyes, bracing her hands against the cool porcelain sink, and gave herself to the heat that suffused her body at the thought of his touch.

She was conscious of her breasts brushing the insides of her arms and imagined Chas's hands on her flesh, his eyes going smoky with desire. Tongue caged between his teeth, now, he took the fullness into his hands and brushed her nipples with his thumbs. Streaks of heat flashed through her and pooled at the center of her body.

She imagined his mouth on her breasts, felt the razor burn, rough with promise, against the smooth slopes, and then the lovely warmth and suction of his lips on her nipples, as he gently tugged and teased.

She felt her hips rotating of their own accord, stirring and folding her sensuality into a creamy languor which drenched her in moisture. She pressed her legs together, only to imagine Chas easing them apart, nibbling his way up her inner thighs.

Her knees went weak, and she clutched at his bare chest, only to find to her chagrin that it was square, devoid of muscle, and had faucets. Her eyes flew open, and she gazed at her face, pulled into a foolish grin.

How embarrassing! If she'd kept her eyes closed, what would she have done, ridden the commode? Nice people didn't have thoughts like this. She shifted from foot to foot. Her nipples stood at attention like torpedoes under her nightie, and she made fists to try to squash them. No results.

Chas lay sleeping at the other end of the hall-way and wasn't having any part of this fantasy. He hadn't touched her since she'd moved into his house, which she found both reassuring and disappointing. Was he a gentleman, or had he tired of her already? So maybe sex in the office was a bad idea—but what was wrong with sex at home?

Should she creep into his room, slip under his covers, and have her way with him while he was asleep? The thought of his long, muscular, warm body made her quiver. She wanted to mess up his hair, take his mouth, and rock his world. She wanted to run her hands over the gorgeous landscape of his chest, and trace his jawline with her tongue. She wanted a big ol' handful of his sexy buns, and then . . .

She took a few steps out of the bathroom and down the hall. Excited hormones buzzed through her body in flight formation, ready to pollinate for the queen bee and the big "O."

Then Cecy remembered what had happened the last time she'd surprised Chas in the dark. Crawling into his bed in the middle of the night might not be such a good idea. She bit her lip, turned on her heel, and made her way back to her own room.

Suddenly, everyday objects seemed throb-bingly phallic. Her hair spray. Her travel umbrella. The cordless phone. This was bad, very bad, and it was all Chas Buchanan's fault.

Mama Sue had warned her long ago what would happen if she entertained thoughts like this. Cecy turned out the lights and climbed into bed, arms folded across her chest and knees clamped. She conjured to mind every lipless, wrinkled, righteous politician she could think of. She imagined them running around naked and limp, with knobby knees and concave, skeletal chests. The last of her hormones rolled over in the air with a disheartened "bzzzz" and retreated back to the hive, while she heaved a sigh of relief.

Maybe—just maybe—she'd be able to sleep now.

Cecy walked into the kitchen the next morning to find Chas muttering invectives over the trash can. He was brushing coffee grounds off a section of the newspaper.

"You threw out the coupons from the Sunday edition!" His tone was accusatory.

"Good morning to you, too." She stared as he began to blot the brown stains with a paper towel.

"Good morning." His tone was grudging. "You still threw out the coupons."

"I didn't realize that you saved them."

"Of course I save them! I don't hurl valuable dollars into the trash." He scrubbed as much of the coffee off as he could, and then brought the coupons to the table with the scissors.

Bemused, she saw that he owned a leather coupon organizer, sectioned alphabetically. She stifled a giggle and went to the coffeemaker.

Frau Buchanan flipped through the pages eagerly.

"So, you save a lot of money with those at the grocery store?" Cecy tossed the question over her shoulder as she stirred sugar into her coffee.

Chas, with pride, told her exactly what he saved.

"Really," she murmured. She bent down and opened the under-sink cabinet. "Is that why you have four different types of disinfectant down here?"

He glared at her. "They were on sale, and I went on Triple Coupon Day. I always do."

"You have a lot of pain relievers, too."

He ignored this statement.

"You know, I was looking through one of your basic economics texts last night, when I couldn't sleep." She wouldn't tell him *why* sleep had eluded her.

"Excellent. I'm so glad."

"And I kept coming across this term they used over and over. *Opportunity cost.*"

Chas froze in the middle of clipping.

"How much do you make an hour? Never mind—it's none of my business. But couldn't you be generating more income, during the hour that you clip coupons, than you save by doing it?"

Her question was greeted with icy silence. Cecy grabbed her coffee cup and backed out of the room. Maybe it was time to whiz through the shower about now. Before his scissors ended up poking out of the back of her head.

She was definitely starting to agree with Grand; her host was in serious danger of becoming Young Stiff-Rump, Jr. It was a crime for a man whose face was covered in gloriously sexy razor stubble to hide it behind the coupon section of the newspaper. Those beautiful strong hands could be employed so much better, too. Her breasts tingled, and she frowned at herself. She had to pull herself together.

That evening Cecy stood, hands on her hips, in the garden section of Home Depot. How could anyone know what all these plants were? They were all green, and looked alike. Well, sure, some had pointy leaves, and some round. Some had flowers, others didn't. Delicate spidery varieties clearly stood apart from hulking, woody-stemmed critters.

And they all had different appetites, like people. Some plants avoided sunlight; others drank great quantities of water. It was all so confusing.

She wandered up and down the aisles with no clue what to buy for Grand's back garden. Cecy was approaching an orange-aproned employee to beg for help when she saw that she could offer some assistance herself.

An older couple stood near the employee, the woman tall, spare, and elegant. The man was a bit on the portly side, and wore a camel jacket covered with cat hairs. They were rapidly firing questions at the girl in orange, whose mouth hung open in consternation. The questions were in broken English and French.

"Do you have a machine *d'arroseur? Une petite douche pour des fleurs? Aussi, notre plante*—she is sick. *L'acidité* in the soil—*c'est trop élevé . . .* "

They were looking for a special type of watering wand, and hadn't been able to find it on the shelves. Cecy discerned also that they had a sick indoor plant, and that the acidity in the soil was too high.

She stepped forward and translated for the clerk, and then spoke to the couple in French. They almost fell upon her in gratitude.

"*Votre français, c'est magnifique.* Where did you study?"

"*À l'université,*" Cecy explained. In college. "Where are you from?" she asked in French.

The couple, Mr. and Mrs. LeBlanc, were from the outskirts of Paris. Had she ever been there? Her accent was very good, for an American.

"Thank you," Cecy said. "I went once to Paris, while I was studying French literature. I have a master's in it."

They seemed impressed, but she made light

of it. They asked if she wished to go on with her studies and complete a doctorate.

Cecy looked down, embarrassed, and then met Mme. LeBlanc's shrewd gaze. "No," she said. "I'm not cut out to be an academic. From now on I want to enjoy reading stories, not pick them apart and drone about the spine of one, the kidney of the next. I'm afraid that I'm not an intellectual."

M. LeBlanc laughed, his sandy grey hair rumpling in the breeze. "You appear to feel guilty about that," he commented.

Cecy smiled in spite of herself. "I feel that I've spent an awful lot of time and scholarship money on this education of mine, and now I don't want to go on with it."

"*Alors,*" he said. "Some of us are cut out to spend our lives buried to the eyeballs in libraries, and others are not. You are to be complimented that your interest took you this far."

Cecy thanked him. "*Et vous?* Do you spend your days buried in a library?"

Mme. LeBlanc laughed merrily. "Yes, you can be sure he does. He's a professor. I have to remove books from his belly in order to make room for a plate of food, in the evenings."

M. LeBlanc looked sheepish. "She stopped asking me to come to the dining table years ago, especially since she could no longer find it, for the books."

"I clear them away, and he replaces them with

towers of new ones," his wife complained. "Me, I cannot work in such a mess. Hideous."

"What do you do?" Cecy asked.

"I'm a graphic artist and illustrator."

Her husband broke in. "Yes, but she is far too organized and neat for her artistic spirit," he teased her. "If only she would suscribe to my very comfortable chaos theory—"

"Comfortable! Etienne, how you can reach any conclusions in that bottomless pit is beyond me."

Cecy was delighted with them. "What brought you to the United States? How long will you stay?"

"I have a research grant from Emory University, you see. I'm a historian. I'm very lucky that my Sylvie can do her work here, too. I'd miss her terribly."

Sylvie put a hand to her hair and rolled her eyes. "*Oui*, in the one hour out of the twenty-four when he's conscious of my existence. . . ."

"*Ma chère*, you know you exaggerate. I'm conscious of you at least three hours out of the day. And you couldn't abide me yapping at your heels for any more than that. You are too busy being organized." Her husband smiled indulgently.

"*Eh bien*. He has a point," Sylvie conceded.

"You have a cat?" Cecy gestured to Etienne's coat sleeve.

"Believe it or not," his wife cut in, "his coat used to be made of camel's hair. But he tosses it on Fleurette's favorite chair every night, and she nests in it."

"Fleurette is your cat?"

"She seemed to come with the house we are renting. She's a grey, and provides us with a luxury of hair in return for her meals. We think it's a point of honor with her."

Cecy chuckled. "I know, I have one, too. Do you enjoy Atlanta?"

"It's not so bad," Sylvie answered. "We miss Paris, however, and our friends and family. It's so good to hear a French-speaking voice. We've picked up some English, of course—he speaks it better than I do, since he must read it for his research. But we're still not so good with the idiomatic phrases, the 'slang,' you call it. And I'm afraid we speak French to each other at home." She hesitated. "Do you know of anyone willing to tutor English? Or would you be interested in it yourself? We had a tutor, but she was so busy that the arrangement didn't work out."

Cecy thought about it. Why not? She could use the money, and she would enjoy these people. "Yes, I would consider tutoring. How many times a week would you like to meet?"

Sylvie looked at Etienne, who shrugged. "Perhaps twice?"

Cecy nodded. "All right. Let me give you my telephone number."

And just like that, she had a second job. She couldn't wait to tell Chas. This was very exciting! And all because she'd come to Home Depot looking for plants. She frowned. Her mission was still far from accomplished.

"Do you know anything about gardening?" She asked Sylvie.

"A bit. *Pourquoi?*"

"I know nothing, and I've got a vast backyard to make presentable."

Sylvie pursed her worldly mouth. "Is it mostly shady, or does it get lots of sun?"

"Mostly shady."

"For the ground, or pots?"

"A few of each."

"Well, then, come along, and I'll show you a few varieties of plants that should thrive under those circumstances. I can't promise you results, since I don't know the condition of your soil, but I can point you in the right direction."

She put impatiens, blue daze, verbena, calladiums, and a small bromeliad in Cecy's basket, while Etienne followed patiently.

"Thank you. I'm so glad we met each other today!" Cecy said.

They all parted ways, well satisfied.

Cecy went to look at pots next, but decided that she couldn't afford any. The price of the plants was already going to be high, and she'd only gotten enough to dot the brick patio. Chas would have to pay for any further landscaping he wanted to do. She paid cash for her new leafy charges and gazed down at them affectionately.

"I'm going to do my best to make you happy," she told them. "But I'm not a very experienced plant mommy, and since you can't howl when you're thirsty or when your pots need changing, we're going to have to find a way to communicate."

14

Cecy poked around the big garage for pots when she got home, and tried not to think about casting Chas's nude body as a garden sculpture.

She found a couple of old containers that cleaned up well. She'd bought a bag of potting soil, and she filled the containers with the moist, crumbly stuff. She eased the impatiens from their temporary flats, and set them firmly in the new homes she'd chosen for them.

That left the verbena, the blue daze, and the bromeliad, for which she had no pots. She sat back on her haunches and brushed the soil from her hands. *All right, Grand, now where are you to tell me what to do with these things? It's your garden, for heaven's sake.* But Grand chose not to render any aid. Perhaps she was busy haunting some unsuspecting soul.

Why was it that Grand, whom she'd never even met in life, had made an appearance in her dreams, but Brock was just . . . gone? Cecy knit her brows. It didn't make any sense. She stared at the plants, as if they had something to do with it.

That's when it came to her. She rose and went into the kitchen, where she quickly washed her hands, and then ran up the stairs to her room.

In the back of the closet she'd shoved the two boxes of Brock's things that she'd kept. She opened one. Inside were the few toys that Brock had saved from his childhood. They hadn't had many to call their own, since most things at Mama Sue's had gone into a big community toy chest, but she and her brother had each had two or three things they'd treasured as theirs alone. Cecy's had been a battered Barbie Doll, a stuffed bear with one eye, and a jigsaw puzzle of the Eiffel Tower.

Brock's favorite things had been a plastic fireman's hat, a yellow Tonka dump truck, and a set of bongo drums that had driven Mama Sue crazy. Cecy reached down and took the fireman's hat into her hands. He'd gotten it one Christmas when they were about eight, and she could still remember him running around wearing it, along with his Mickey Mouse pajamas. His smile had been a little crooked even back then.

She set the hat down next to her on the floor and pulled out the heavy Tonka truck. Barbie had driven it in the sandbox behind the house, though she was only allowed to do so when Donald Duck was tired. Brock had reluctantly agreed that Barbie could learn how to operate heavy construction equipment since she wasn't rich enough to own her own camper or sports car.

The bongo drums Brock had played when he was a little older—maybe twelve. He'd beaten on them to any kind of music available, whether it was *Jesus Christ Superstar*, the *Star Wars* sound track, or the BeeGees. He'd made up his own rhythms and secret coded messages.

Cecy took the three items downstairs. They weren't doing anyone any good, sitting in a cardboard box in the back of a dark closet. They might as well be put to some use. She carried them outside onto the patio and set them on the table, then rooted in Chas's toolbox in the garage. She returned with a cordless drill.

She fired it up and used it to make three small holes in the top of the fireman's hat. Then she made one small hole in each bongo drum, and a couple in the load-bearing bottom of the truck. That done, she filled each item with potting soil, then planted the blue daze in the Tonka truck, the bromeliad in the fireman's hat, and the verbena in the bongo drums. She arranged them in a half circle around the two-tiered birdbath in the center of the brick patio. The patio got no direct light, shaded by the house and thick clusters of huge old trees. She hoped the plants would be happy there, and she'd created an impromptu tribute to Brock. Perhaps he would come to visit, if only to yell at her for puncturing his things.

Cecy brushed off her hands again, put everything away in the garage, and went back into the kitchen. She gazed outside through the mullioned window at the little shrine to childhood. It was really very charming. Maybe she could find some other unusual containers to plant in.

As she turned away from the window, an old recipe card caught her eye. It was lying in plain sight on the scarred old table, and she hadn't noticed it before. She picked it up.

"Hildy's Beef Bourgignon," she read. Chas must have left it there, planning to cook it that night. She looked down the list of ingredients. She didn't think the kitchen was stocked with any of them, so she tucked the card into her jeans pocket and went to get her purse. She could follow a recipe; Mama Sue had let her help in the kitchen some. The only really expensive ingredient was the beef, and since she'd just acquired a tutoring job, she'd splurge. It was another way to thank Chas for all he was doing for her.

"I'm going to take the Jeep to the store," she called up the stairs. He'd been holed up with his laptop in his room all day.

"Fine," she heard him call down. "Just don't park it in front of any emergency exits, okay?"

"Very funny," she muttered, as she snared the keys off their hook. "Wiseass."

Chas came out of isolation three hours later. He congratulated himself on not once thinking of Cecy naked. He was, after all, a man of discipline and dignity. He could respect himself once again.

He sniffed the air around him hungrily. The most delicious aroma wafted up the stairs, one he hadn't smelled since he was in his late teens. He followed the enticing scent downstairs and into the kitchen. Cecy stood over a large pot, sampling some sauce from a shallow ladle.

"Mmmm. This smells *exactly* like Hildy's recipe," Chas said.

"Naturally, since it *is* Hildy's recipe—as you very well know."

"Huh?"

"You're the one who left it lying on the kitchen table. It's not like I dreamed it out of thin air." She set the lid back on the pot and put the ladle in the sink.

"What are you talking about? I don't have any of Hildy's recipes. My mother had them, and I would assume they're somewhere in my stepmother's kitchen, now."

"Chas, somebody left this recipe on the table. Since I didn't, and it's just you, me, and Barney living here, you must have."

"But I didn't." He stared at her.

"Then where did it come from?"

"I don't know."

"Chas, that's just plain weird." A ripple of emotion disturbed her expression.

He decided it must be hidden amusement. "Okay, stop pulling my leg. The recipe was stuck inside one of the cabinets, right?"

"No. It was just sitting on the table, like I said."

Uneasiness crept over Chas as he recognized his grandmother's handwriting. How had a recipe in her hand gotten here, years after her death?

A logical explanation existed, he was sure, but he was damned if he could think of it at the moment. "Well," he said, rubbing his hands together, "regardless of where the recipe came from, it sure smells good. I didn't know you could cook, or I would have chained you to the stove barefoot days ago."

That put a martial light into her eyes.

Chas got two plates out of one of the kitchen cabinets and started to hand them to her. He stopped mid-gesture, and asked her suspiciously, "You haven't dropped anything, er, strange in here, have you?"

"Nope. I snapped the last acrylic fingernail off a week ago." Cecy grinned at him.

He lifted her hand and inspected her nails. They looked a little weak and puny, but much better than before. They'd resembled fat, ceramic drawer pulls, in his opinion: thick and shiny and obviously stuck onto the surface.

Cecy pulled her hand back. "I know, they look terrible."

He frowned at her. "I think they're a vast improvement. Your hands look like they belong to you now, not some department-store mannequin."

"I thought men liked women with all the trimmings."

"Some men do. I don't happen to be one of them. Too much fancy wrapping makes me suspect that there's nothing but a big empty box underneath, not a real woman."

"Why? Is that what Maria was like?"

Chas dug his hands into the pockets of his faded jeans. "Yeah. That's what Maria was like. Though who knows—maybe her neurosurgeon's discovered a soul under the tinsel somewhere." He watched Cecy place a healthy portion of beef on his plate, then heap peas and potatoes next to it. She ladled extra sauce on top. His stomach growled.

"I heard that," she announced. She spoke straight to his gut, as some men talked to a woman's breasts. "You only have a minute or so to go, so calm yourself, you big cavern." She put much less food on her own plate and followed him to the battered old table.

She'd already set it with utensils, and some small blue flowers floated on the surface of water in a plain glass bowl. She'd put this in the center, along with two candles in glass holders. The effect was warm and charming.

Cecy sat with one foot tucked under her and nipped into her food. She had her fork in her mouth before he'd even picked his up. His lips quirked at that. Maria had waited for him to take a bite—he'd had to savor it with drama— and compliment her effusively before she'd pick at her food herself.

Cecy swallowed her first bite and rolled her eyes heavenward in appreciation. "Wow. This is incredible. Hildy deserved a full-length mink, not just a stole!"

He laughed. "I think she did end up with a full-length silver fox. But, Cecy, you made this, not Hildy."

She shrugged. "It's her recipe."

"Not everyone has the right touch for cooking, though. You do. This is wonderful. Thank you."

"It's no big thing," she muttered.

"Yes, it is. And it's the first meal we've cooked in Grand's house. This calls for a toast. I've got a bottle of wine somewhere." He rose and went in search of it among the boxes in the dining room. "Aha." He found two wineglasses and a corkscrew and brought the works to the table, where she watched him open the bottle.

"Silver Oak, 1993," she read aloud.

"It's a very nice cabernet." He handed her a glass, and their fingers brushed as she accepted it. A little lightning streak of electricity shot up his arm. Zing, bada boom. Damn, how did she do that to him?

Chas sat and lifted his own glass in preparation for a toast. *To licking this gravy off of your bare breasts.* He banished the thought. "To a lovely meal, prepared by a lovelier woman," he said.

Cecy's face was tinged with pink as she drank. "Th—thank you."

"You act like you've never been toasted before, silly." He smiled at her.

She swallowed and gave him a wobbly smile in return. "I haven't. This is a first."

"You're kidding."

"Nope."

"Not even on your birthday?"

"Not unless you count clinking beer mugs."

"Well, I suppose that works."

They ate for a while in companionable silence, and Chas studied her covertly. She had a natural grace that charmed him. Her coloring, her naïveté, the soft, barely visible downy hairs on her cheek in the candlelight—it all made him think of a baby gosling. He wanted to reach out and stroke her face with his finger.

Cecy, oblivious, folded an onion slice into a figure eight on top of a morsel of beef, swirled it in sauce, and popped it into her mouth. Her eyebrows wiggled in appreciation, and she closed her eyes for a moment.

He liked to watch her eat. Every time he thought of his squashed McDonald's leftovers in her purse, it made him sick. He never, ever wanted to see her in that position again. And if she followed the financial plan he'd worked out for her, she wouldn't be. She might never be rich, but at least she wouldn't starve.

As he mused, she speared her last piece of potato and swabbed it all over her plate, mopping up every last trickle of gravy she could find. She froze as she caught him looking at her, and he grinned.

"Sorry," she said. "Is that bad manners?"

He shook his head. "Not as far as I'm concerned. I like to see a woman enjoy her food." He rose and picked up the plates. "Have some more wine. Do you want me to bring you seconds?"

She thought about it—he could tell. But she shook her head. "No, thanks." He took the plates to the kitchen counter and rinsed them off in the sink. Then he walked through the dining room to the foot of the stairs, where he'd left a legal pad and some computer printouts earlier.

When he brought them to the table, she was staring into the ruby red liquid in her glass. She looked up, saw the sheets of numbers he held, and took a quick gulp of the wine as he sat down.

"What's that?" she asked.

"This is a plan I've been working on for you today. A financial plan. Some of this may change, depending on what kind of debt-consolidation loan I can get for you."

Cecy clasped both hands around the heavy cut-crystal glass. "Okay." She took a deep breath.

"Relax. I'm not going to sit here and criticize

you. I'm just going to make some suggestions as to how you can save. Okay?" Chas smiled at her reassuringly.

"Okay."

"All right. Here's what I'm paying you in salary for the next year, if you can make the commitment to stay that long."

She nodded.

"I'm going to ask you to sign an informal contract that you'll do so, just so I'll feel better about giving you a reference to the loan company. What do you think about that?"

"Sounds . . . fair," she said cautiously.

"If you live here for six months, you should be able to save enough money to put a decent down payment on a small car and get yourself an apartment. I'd put those funds in a checking account. I'd also put a hundred dollars per paycheck in a savings account that you swear not to touch for any reason at all."

"Okay."

"Now. I want you to write down everything you can think of that costs you money. Everything, from chewing gum to clothing to gasoline."

She did so, and Chas watched her scrawl a long list on the yellow paper. He took another swallow of wine and tried to ignore the subtle scents of her body and hair. Peaches and hydrangea again, damn it. Her smooth skin glowed in the candlelight.

She distracted him by pushing the list at him.

He ran his eyes down it, looking for things to eliminate. "Ah-ha!"

Cecy jumped. "What?"

"Panty hose. You're working in my office, now, and I don't see the need for them." *You could save money on underwear, too,* said the horny lust devil that possessed him lately.

"But they're only about three dollars," she argued.

"How long do they last before they run?"

"Usually only one or two wearings," she admitted.

"Ax them. Fifteen dollars a week is sixty dollars a month is seven hundred and twenty dollars a year in useless petroleum product."

Her mouth hung open.

"Yeah, seven hundred and twenty bucks a year," he reiterated.

"They're a petroleum product?"

"Yup."

"So I'd actually be helping the environment if I didn't wear them. Okay. No more panty hose."

Helping the environment? Chas didn't know about that. But he moved on to the next item on the list.

"Cat litter and cat toys," he read. "Can't that beast do his business outside?"

"He does, sometimes. But not all the time."

"Okay." Chas left cat litter on the list. "But the toys have got to go."

"Barney needs his toys. You don't want to know what happens if he doesn't have them."

Chas waved his hand in dismissal. "Cat toys get the ax."

"Okay, but don't say I didn't—"

"Magazines? Why do you need to read fashion magazines?"

"Chas, that's a very normal thing for a woman to do," Cecy protested.

"Normal or not, they're dangerous. They convince females that they're fat, shabby, and not in the correct swing of things. That means money spent on weird diet programs, new wardrobes, and all sorts of excursions they'd never have dreamed of on their own."

"Hey, wait a minute!"

"Worst of all, they provide you with those damned quizzes on everything under the sun. The magazines get the ax."

"I'm keeping one," Cecy insisted.

He ignored her. "Hair color!" He found that ridiculous. She didn't need to dye her hair. It looked fine. "Ax," he muttered. "Makeup—ax. Non-necessary items."

Cecy rolled her eyes. "Leave those on the list, Chas. I've cut down from department-store makeup to drugstore makeup, and from salon treatments to home hair care. That's as low as I go."

He grunted at her. "Bottled water! Now, if that's not a waste of money, I don't know what is. Next they're going to start selling air with designer oxygen in it, and people will line up to order the stuff by the case."

"Okay, Chas, that's enough. Next you'll be telling me to use a cloth diaper instead of feminine protection." She grabbed the legal pad from him, and he felt heat flush his cheeks.

"Look," she said gently. "I'd really appreciate your help with the big stuff, but leave me alone on the minute details, okay?"

He nodded gruffly, and reached for his wine. He'd never understand the things women spent money on, never in a lifetime.

Cecy put the yellow pad on the other side of the table and came around to touch his shoulder. "I know you're just trying to be nice," she said.

He *was* trying to be nice, he thought, as he inhaled peaches and hydrangea. The problem was, he didn't feel like being nice. He felt like pushing her back onto the table and having her, with whipped topping, for dessert.

He willed the thought to go away, to stop torturing him. Unfortunately, his effort must have shown on his face, for Cecy seemed to think his feelings were hurt. She touched his cheek, next.

"Chas," she said, softly. "I didn't mean—"

He wasn't even conscious that he'd pulled her onto his lap, that he'd covered her mouth with his own, until they both gasped for air. Her arms were twined around his neck, and his face was buried in her hair as he sucked in oxygen. Her scent drove him crazy, sent his lips skittering over the smooth skin of her neck and shoulder. He couldn't get enough of her.

He ran his fingers under the placket of her shirt, unfastened the top button, and spread the fabric wide to access more of her warm, silken skin. He felt the vibrations of a tiny moan under her breastbone. She arched her body closer to his. With his tongue, he tasted the hollow between her breasts, cupped the swell of each through her bra. She wasn't wearing racy red lace today, but plain white cotton that was lovely in its simplicity. Cecy herself was the ornament, and this turned him on more than the lace had.

He groaned and bit gently at her nipples through the stretchy fabric. They hardened immediately, and so did he. He ripped open the rest of her buttons.

God, she had beautiful breasts. Not too large, not too small. He tugged at the top of her bra and dragged it down until it rested under both swells, and her nipples poked toward him with sexy impudence. He licked first one and then the other.

Cecy gasped and bit her bottom lip, hard, straining against him. She wanted more. Instead, he teased her by taking that plump lip in his own teeth, wresting it away from her, and sucking hard.

She rubbed her cherry peaks against the fabric of his shirt, the expression on her face one of shameless pleasure. He didn't think it possible for him to become harder, but he did. He shot down with his mouth and caught her left breast. He kneaded, bit, sucked until she whimpered, and then he commandeered the other one.

Cecy quivered against him. He kissed each flushed, excited nipple, then pinched them lightly before he tore off her shirt completely and yanked the bra over her head. He set her on her feet, flipped the kitchen light off, and was back and unfastening her slacks before she could miss him. They dropped and pooled around her ankles; his own followed suit.

She stood before him in nothing but plain white-cotton panties and tousled hair. Chas kissed her and skimmed his hands down her sides. When he reached her hips he discovered the panties were virtually backless. Immediately, each hand held a warm, creamy handful of female bottom. He hauled her against him and squeezed. He wanted some more of that. "Full of surprises, aren't you, baby?" He growled the words against her ear, then turned her around so he could enjoy the view.

A narrow band of elastic traveled round her waist and connected to a tiny swatch of fabric that plunged down and disappeared between her buttocks. He wanted to follow it. God, she was sexy. Chas ran his hands back up her tummy to her full breasts and stepped up close behind her, lodging his erection between her legs, right under that luscious ass. He bent forward until she lay cheek down on the kitchen table, quivering under him.

Slowly he eased back, running his hands up and down her back, massaging her with his thumbs, his fingers, his palms. He moved down to her buttocks and gave them the same treatment, then her thighs, which he spread, and her calves. He knelt on the floor behind her, fingering the lines of the thong. He bit gently at one cheek. She squirmed, and he laughed, tugging upward a bit on her thong. Then he sent his fingers exploring beneath it, and plunged his finger into her hot, wet female core.

He dragged the panties down and off and tossed them away, all the while pulsing inside her with his finger. Cecy writhed on the table, and soon bucked against him with escalating cries until she came. Then he replaced his finger with the hardest part of him, moved his hands back to her breasts, and kissed her shoulder while he drove into her from behind. She was a slick, hot glove for him, her body sucking and pulling in wild abandon. He felt her breasts, engorged for him. He felt her hot core surrounding him. He felt her delicious soft ass slapping against him while tension raged and coiled within him. It built to a frightening peak—he staggered—and then spilled out of him and into her depths while he collapsed against her, burying his face in her hair. She cried out again and clenched around him over and over as he caught his runaway breath.

They lay together, panting, their bodies damp and satiated. He wished he could stay inside her all night. As he snuggled her close to him, he decided he would. A light breeze from the overhead vents blew around them, and between his legs. It felt wonderful, until the breeze turned into a tickle, and the tickle suddenly took a furry "whack" at his family jewels.

Chas yelped, leaped back, and took a wild swing at whatever it was. Cecy screamed and scrambled onto the table. A chair next to them went flying.

He heard a loud hiss and the unmistakable sound of feline paws in a dead gallop over hardwood floors.

"That goddammned rodent of yours!" Chas thundered. "He tried to snack on my balls!"

15

"Barney is not a rodent!" Cecy stood with her hands on her hips, naked and indignant in the candlelight.

"He's a menace!" Chas stalked to his pants and grabbed them from the floor.

"He was curious, that's all. He lost his own fuzzy little yarbles at an early age." Cecy tried to inject her tone with reason.

Chas was having none of it. "That's no excuse to sniff mine. He's a perverted little rat."

"He's a sweet, innocent little kitty." Her voice rose again.

"Next time your sweet innocent comes near my balls, curiosity won't have time to kill the cat—*I* will. And then I'll make cat cassoulet."

"You're a very sick person," Cecy said severely. She watched him stuff himself back into his pants. "Why is it that men have such an overinflated concept of their appendages?" She fished around for her own scattered clothing.

Now it was Chas's turn to take offense. He reached out, pulled her to him, and towered over her. His eyebrows formed angry black squiggles.

"You just experienced my appendages," he reminded her. "Did they seem overinflated to you?"

"N-not at all," she stammered. She stood close against him, wearing nothing but her open oxford cloth shirt. She could hear his heart beating in the silence of the evening. A fresh streak of desire flashed through her as she felt him hardening again through his jeans. Great. The man had just threatened to make stew out of her cat, and she still had the hots for him. What kind of a woman was she?

"I didn't think so," he rumbled. "You seemed to find my body, and everything I did, highly . . . stimulating." He ran those big hands of his down her back. She sighed into his chest. It was warm, and fuzzy with hair, and so wonderfully male. He played the muscles along her spine like a musical instrument, reducing her to jelly. She decided, in a wanton wave, that Chas just talked tough. He wouldn't hurt poor Barney. He had a reluctantly soft heart and a relentlessly hard trouser snake. She smiled. She was up for a few more hours of snake-charming, where this man was concerned.

He seemed to have the same idea, for he picked her up so that she straddled him and made for the stairs with his booty. Well, it was really her booty, but she'd let him borrow it. She wriggled and shifted position. The button on his Levi's was cold!

"Cecy," he said into her ear, "will you talk dirty French to me?"

Oooh, she'd never done *that* before.

He mounted the stairs with her, and she whispered into his ear. *"Mon autre chagatte, elle t'aime aussi."* My other cat loves you, too.

"Yeah?"

"Oui. Elle aime ton boudin blanc." She likes your white sausage.

"God, that's sexy, baby! Talk to me some more."

"Je voudrais a jouer ta cornemuse grande, chéri." I want to play your big bagpipe, baby. *"Je voudrais te faire grimper au septième ciel,"* she continued huskily. I want to spread your toes apart.

Chas had her shirt wide-open now, and was rolling his tongue over her nipples.

"Oui, chéri, léche mes ananas. Oohhhh." Yes, baby, suck my pineapples. *"Tu me fais vibrer."* You turn me on. *"Tu me fais mouiller ma petite culotte."* I'm so hot for you.

He growled and clutched her bottom, turned on the landing, and had her in his bedroom in seconds flat. There he tossed her on the bed and unfastened his jeans.

"Ah, c'est magnifique! Tu es au garde-à-vous, mon mousquetaire." Ah, it's magnificent! You are at attention, my musketeer. *"Tu as un boulet dans ton canon."* You have a bullet in your cannon. *"Alors, viens et fais exploser ce boulet à l'intérieur de ma petite chatte, chéri."* Come here and fire it into my darkness, sweetie.

Chas seemed to have no problem with her being his superior officer. He brought his cannon to her for inspection, and, under her attention, it began to smoke.

He fired and reloaded many times that night, seeming to find it very pleasurable to be a musketeer. Cecy fell asleep in his arms, her body exhausted and satiated with loving. She murmured one last phrase to him in French.

"J'ai peur de tomber amoreuse de toi." I'm afraid of falling in love with you.

She awoke before Chas the next morning and gazed at his face, relaxed in sleep. The firm planes of his cheeks and jaw were covered in dark stubble; his long eyelashes rested in the hollows beneath his eyes. His breath came deep and even.

She lightly traced the outline of his chiseled lips with her finger. He had a full, sexy mouth. It was not a mouth that looked as if it belonged to an accountant.

Chas's mouth hinted at the sensual side of

him—the midnight lover who'd shaken her to the core and made the world drop away. Was this really the same man who had lectured to her about the expense of panty hose? It was hard to believe.

He clipped coupons, but opened his home to her. He lectured about the expense of bottled water, yet served her expensive wine. He told her makeup was an unnecessary item, but had bought her bath oil and body lotion after she'd slaved in the garden.

He dressed like a businessman, but made love like an artist. She'd never, ever, in her life experienced sex as Chas Buchanan served it. She'd never talked dirty to a man in English, much less French. Never spread herself so vulnerably wide or languorously for such a thorough invasion of prime virility. He'd made love to her until her eyeballs rattled and all sensation had shattered around her in a mindless explosion.

Though she'd had a couple of serious boyfriends, they certainly hadn't made her feel like *this*.

Chas wasn't a boyfriend, though. He was a . . . what *was* he? They'd never been on a date; she couldn't say she was "seeing" the man. He wasn't even a friend of hers, to be brutally honest.

Chas was her temporary boss. He was her temporary landlord. She hoped it didn't follow that he was her temporary lover; the thought depressed her.

Her job, her housing arrangement, the people in her life, even the very bed she slept in—all were tentative, ephemeral. She needed roots even more than she needed solvency.

Oh, where was Brock when she needed to talk to him? At least they'd been rootless together. Cecy slipped out of bed and stood looking down at Chas for a moment. She smoothed back some curling hairs at his temple, then withdrew her hand. She found her discarded oxford cloth shirt, shrugged it on, and tiptoed down the stairs.

She started some coffee, then opened the kitchen door into the early dawn and padded outside barefoot to the little shrine she'd planted the day before. She wrapped her arms around herself. The fireman's hat, the Tonka truck, and the bongo drums were dappled with morning dew, and still cradled their flowers.

"Brock," she whispered into the damp air. "I miss you." A few birds answered her, and a light breeze rustled the leaves in the trees. Cecy tucked her hair behind her ears and swallowed. She wandered to one of the wrought-iron chairs around the patio table, and sat down in it. Wherever Brock was, whatever he was doing, she hoped he was happy.

Chas awoke to find Cecy's side of the bed empty, and his conscience full. He had done exactly what he'd sworn not to do: thoroughly boinked her while she was dependent on him.

What did that say about his morals, not to mention his resolve? The poor woman was trying to stand on her own two feet, and didn't need him knocking her off them with his prong.

That part of him woke and stirred, popping out the fly of his boxers as if to mock him.

"Who asked you to rear your ugly head?" Chas growled, smacking it down. "You're nothing but trouble." He irritably swung his legs out of bed.

What on earth was he going to say to Cecy when he saw her? *Gee, thanks for a wonderful evening, but I think you should stay with your cat tonight?* Oh, yeah, that was suave.

Would she be all clingy and emotional this morning? Or—worse—had she slept with him out of a sense of obligation? Had she felt she owed him, since she was staying in his home?

He groaned. One thing was for sure. He'd have to create some distance between them after last night. He made his way into the bathroom, grabbed his toothbrush, and attempted to scrub some of the bad taste out of his mouth.

Cecy hummed as she cut a cantaloupe in half, then scooped out the seeds. She and Chas had time to have an intimate, relaxed breakfast together before they had to go in to the office. She sliced the canteloupe into sections, then cut it into chunks and arranged it on a large plate.

Next she found some bacon and set several strips to sizzling in a heavy old frying pan. She mixed pancake batter and set it beside the stove to wait until Chas appeared.

She was pouring two mugs of coffee when he lurched into the kitchen looking very peculiar.

"Hi," she smiled, and kissed him on the cheek. "Sleep well?"

He shot backwards as if burned. "Uh, yeah. You?"

She blinked rapidly to hide her hurt. "Fine."

He nodded. "Good. What's all this?" He gestured at the food she'd prepared.

"I thought we'd have a nice breakfast before going to the office." She stared at him. He had the oddest expression on his face.

"Thanks, Cecy. But I'm really not hungry. The coffee looks great, though. I'll just take it outside." He grabbed the paper and one of the mugs and made for the back door.

Well. So much for a romantic morning after. He obviously didn't want to get cozy with her. It was wham, bam, thank you ma'am, scram. Men were *warthogs*.

She turned the bacon, fantasizing that it was Buchanan's innards. Just for good measure, she cranked up the heat under it and watched it hiss, sputter, and pop. She burned the edges of it on purpose. When it was done, she threw it on a plate and mashed any remaining life out of it with a paper towel to soak up the grease.

Pig. Hairy pig. Insensitive hairy pig. How could he make love to her all night, murmuring endearments and exchanging kisses of the most intimate variety, and then treat her as if she were hired help in the morning?

Cecy left the bacon on the plate, shoved the pancake batter into the refrigerator, and sat down with a bowl of cantaloupe. She speared a chunk savagely, watching the tines of her fork drive through the melon to clink against the bowl below. Once in her mouth the sweet chill of the fruit soothed her, and she let it slide over her tongue and tickle the roof of her mouth.

She turned her head to peer out the window at Chas. His dark head was bent over the newspaper he was apparently reading, but he still hovered over the same folded section of the front page. He drank his coffee with a slightly unsteady hand.

Perhaps he was feeling sick. She could give him the benefit of the doubt instead of sulking and pretending she was frying his intestines in a pan. How many times had Brock told her she was too impulsive and emotional?

Was she miffed because Chas hadn't cuddled her this morning? Well, *she'd* gotten up early. She needed to be an adult about this. She picked up her coffee and made for the garden door.

Chas looked up as Cecy emerged to join him. She was rumpled, tousled, and sexy as hell. Those long legs of hers taunted him from under the hem of her shirt, and he had a bizarre urge to suck on her kneecaps. Christ, that was a first. He'd never even *noticed* a woman's knees before. He'd always been a red-blooded, self-respecting T & A man.

Just shoot me. I have no desire to get in touch with my sensitive side. Next he'd be getting season tickets to the ballet. The idea of gazing raptly at men in tights was too much for him, and it drove him to conversation.

"So," he said, expansively. "You going to eat all that bacon by yourself?"

She shook her head. "No, the sizzling pig strips were for you."

"Ah. Now that you make it sound so appetizing, I may have to eat some."

"Okay. I thought maybe you weren't feeling well." She peered at him, concern in her blue eyes.

"Who me? Never felt better." He patted her shoulder and retreated inside, where he found the batter, poured some into the frying pan and stood guard over it with a spatula. When he looked over his shoulder out the window, she was still sitting there, her face wiped clean of all expression. She took a sip of coffee.

Chas finished cooking a large pancake, flipped it onto his plate, and heaped bacon on top of it. He drenched the whole with syrup and sat down at the kitchen table to eat. He'd gotten about two mouthfuls down when Cecy opened the door and came back in. She walked to the stove and poured a small amount of batter into the pan for herself.

The silence between them was pregnant. Chas

broke it first. "It's so nice outside, I think I'll take my plate back out there." Out of the corner of his eye, he saw Cecy drop the spatula on the stove and put her hands on her hips. The movement pulled the shirt tight around her small firm bottom, so he fixed his gaze firmly on his plate and hustled outside. He watched her covertly.

Cecy's shoulders were stiff, her movements deliberate. She flipped her hotcake and scowled down at it. Why did he have the feeling that she was imagining *him* in that frying pan?

Maybe because he was behaving like a royal peckerhead. But what choice did he have? Cecy needed to find herself, not get emotionally hung up on him.

Cecy sat at her desk in the office, working on a client presentation. She had showered most of the hurt away, and then slapped powder, deodorant, and freshly pressed linen over the rest of it. She smoothed her hair, which she knew was immaculate, and pursed her lips in their fresh coating of mauve. She was a professional working in another professional's office, and her feelings did not belong here with the paper shredder, water cooler, and fax machine. She had unplugged her emotions, wrapped the cord tightly around them, and stored them in the credenza.

Her fingers clicked over the keyboard, and she refused to look at the green leather couch where she and Chas had made love. It was for seating the uptight rumps of his clientele, and that was all.

The telephone interrupted her cool efficiency, and she turned to answer it. "Chas Buchanan's office, may I help you?"

"Cecy," said a familiar voice. "Is that you?"

"Pam?" What was her hairstylist calling here for? How had she gotten the number?

"Yes. Hi! I've been worried about you. I guess that guy Buchanan tracked you down, after all. How've you been?"

"Fine. Great. What do you mean, he tracked me down?"

"He came here looking for you, a few weeks back."

"He what?" The very idea of Chas inside Daisy Darling's Day Spa made her laugh.

"I'm serious. He came in, desperate to find you, and left his business card. That's how I got the number."

Chas had entered the hooker pink portals of Daisy Darling's, in search of her? If the thought weren't so entertaining, it would have been almost sweet. "Hah," said Cecy. "You're pulling my chain."

"No, girl, I'm not. So are you doing okay? Are you working full-time, now?" Pam's voice exuded genuine and unexpected concern.

Cecy straightened in her chair. "Yes, I am—as a matter of fact, I have two jobs now. I'm going to be tutoring a French couple in English, starting tonight. How about that? I'll be able to come in for a haircut and some highlights, and actually pay in cash. No more shampoo girl."

"Oh, Cecy, don't you feel bad about that. Just about everyone's bounced a check at some time or another, and you worked your butt off to make it good. I'm glad you're doing so well. You want to meet for a drink sometime?"

"I'd really like that, Pam. Thanks."

"Why don't you come by the ole pink shack Thursday after work, and we'll take it from there."

"Great. See you around six, then?"

"That works for me."

Cecy replaced the receiver with a warm feeling in her heart. Somebody in Atlanta cared what happened to her. She was truly touched by Pam's call.

She began typing again, but her thoughts were distracted by the idea of Chas braving the daisy-dotted gaggle at the salon. He'd been looking for her? Why? Had he wanted to apologize for the scene between them that morning she'd run out of his office? Had he felt bad? Or had he just wanted an instant replacement for Jamie?

She decided it was the latter. Buchanan was ruled by pragmatism, not emotion. She'd do well to remember that.

16

"The quick brown fox jumped over the stupid man," Cecy said, in encouraging tones, "because she was far too intelligent to be caught by such a moron." She paused, and looked at Etienne and Sylvie. "Now you repeat it."

"Ze queek browwn fohx jahmpd ovehr ze styupid mahn," Etienne parroted, with a twinkle. Sylvie finished the sentence. "Becohse she wohse far too eentelligent to be coht by such a morohn."

They sat in the living room of the couple's rented house in Inman Park. It was a beautiful mellow Victorian with gingerbread trim, furnished with lots of dark hardwood and needlework. Etienne lounged comfortably in a threadbare wing chair, while Sylvie crossed her thin, elegant legs and sat upright on the camel-backed sofa.

Fleurette, their cat, was curled—true to form—on Etienne's jacket in another armchair. Periodically she awoke long enough to tease another greyish tuft of hair from her own coat and drop it onto his.

"Very good. Now let's work some more on your accents. Watch my lips. 'Bye, bye, Miss American Pie.' "

"Bye, bye, Mees Americahn Pie."

Cecy nodded. "Say, 'I'd like grits with that, please.' "

Sylvie drew her brows together. "Greets? *Mais non*, I have experienced zeez greets of yours. *Ces sont horrible!* Pah!"

Cecy gurgled with laughter. "Okay, how about this? 'You think your grits are groovy, but they're god-awful and gross.' "

"Etienne, she has fun at our expense," Sylvie complained, but laughed with Cecy. She and her husband both began in a singsong. "You theenk your greets are groofy, baht zey're god-offal ahnd grohss."

"Groovy," Cecy corrected.

"Groovvvee," said Etienne and Sylvie.

"Do you want to take a break?" Cecy asked.

"*Eh bien.* You will have some wine?"

"As long as I won't be arrested for teaching under the influence," Cecy quipped.

They looked blank. She explained to them in

French, and Etienne got up to get a bottle, waving his hand. "*Non, non*, we will not arrest you! Perhaps for dinner, only. Then we set you free." He sent a shrewd smile her way. "*Alors*, tell us about zees so stupid man zat the fox, she jump over."

Cecy opened her mouth and then closed it. Damn, but he was perceptive! Or was she that transparent? She had no idea what to say. She really didn't know the couple well enough to be pouring out her romantic problems to them.

"Ah!" He clapped his hands. "I am correct. You, my dear, are the leetle silver-teeped fox, eh? The beeg lout, we don' know who is he, yet. Baht he chase the leetle fox. Yes? However, he knows not what to do with her, when he catch her, hmmmm?"

Cecy felt heat rise in her face and was happy when Sylvie stepped in.

"Etienne! You are waxing metaphorical again, *chéri*. You make the *jeune fille* feel awkward."

"No, no!" Cecy protested. "It's fine. What he says—it's true. I just didn't expect him to see it, that's all."

"Etienne sees everything," he said, handing her a glass of wine with a wink. "*Vraiment*, he is a wise man."

Sylvie rolled her eyes. "Do not get high on yourself," she warned, "or I will serve to you the god-offal greets for dinner."

"My wife, she terrorizes me," Etienne mourned. "I live in fear."

Cecy grinned.

"So," he continued, "when deed ze leetle fox jump over ze styupid mahn?"

Cecy took a sip of wine and raised her chin. "Today," she said, firmly.

"*Aujourd'hui*. And zen, deed he trip over heemself, trying to catch her?" His shrewd little eyes searched her face.

"No, he ate pig strips and behaved as if I were the maid."

Both sets of French brows wrinkled at her. "What is it, the peeg streeps?"

Cecy apologized. "Sorry—bacon. I try to make it sound as gruesome as possible, so that I won't eat it. Bacon's so fattening."

"*C'est vrai*," Sylvie nodded. She patted a hip. "Me, I cannot eat that either."

Etienne waved an impatient hand. "So zees man, you are *amoureux de lui*—in love with him? And he does not see? Or he is a jerk?"

In love. Cecy balked at the words. Was she in love with Chas? Her breath caught in her throat. Images flashed through her head. Chas, catching her as she tripped over his boot in the emergency center. Chas, paying her bill. Driving her home when her car was gone. Giving her a job. Accepting Barney into his office. Not skinning him after what he'd done to the Jeep's leather seats.

Chas with his head bashed in, making love to her with fierce possession—then passing out in the emergency center. Working up a financial plan for her. Chas, last night. She'd thought she'd died and gone to heaven, until she woke to his cold attitude this morning.

Was she in love with Chas Buchanan? Absolutely not! The idea was laughable. She was grateful to him, and she had the hots for him—that's all.

And though he was obviously sexually attracted to her as well, he'd made it absolutely crystal this morning that romance had nothing to do with their sheet-twisting.

"Cecy?"

"*Oui.*" She snapped out of her musing to find Etienne's eyes on her, and Sylvie's as well. She tossed back some wine, sucked in some attitude, and gave a slight shrug. She hoped it conveyed her gentle amusement, her *ennui*, with the silly vagaries of human nature. "Love? Chas? Of course not."

Etienne frowned at her. "*Zut alors,*" he said to Sylvie, "our leetle teacher, she's broken of ze heart."

"*C'est vrai,*" Sylvie agreed. She poured her guest some more wine. "We have a daughter your age. Tell to us everytheeng."

Cecy attempted a subject change. "You have a daughter?"

"Ah, yes. But it's most distressing—she has no problems for us to solve. We are unnecessary." They waited for her to tell her tale of woe.

Where was the famous French reserve? Etienne and Sylvie seemed to have shed it with their airline stubs once they'd set foot on American soil. She wasn't used to such interest in her life, and she wondered how they'd gotten onto so personal a subject. But their kind faces were expectant. They would be crushed if she denied them.

"I tripped over Chas Buchanan while I was stoned on Midol and Veuve Cliquot."

Sylvie brightened. "You fell over him—Etienne, note the symbolism, *mon chéri*." She turned back to Cecy and gestured for her to continue.

Cecy told the whole sorry tale, with the exception of the very personal parts. Her students poured her more wine and encouraged her. They analyzed Chas's every action together. After an hour or so, Etienne pulled on his earlobe and contemplated his portly belly for a moment. "I seenk," he said sagely, "zat zis man, he care for you. Hees actions, they speak so."

She looked up at him. "You really think that?" The wine was making everything pleasant and fuzzy.

He nodded. "*Mais oui*. Zees man, he still tolerate you, aftehr you pour ze abominable drink de l'orange on his bourbon." He shook his head, as if to banish the image of such heresy. "Oh, yes— he care for you."

Cecy threw up her hands and appealed to Sylvie. "What is it with men and their liquor? I'll never understand."

Sylvie looked grave. "It was very bad of you.

Eez like Ugly American demanding 'ketchup' for *le coq au vin*."

Cecy gave a reluctant chuckle.

Sylvie changed the subject. "And do you know how we met, he and I?" She pointed to Etienne.

Cecy shook her head.

"I keeck him, on ze train!"

Etienne laughed sheepishly.

"He deserve it, oh yes. I ride ze horses, in my youth, eh? And I am on ze train, een ze breeches."

Her husband waggled his brows and growled. "Mmm, mmm, mmmh. She had ze posterieur to make a man howl at ze moon. I could not help myself, *vous comprendez*? I only want a morsel . . . just a small one . . ."

"He peench me, ze goat!"

Etienne spread his hands helplessly and looked for sympathy.

"I am wearing ze boots," said Sylvie, "*avec* how you say—"

"Spurs?" Cecy supplied.

"*Oui*. I keeck to behind, very hard. He howl, but not at ze moon."

"I stagger, I am in pain! She is weethout re- morse."

Sylvie was indignant. "Remorse! Hah."

"I still have *la cicatrice*—ze scar." Etienne pulled up his left pant leg, and displayed a white mark on his shin.

Cecy was puzzled. "However did you get her to talk to you, after what you did?"

Sylvie laughed. "Next day, he is on ze train, same hour. I board at my station, I stand. He worms his way over, and he holds up his hands. They are tied at the wrist, with twine! I cannot help myself, I laugh and laugh. He begs me to have a drink with him. What can I say?"

Cecy shook her head, charmed. Etienne's expression was smug; Sylvie's arch. She'd been so lucky to meet them.

Chas monitored the markets and made some adjustments in a client's forecast. He was finding it hard to concentrate today.

The tension between him and Cecy was growing, they batted it back and forth between them like a tennis ball. He was ever so polite to her, though completely standoffish. He'd gotten her the debt-consolidation loan. He patted her on the back every once in a while, just to make sure she knew they were friends.

But every time he saw Cecy, he wanted to take her in his arms and kiss the top of her head. And then her ears, her lips, and so on. But he behaved himself, trying to be a gentleman, even if the horny Yankee inside wanted to toss his modern-day Scarlett on the nearest flat surface and dive beneath her petticoats. Did that mean he was in love with her? Nah. He was old enough to know the difference between love and hot tail.

She was a sexy little armful, but he'd thought the same of Maria, and boy, had that faded quick. Along with three columns of numbers in his checkbook and the last of his illusions about women.

Cecy was very cute, and in a desperate situation. He had to be realistic. He'd invited a woman without a penny to her name to live in a beautiful house on West Paces Ferry, and then he'd asked—well, tossed—her into his bed. He couldn't blame her for wanting to stay there, could he? She was human, so the cogs were turning behind those soulful blue eyes of hers.

He had no idea how she'd found that recipe of Hildy's, but that delicious dinner, dredged from the carefree days of his boyhood, had to have been engineered. It was a piece of brilliant manipulation. Tom Barry was right to warn him.

He'd be watching Cecy carefully. She'd taken up cooking for him, and next would be the laundry. Perhaps a little home decorating. Uh-huh. She'd be making herself indispensable, sewing herself seamlessly into the fabric of his life until presto! He wouldn't make the effort to rip her out. Meanwhile, all her financial problems would be solved, and she'd live happily ever after.

So call him a cynic—he had cause. He liked Cecy, he loved going to bed with her, but he wasn't going to be her sugar daddy. Maybe he should try setting her up with another guy, so that they could avoid the inevitable ugly scene when she found her plans to snare him weren't going to work.

Chas ground his teeth at the thought. Could he stand watching her flirt with another man? Of course he could. He'd feel that basic thump-on-the-chest jealousy that any man would experience upon watching his sexual territory invaded, but he'd get over it in a heartbeat, and get on with his life.

He reflected on the idea, and began to plan a Southern-style barbecue dinner. Ribs, he thought. Ribs, chicken, mustard-based potato salad, and Tom Barry would be on the menu. But the pièce de résistance would be an old business school buddy of his, who'd just moved back to Atlanta after an absence of years. Blond, blue-eyed, single Christian Cox. He and Cecy would make a handsome couple. Chas flipped through his day planner for a suitable barbecue date. Cecy could invite a couple of girlfriends, if she had any, or he could dig up some women all too eager to round out the ratio.

He'd have to shell out some money for the whole affair, but he had to look at it as a charitable cause—and an exorcism. He couldn't have Cecy getting all hung up on him, simply because they'd shared a few bouts of great sex.

Cecy took a bus to a corner near Daisy Darling's Day Spa and walked the few remaining blocks. She stepped inside to find Daisy, wearing her trademark yellow-ceramic flower pin, sweeping up hair from the linoleum floor. Pam was soaking her feet in a pedicure tub, and the sound track from *Evita* thundered on the tinny sound system. One of the girls lip-synched into a metal-wrapped circular brush, her other hand reaching with drama out to her imaginary masses.

"Hi!" Cecy hollered, above the din.

"Hey, girl! Good to see you," Pam shouted back. "Are you ready to have some fun?"

Cecy gave her a hug. "I am, but you look tired."

"Just soaking my throbbing feet. I'll be good as new in a second, and ready for a margarita."

Within a few minutes, they were all piling into Pam's yellow Corvette. The motor roared, Cecy braced herself, and they shot into the street.

Cecy had never ridden in a Corvette, much less a bright yellow one with a punctured pack of birth-control pills dangling from the rearview mirror.

Pam caught her looking at them and grinned. "It's the only way I remember to take them, hon."

"Sure," Cecy said. "That works." She sat in the backseat with Daisy, who fluffed her layered hair and reapplied a bloodthirsty shade of dark red to her mouth.

The lip-synching girl, Suki, rode shotgun, with her silver-sandaled feet dangling out the window. Her toenails were a metallic blue.

Pam cranked up the tunes and ogled a twentysomething guy at the next stoplight. He grinned and scratched his forehead through the opening of his backwards baseball cap.

How suave, Cecy thought. The car rumbled forward as the light turned green, and Pam left Mr. Cool eating her dust. They rounded a few more corners and flew down a couple more stretches of road. Pam took a hard right into a strip mall, which featured a bar called Hot Diggety's. Judging from the boots and wide-brimmed hats of two men walking through the door, it was a country place.

Cecy's suspicions were confirmed as they approached and had the hair blown off their heads by the voice of Billy Ray Cyrus. This was not her scene, but she squared her shoulders and resolved to have a good time. She would enjoy a nice imported beer and talk to a tall cowboy who'd make her forget all about Chas Buchanan.

An hour later, Cecy had to admit her plan wasn't working. A slick hick called Harvey was exerting his dubious charms on her behalf, and all but humping her leg in rhythm to the howls of yet another country voice. This artist boohooed that he'd lost his ranch, his truck, his woman, and his dog to cruel fate. Cecy wished he'd find a gun and put an end to his misery and his song.

Harvey decided to bewitch her with a litany of his cunning strategies on raising blue-ribbon hogs. He seemed to feel he communicated more soulfully with his hand over hers on the bar. She disentangled her fingers quickly and wrapped them around her glass of lager.

Harvey inched himself closer to her and pressed his knee against hers. Cecy scooted as far back on the barstool as she could to avoid the contact. Where was Pam? She glanced around to see her talking to a couple of normal-seeming guys at a small table in the back. "Excuse me, Harvey. It's been nice talking with you," she said, "but I've got to find my friend."

"Aw, baby, I'm your friend, too." Harvey looked mournful.

Cecy felt a twinge of guilt for unloading him, not liking to hurt his feelings. But she hadn't started the conversation, and she really couldn't stand any more of his very unsubtle advances. She had to retreat now, or he'd be nibbling on her ear and telling her about the wonders of modern fertilizers.

She extricated herself and made her way back to Pam's table. One of the men sitting there reminded her of Chas, though he wasn't nearly as good-looking. She wondered what Chas was doing tonight. She hadn't seen much of him during the day—he'd holed up in his inner office. Before she'd left, she'd simply called to him that she was meeting a friend for a drink.

She looked around at the selection of men in Hot Diggety's. None of them had the kind of presence or sexual magnetism Chas had. Most were absurdly cocky, not quietly confident, as he was. They strutted and bobbed their heads like ridiculous roosters, except most roosters didn't sport belt buckles the size of satellite dishes or wear their names engraved in leather over their buns.

Cecy sighed and cupped an ear for the shouted introductions at Pam's table. The Chas knockoff called himself Zeke. She gave him a perfunctory smile and settled down to see just how bad *his* lines would be. While he got started on them, she dissected his appearance. The guy had Chas's dark hair, but it didn't read blue under the light the way Chas's did. Zeke's eyes were brown, not coal black, and they had a funny scrunched shape instead of Buchanan's ode to almond.

Inch by inch, she found him sadly lacking. His jaw, for example, was too narrow, and his Adam's apple too bony. It bobbed in an odd rhythm as he spoke.

He had short fingers, and snaps instead of buttons on his shirt. She also had no tolerance for plaid in those particular shades. Cecy's scrutiny was interrupted by the waitress, who set a peculiar-looking drink down in front of her.

"From him." She jerked her head back toward Harvey. "It's a Slow Comfortable Screw up against the Wall."

Harvey, across the room, waggled his eyebrows at her and raised his beer in salute.

Cecy felt *her* eyebrows crawling up into her

hair, and her cheeks lit with embarrassment. "I don't think so," she said. "Would you please take it back to him?"

The waitress rolled her eyes and picked it up again. "Whatever you say." She trudged over to Harvey, who apparently refused it, because it came slogging back to her on the waitress's tray.

"He says," the woman sighed, "that you can do whatever you want with it, but he's not taking it back."

Cecy frowned. She looked at the waitress, who seemed harried. She wore three Band-Aids on each ankle under the support hose. It would be unkind to keep playing Ping-Pong with the sexually loaded drink. "Okay. Thank you." She took it and set it down on the table, but pushed it far into the middle and didn't touch it.

To ignore Harvey's salacious glances, she paid more attention to what Zeke was saying, and discovered to her shame that he was a nice person. Now she felt horrible for deciding that he was Sears compared to Saks Fifth Avenue Chas. When had she turned into such a snob?

She supposed it was when she had fifty thousand dollars of insurance money, no knowlege of a thirty-thousand-dollar medical bill, and too much time on her hands. She'd learned to scrutinize labels, quality, design—anything but herself and what she was going to do with the rest of her life.

While Zeke told her about his day-to-day challenges as an insurance agent, she revised her opinion of him. Okay, Chas was better-looking. Someone should bronze him, like a pair of baby shoes, and stick him in the foyer of his office building.

But this guy was nice. He had a warmth that was much more appealing than the polite mask Chas wore around her these days.

They chatted for a while, and Zeke told her she reminded him of his sister Julie. Julie was in college, studying urban planning. Zeke sent her money when he could, and—

The flow of conversation was interrupted by the Band-Aid-clad waitress, who set another weird-looking drink in front of Cecy.

"A Blow Job," the harassed woman said succinctly. "Same guy." She disappeared.

Cecy stared down at it, more than annoyed. She refused to even look at Harvey. "What is he doing?" she hissed to Zeke.

He cast a dark glance at the jerk. "Licking his lips. You want me to put a stop to this? I'd be glad to."

"No, no," she said hastily. "He's just an idiot."

They resumed conversation. Pam, across the table, was flirting wildly with Zeke's blond friend. Daisy and Suki were somewhere in the crowd.

Cecy shared some of her own background and learned that Zeke and his sister Julie had grown up in a small Texas town not far from Mama Sue's. "You're kidding," she exclaimed. "Salado? I grew up in New Braunfels." They reminisced fondly about the central portion of the Lone Star State. She'd been antiquing in Salado, and he'd been "tubing" on the river in New Braunfels.

By the time the waitress showed up at their table again, they were becoming friends. The woman balanced her tray on one hand and plucked a third drink from it for Cecy. "Sorry about this," she muttered, setting it down. "Uh, it's a Screaming Orgasm. From you know who."

Cecy jumped up, livid, and turned toward Harvey with a death look. She grabbed two of the drinks and started for him, determined to give him a piece of her mind and a cold sticky shower.

Zeke unfortunately got to him first, and yanked him up by the collar. "You wanna stop bein' obnoxious and leave the lady alone?"

Harvey unwisely invited Zeke to do something anatomically impossible.

The next thing Cecy knew, Harvey was repeatedly kissing the floor. Zeke had forcefully inspired him with affection for the dirt that walked in on the boots of customers.

With a final shove, Zeke plastered Harvey's lips to a greenish brown piece of discarded chewing gum, and left them there.

Then he got up, dusted his hands, and turned to Cecy. "Would you like me to take you home?"

17

Chas paced moodily about the house. Where was Cecy? The only trace of her in the silent house was the leftovers of Hildy's beef bourgignon. Well, that and her ugly, broken-tailed, perverted hair ball of a cat. As soon as Chas hauled the cold beef out of the refrigerator and set about making himself a plate, Barney came striding into the kitchen as if he owned the place. Chas reached down and adjusted himself, memory making him protective.

The cat seemed to believe that Chas was heaping up the healthy portion for his own feline delectation. His whiskers twitched, and he waved his bent tail back and forth, though he stopped short at wrapping himself around

Chas's legs. Too much mutual distrust existed between them. He did yowl and wait for beef to be placed before him.

"In your dreams, buddy," Chas said.

Barney looked offended. His crooked little jaw and pointed snaggle teeth snapped shut, and he blinked once. Then he parked his haunches on Grand's black-and-white-checked kitchen floor, and waited.

Chas rewrapped the leftovers in plastic and stuck them in the refrigerator. He turned to find Barney mid-leap toward his plate, and blocked him like a goalie. "Nice try," he had to admit. "You're no pussy."

Barney lashed his tail, displeased at being outmaneuvered. He trotted out of the kitchen and lurked under a side table, spying on the victor while he ate.

"If you think," Chas said conversationally, "that I'm going to give you expensive gourmet food after what you did to my leather seats, my office, and my *huevos*, you have another think coming."

Barney got up and took a swipe at a paper wad, for all the world like a surly teenager kicking a tin can. He sent it skittering across the living room, then launched himself after it. He fell on the paper and tumbled with it, securing the wad between his front paws and putting a whipping on it with his back ones.

Chas laughed.

The cat cocked his head at the sound and

spun on the polished wood floor. He regarded Chas intently. Then, by God, he picked up the paper wad in his teeth and brought it over, dropping it between Chas's feet.

Chas stopped munching. He reached down, snagged the paper wad, and tossed it in the direction of the fireplace. Barney galloped after it, batted it twice, then brought it back.

"I'll be damned," Chas said. "Where'd you learn to retrieve?"

Barney hunkered down and waited until he tossed the wad again. He brought it back like a Labrador.

"I have to tell you, cat, I'm impressed."

Barney rubbed up against the leg of the coffee table. They played armchair ball for a good ten minutes before Chas got inspired to find some fishing line and hang Barney's toy from a doorknob. In the meantime, he let him lick his plate.

That done, Chas's thoughts returned to dwell on Cecy. What kind of drink was she having with what kind of friend? She hadn't even invited him along. She'd seemed happy to get away from him and the office, despite the fact that he'd gone out of his way to be polite, affable, and charming. He'd made sure to pat her arm and thank her for a particularly good set of presentation materials.

It was all very disturbing. Not to mention that it was past eleven o'clock, and she hadn't bothered to call him and let him know she was alive.

He forced himself to focus on the old *King Kong* movie that unfolded with stilted cheesiness across the television screen. But Fay Wray reminded him of Cecy, damn it all.

When he heard the rumble of a vehicle pulling into the semicircular drive, he jumped out of his chair and stalked to the window. He pulled a corner of the drape aside and watched as a tall cowboy helped Cecy out of his blue Dodge pickup. The bastard held on to her arm far longer than necessary, and she had the nerve to laugh up at him in the moonlight.

Then she kissed him on the cheek. Why, the shameless tease! The cowboy stood a little taller, released her arm, and began to walk back to the driver's door. Chas fought the urge to run for a potato peeler and skin that kiss off the asshole's cheek before he could get away with it.

Cecy was coming closer to the front door. Chas dropped the curtain, sprinted back to his chair, and arranged himself in a studied masculine sprawl before her key touched the lock. He pointed the remote at the television and increased the volume.

The door opened and shut behind him. She jingled her keys, unzipped her purse, and said, "Hi, there."

Hi, there? What kind of lame greeting was that, after her scandalous behavior? But Chas was damned if he'd let her see she'd gotten to him. He yawned, long and wide, cast one lazy eye in her direction, and grunted. "Hey." He rotated his eyeball toward *Kong* again.

"I went to a country-western bar," she said. "It was fun."

"Really." He let disinterest roll off him in waves. "Good."

"What did you do tonight?"

Played a mean game of paper wad with your cat. Hell if he'd admit that. No way. "Oh, I had a lot of work to do," he lied.

"Chas, do you ever do anything fun?"

He blinked. "What kind of question is that? Of course I have fun. I . . . play golf. That's fun."

"No, I mean really."

Chas rubbed his hands on his knees, feeling defensive. "I do have fun," he insisted. "All the time."

"Impulsive, wind-in-the-hair, laughing-out-loud fun?"

He ran his hand through his hair impatiently. "Yeah. That's me. All the time. I'm the Chasmanian Devil."

"Uh-huh."

Maybe it was her dubious tone of voice. Or the questions she was asking him. Or the fact that she'd just picked up another man and kissed him in the moonlight, even if it was only on the cheek. Chas didn't know why, but he found himself irate. "What do *you* do for fun," he exploded, "besides give new meaning to the word 'irresponsible'?"

Cecy stood perfectly still for a long moment. Then she mounted the stairs without a word. He heard the door of her bedroom shut, and that was that.

He muttered curses to himself, watched Kong get shot off the Empire State Building, and thumped his head against the back of his chair. He had fun. He'd just had a great time being a dickhead again to poor Cecy. He was a helluva guy.

Cecy sought refuge at Target the next day after work. She wandered the aisles with a shopping cart and lost herself among the merchandise, occasionally dropping in an item that looked irresistible. So far she had quite a pile. The metal basket carried ten pairs of her favorite brand of panty hose, some mascara, assorted lipsticks, hair accessories, six different cat toys, and a case of bottled water.

In the clothing section, she added a purple bra-and-panty set, then hesitated over a turquoise one. Hey, she was irresponsible, right? And she needed a turquoise bra. Desperately, if only for the mood lift it would bring. She threw it and the panties into her basket, and kept on rollin', rollin', rollin'.

She was comforted by the smell of newness in the air all around her. So many products to explore, with bright seductive packaging that announced they were Ultra! and Improved! Her heels clicked on the shiny white floor, and she moved into the toy section. Wow, look at all those Barbies. Barbie had lately discovered the wonders of both hair dye *and* education, in that order. That pert, perfect face of hers now appeared under coiffeurs of red, black, and brown. Barbie was employed these days as a doctor, a horse trainer, an aerobics instructor. Goodness, wasn't Barbie multitalented. They ought to rename her Sibyl.

Cecy pored over Barbie's outfits anyway, and sighed with gentle avarice. Look at the ball gowns! The swank city suits. And hot damn, those shoes. Barbie was one lucky chick. Her designer shoes didn't cost hundreds of dollars, like the Manolo Blahniks Cecy coveted. Barbie's probably cost an average of sixty-nine cents. It wasn't fair.

Out of this injustice, an idea was born in Cecy's head. The next time she really, really wanted to buy a new outfit for herself on her nonexistent budget, she would buy one for Barbie, instead, at a fraction of the cost. This was a brilliant plan! She'd save all that money on dry cleaning, too, since Barbie had no body odor and didn't usually spill coffee on herself or collect cat hairs on her butt.

She might be a little old to play Barbies, but it was all in the name of saving money. And what was clothes shopping, anyway? If the truth be told, it was really just an adult version of playing dolls.

She plucked a redheaded Barbie whose shoes

she particularly admired off the shelf. Next she selected two different outfits.

Using her newfound logic, she put the turquoise and purple underwear back, along with a few other things that had migrated into her cart in the women's clothing section. Then she stared down at the ten packages of panty hose. Okay, so she'd gone a little hog-wild, and all because Mr. Fun had told her *not* to buy them. If she really didn't need panty hose in his office, then she supposed they were a flagrant waste of money. She unloaded them and put them back. She raised her chin. She was not passing up the makeup, though.

Then she eyed the seven lipsticks she'd tossed into the cart. They were five dollars apiece. Did she really need all of them? Cecy prayed for discipline, for stoicism, for just a tiny minimalist impulse to come shooting out of nowhere and set her straight. She'd always been a pink lipstick kind of girl.

Peach, plum, burgundy, slut red, beige, and white she could do without. She scooped them out of the cart and stuck them back in their various holes in the plastic display. Yes! She was strong. Cecy put a hand to her breast and inhaled deeply in a self-congratulatory moment.

She looked back down at her cart. Damn it, Buchanan was right. Why should she pay for designer water? She could drink tap slop, at least until she paid down that debt-consolidation loan. She pitched the hair accessories for good measure. The toys for Barney caused her to hesitate. Did he really need all six? Surely not. She was appalled at what the manufacturers charged for a feline-sized stuffed animal, anyway. She kept one little striped ball for him.

Cecy checked out at the register for less than forty dollars, feeling very pleased with herself.

A week later, after a very entertaining tutoring session with Etienne and Sylvie, Cecy realized what she wanted to do with the rest of her life. She was a damned good teacher. Though her methods might be a little unconventional, she made learning enjoyable for her students by relating the subject matter to their lives. She was patient. She was kind. She liked people of all types and ages.

Chas had asked her an obnoxious question two months ago, when they'd first met. *Why Frog Tales? Why didn't you study something useful?*

Because I loved it, she'd answered. And therein lay the key. She still loved French, and French literature. But she loved it on a visceral level, a passionate one, not an analytical, intellectual one. She loved the cadence and the rhythm of the language, the shared emotional experiences of the stories. She didn't give a flip about what she'd been forced to study in graduate school: postmodern and poststructuralist philosophy. She liked beginnings, middles, and satisfying ends. Why would anyone want to remove structure and stability from literature, or from life, which had so little of it to begin with? She didn't want to deconstruct language and literature and send their entrails flying into abstruse chaos theories. So there.

Why had she felt obligated to earn a Ph.D. she didn't want? Perhaps she was meant to teach on a different level. She didn't need a Ph.D. to teach high-school French; what she needed was training and certification.

She resolved to look into Georgia's teaching programs the very next day.

Chas rubbed his hands and surveyed the big spread of food on the dining-room table. Creamy Southern-style potato salad stood in one silver bowl, winking at the mother lode of baked beans in a chafing dish. Fresh coleslaw and green salad rounded out the side dishes.

Each place setting sparkled in the afternoon sunlight, and a large bouquet of multicolored blooms graced the center of the feast. His top-secret, hot-damn, homemade barbeque sauce awaited the finishing touches. The pork ribs and chicken had been marinating since the night before, and a nice pinot grigio was chilling with the dark beer in the refrigerator.

Chas was well satisfied. He'd spent some dough on this affair, but by hosting it he would, number one, prove that he could have fun, and number two, begin to unload Cecy onto her new sugar daddy. He hadn't seen Christian Cox since business school, but he knew Cecy wouldn't be able to resist his considerable charm. And if she did, by any chance, there was always Tom Barry. Chas chose not to remember what he'd done to Tom the last time he'd displayed any interest in his houseguest.

He wondered what these two friends of Cecy's would be like, and checked his watch. Everyone was due any minute, and she hadn't made an appearance yet.

As if on cue, he heard her heels on the landing and turned to look up at her. Ooooooo-eeeeee. Chas felt unbalanced suddenly, dizzy—as if he had backwards vertigo. She stood looking down at him, fastening the French cuff of a completely sheer blue-green blouse. It did have one of those tiny things under it—he believed women called them camisoles—but the overall effect was calculated to make a man drool on himself and trip over his dick. You could see straight through the damned shirt and imagine her in it alone, without any panties on, gyrating to some soft music.

But the vision didn't stop there. Oh, no. Cecy had had the malice aforethought to tuck this sheer, wispy article of torture into some form-fitting black leggings that left him breathless, and had slipped her feet into sexy, strappy sandals that presented her toes like hors d'oeuvres to tempt him. He wanted to suck on them.

Oh, hell. Now he'd gone from kneecaps to *toes*. Chas swore under his breath. He needed a drink, a stiff one.

She'd done something different to her hair,

too. It was big and fluffy and artfully brushed so that she looked as if she'd just tumbled out of bed after a shattering orgasm. He rubbed a hand over his face and turned away for that drink.

Cecy came down the stairs, and asked in a small voice, "Do I look okay?"

Chas headed for the bourbon. No, she didn't look okay. She looked staggering, hot, phenomenally beautiful. He wanted to Velcro her to a wall and do unmentionable things to her. He poured himself two fingers and tossed the liquor back. Then he managed to speak.

"Yeah," he said. "You look . . . nice." The woman was driving him to drink, to madness, to having premeditated fun. He wished she would keep away from him until the guests got there.

"Oh." Cecy pushed her sleeves up her arms just a little. "Well. Thanks."

"I've invited this great guy tonight," Chas enthused. "You'll like him. His name is Christian Cox, and he's good-looking, makes tons of money, and single."

Cecy narrowed her eyes at him. "Really."

"Yeah. I thought you might like to meet him." Chas saw a flash of anger in her beautiful eyes. Why was that? He was doing her a favor.

"Did you, now. Thanks for thinking of me." She shot him a dark, enigmatic look.

Chas shifted uncomfortably. The doorbell rang, and he went to answer it like a good host. He found two women on the other side of the door. The older one wore a ceramic yellow flower and a short, tight, leopard-print skirt. She appeared to have put on her makeup with a trowel. The other girl was quite pretty, and dressed more tastefully in brown boot-legged pants, the requisite boots, and a simple cream-colored top. "Hi, Handsome," the two said simulataneously.

He stood back to allow them entrance. "Er, hello."

Madam Leopard pushed forward. "Remember me? I'm Daisy. And this is Pam. You came by the Day Spa looking for Cecy one day."

"Of course," Chas said smoothly. "How could I forget? Two such lovely ladies, that is."

They giggled. "We brought dessert," Pam said, handing him a package of Ding Dongs.

"How thoughtful of you." Chas accepted the dreadful things with courtesy. "I'll just put these in the kitchen. Come on back."

Daisy let out a low whistle at the interior as it unfolded before her. "Nice digs," she commented. "Not much furniture, though. If you're looking, Rooms to Go has a big sale on now."

"Thanks. I may check it out," replied Chas. "What can I get you to drink?"

"D'you have any strawberry wine coolers? Or Zima?"

Chas restrained a shudder. "I'm sorry, I don't. I have a nice pinot grigio, if you'd like that."

"Oh, sure." The girls spied Cecy. "Hey, sweetie!" They hugged her. "You look hot."

"Thanks! You, too."

The doorbell rang again, and Tom Barry sauntered in without waiting for Chas to invite him. He dangled a six-pack of Miller Genuine Draft from one finger. "Howdy, all."

"Howdy," Pam replied, in breathless tones.

"Hi," said everyone else.

Tom swung the six-pack on the crook of his finger and gazed at Pam. Then he blinked three or four times in rapid succession and set the cans on the kitchen table. "Whose 'Vette is that, out there?"

"Mine," said Pam, almost shyly.

"Is that right?" murmured Tom, allowing his eyes to rove over her curves. "She's mighty nice-looking."

"Why, thank you." Pam accepted a glass of wine from Chas without even looking in his direction.

"Appears to be in great shape," Tom continued.

"Oh, she is. I keep her tuned up and change her oil often."

"Sweet. What year is she?"

" 'Eighty-six."

The doorbell chimed again, and Chas went to answer it, rolling his cuffs back as he walked. He all but rubbed his hands. This would be Christian, the answer to his prayers.

Chas swung the door wide and opened his mouth to welcome his old business-school buddy. The greeting died in his throat. The

Christian Cox he remembered had worn Brooks Brothers trousers, argyle socks, and blue button-down oxford cloth shirts. He'd climbed to the top of the class in hand-made tasseled loafers.

The man standing in front of him wore form-fitting black leather pants, a T-shirt, and a black leather vest festooned with zippers. His loafers had morphed into shiny black motorcycle boots. Instead of the Rolex Chas remembered, he wore a heavy hammered-silver bracelet, and an ear-ring in one lobe. He was so tan he appeared or-ange, and his hair had been sculpted into some sort of violently blond art form. Worse, he was spreading his arms wide for a hug.

"Buchanan! Good to see you. I was *thrilled* to get your e-mail after all this time."

Chas stuck out his hand. "Cox—you're look-ing, ah, good. Welcome back to Atlanta." He stood there, staring, until Christian bypassed his proffered hand and grabbed him in a bear hug. He was enveloped by the alarming smell of the leather, and a sickening, spicy-sweet cologne that conjured images of men enjoying hot tubs together, naked. Chas backed rapidly out of the hug. "Come on in, let me get you a beer."

"Oh, white wine, please."

Had Christian always had that lisp?

"So tell me all about you," his old friend urged.

Chas wanted urgently to know the same about Christian. Well—not in lurid detail. Just the basics. Like how he'd become Boy George in eight short years. He swallowed. Christian Cox didn't look like anybody's sugar daddy. He looked more like . . . like . . . the owner of an S & M club. Great—dinner was going to be interesting. He'd be surrounded by a shopaholic, an aging beauty queen, a young nymph, a good ole boy, and a bondage boy. He needed another drink.

Christian threw an arm around him on their way toward the kitchen. "Been working out lately? You're one rock-solid hunk, dude." He squeezed Chas's shoulder with his bracelet-clad hand.

Chas stiffened from cranium to tailbone. Nobody, but nobody called him dude. Man, maybe, but not dude. They entered the kitchen, and he made the introductions all around. He ducked under Cox's arm on the pretense of checking the marinade.

"Divine," said Daisy. "*Who* did your highlights, Christian? They're fabulous."

"Awesome," Pam agreed.

"That's such a personal question," Cox simpered. He poured himself some pinot grigio. "God gave me this hair color."

"Don't try to shit *me*." Daisy waggled a finger at him. "I'm in the business."

"I'm unmasked," Christian declared. "My stylist is Justin James. He's an absolute wizard."

"Oh, I've heard of him. He has quite the reputation around town."

"Yes," Christian said with a wicked grin. "He *does*. All true."

Chas was sure that they weren't discussing hair any longer, and hastened to change the subject.

Cecy eyed him quizzically and folded her arms. His right eyelid began to twitch, and he busied himself with finding the tools he needed for the grill. As he reached for the long toasting fork, he noticed that Christian was giving his body an appreciative once-over. Make that a twice-over. *Oh, Jesus, no.* Chas dropped the fork with a clatter, then realized he had to bend over to pick it up.

Damned if he would. Avoiding Christian's eyes, which had brightened, he stuck his foot out and slid the utensil across the floor. He backed, dragging it, against the stove, and then reached down.

"Let me wash that for you, Chazzy," said Cox. "I love hot, soapy water. And long prongs."

Chas dropped the fork again. Sweat beaded across his forehead.

"Yes, *Chazzy*," Cecy put in. "Let him scrub it for you. So nice of him to offer. You told me I'd like him, and I do." She laid a hand on Christian's arm. "Chazzy told me all about you."

"All good things, I hope." Christian touched a hand to his hair.

"Oh, yes," Cecy purred. "He told me he's

been thinking about you a lot lately. He even had a dream about you."

A lascivious grin spread across Cox's handsome face. "Do tell."

Chas rolled his eyes violently at Cecy, but she ignored him.

"Well," she began. "He dreamed you were both stranded on the Isle of Corfu, with nothing but your swim trunks and a bottle of suntan oil—"

Chas coughed violently to drown out her voice.

"Oh, Chazzy," she broke off, concerned. "Are you hacking up a hair ball again? I told you to take your medicine." She turned back to Christian. "He can be stubborn as a mule, you know," she cooed. She took his arm and opened the garden door, whispering in his ear all the while.

Christian expelled his breath in a whooosh. "You don't say? He's hung like a mule, too?" The door closed on them.

Chas reached down again for the fork, horrified. Why was the little vixen doing this to him, all because he'd tried to set her up with a date? He'd hang her from the foyer chandelier when everyone left, by God.

Luckily Pam and Tom Barry were utterly immersed in conversation with each other, and only Daisy eyed him with speculation plain on her face. He knew he was tomato red, and it made him all the more furious.

"It's okay, Handsome." Daisy reassured him. "It's genetic, after all. You can't help being gay, and it certainly isn't anything to be ashamed of."

"But I'm not!" Chas insisted.

"If you want to keep your cover story, that's fine. But when you come out of that closet, you'll feel a million times better. Be who you are," Daisy told him. "This is the millennium, sweetie, not the Victorian Era."

He opened his mouth to refute again that he was gay, but decided it was useless. Daisy's generous, serene expression told him she was enjoying her role as therapist. She continued to expound for several minutes on the benefits of letting one's inner soul unfold like a blossom in spring.

Chas escaped to the grill, where he charred his feelings, along with the edges of the chicken and ribs, and prayed that the evening would end early.

A couple of rounds of drinks later, they all sat around the Duncan Phyfe dining table. He would swear Tom and Pam played footsie together during the entire meal.

"You don't wanna know," Tom said softly to her, "what I used to do in the backseat of *my* 'Vette in high school."

Pam fluttered her eyelashes at him, and Chas felt distinctly nauseous.

Across from him Cecy and Christian chatted in a cozy twosome, which the latter occasionally interrupted with a long speculative stare at Chas. He gnawed suggestively on a pork rib, and licked the sauce off his lips.

Chas averted his gaze, and asked Daisy what had led her into the hairstyling field.

"Well, Handsome," she began, "it all started with my long curly hair and an ironing board . . ."

Her teenage travails paled in comparison with Christian's story, though. He loaned half an ear to Daisy while Cox unfolded his life change to Cecy.

"I went to a massage therapist," he told her. "I was working my ass off in a start-up technology business, and barely sleeping. I had more knots in my shoulders and lower back than we had clients. This guy made me feel like I'd died and gone to heaven, and was hot-looking to boot. He worked all the kinks and hang-ups out of my body, and introduced me to a different way of life.

"To make a long story short, I ended up investing in a video business he had on the side. It's one of the biggest chains in the Southeast now." He turned to shoot a meaningful look at Chas across the table. "We're enormously successful. I've hired a CEO to run the business end, which frees me up to be the idea man and to travel. I'm always on scouting trips for new locations, Chazzy. You must come with me on one. We'll have a *fabulous* time, I promise you." He winked.

Chas managed to lodge a baked bean between his tonsils, and suck it into his windpipe. He was forced to leave the table to clear up the problem.

He returned to find Daisy, Christian, and Cecy discussing the horrors of single life and dating.

"All these divorced men want is a biddable twenty-year-old," Daisy complained. "They're not bright enough to realize they'd be happier with an interesting personality."

"Oh, I *know*," Christian put in, nodding his too-blond head. "I've done the twenty-year-olds, myself. It's tempting, but I'm really ready for a more mature lover, someone I can have a dialogue with." He looked pointedly at Chas. "I'm good-looking, successful, rich, and ready to treat my sweetie right."

"Chas *told* me," enthused Cecy, patting Christian's arm. "Isn't it lucky that you rediscovered each other, after all this time?"

"What about you, Cecy?" Daisy asked. "Are you dating anyone?"

Cecy shook her head. "Not really. Though I've had the bad luck to"—she raised her chin—"to fall in love with someone."

Chas gripped the underside of his chair, hard, and guillotined a morsel of potato.

"Someone who doesn't think I'm that special, apparently, because he keeps me at a polite distance." Cecy wouldn't look at him.

Daisy and Christian clucked in consolation.

"How do you know he's not just reserved, or shy, honey?" Daisy asked.

"Because he just tried to set me up with another man," Cecy blurted. Her hurt hung in the air, a tangible thing.

Chas looked straight down at his napkin, unable to think of a word to say. He was a complete asshole, and wished he could just pull his pants up over his head. Would this party never end?

18

Cecy held her head high and cleared dirty wineglasses and plates from the table after the party broke up.

"Get a room," she heard Chas mutter at Tom Barry. "You've been playing footsie all night." He all but shoved him out the door after Pam and Daisy.

"Yeah, well I know someone who wants to play bootsie with *you*. Pin the tail on the ass, ya know?" Tom replied.

"Shut up!" Chas hissed.

"Who woulda guessed it of Cox?" Tom laughed. "Anyway, thanks for a very entertaining evening. I got Pam's number."

"The way you were carrying on, you could

have gotten her bra as a keepsake. Get out of here. I'll see you on the golf course."

Cecy heard the door close, and then a thump—as if Chas had banged his forehead against it. *Good. Hah. The low-down, rotten, scum-sucking pig.* So she was his charity case, was she? And he'd decided it was time to unload her onto another guy, whose income he'd dangled in front of her like a carrot.

He thought that she'd jump like a bunny for bucks, and then he'd see the last of her little fluffy tail. *God!* She ground her teeth and took another load of dishes to the sink.

Chas Buchanan wasn't kind. He didn't have feelings for her. He certainly didn't *love* her. A four-letter word, that. Four festering, foolish, foul letters that really spelled d-i-p-s-t-i-c-k. Or s-t-u-p-i-d. Or w-a-k-e u-p!

So why was she standing there, doing the dishes from his bomb of a party? Cecy grabbed the platter of leftover pork ribs and shoved the contents into the disposal, then mashed them down as far as she could. That should fix his little red wagon.

She was doing the dishes because she felt obligated. She'd eaten his food. She slept and bathed in his house. She worked in his office. *Aaaaaargh.* Was there anything she didn't owe him for?

She hated the man. She'd wanted love, and he'd given her charity. How humiliating. She'd lived on other people's charity all her life. It had never been mentioned, but she knew Mama Sue received some small pittance from the state for taking care of unwanted children.

And now she was an unwanted adult. An unwanted, debt-ridden, clueless basket case with a fondness for purple underwear.

Cecy took a large scoop of potato salad, opened Chas's utility drawer, and plopped it inside. She banged the drawer shut. That should smell nice in two or three days.

She knew it was an awful thing to do. Immature, ungrateful, and petty. So who cared? What else could she do to relieve her feelings?

Chas's footsteps crossed the kitchen floor behind her. He cleared his throat. "Cecy?"

She ratcheted her chin up another notch and ignored him. Baked beans could do wonders in the clothes dryer.

"Cecy, you don't have to do that. You're not obligated."

She whirled on him, wielding a dripping, long-handled scrub brush. "The hell I'm not!" With each word, she shook the brush at him, showering him with droplets.

Chas wiped at his face with the heel of his hand. A couple of soap bubbles still clung to the five o'clock shadow that grew over his jaw and cheeks like . . . like benday dots. Her onetime dream lover had faded into an overblown Roy Lichtenstein cartoon.

He took a deep breath. "Cecy, please leave the dishes alone. You don't owe me anything. I don't want you to feel that way."

"What way? You don't want me to be in love with you? You don't want me to be upset? You don't want me to *feel*, period! You want to hold your hand over your heart, the Smug Samaritan, and breathe deeply of your goodness and charity. This *has* all been very big of you, truly. I can't ask any more of you—not even a couple of grains of sentiment."

"I don't want you confusing love with gratitude." Chas rubbed his palms on his trousers.

Cecy drew in her breath with a hiss.

"You are in no way obligated to me," Chas continued. "Is that clear?"

She turned off the faucet with a jerk. "I don't owe you anything? Is that so."

"No," he said. "You don't."

She could feel her face snapping into hard, rigid lines. "Well, Chas, you're the accountant. You keep the ledger and balance those columns. I shouldn't question your professional judgment."

"What are you talking about?"

"Oh, just a simple formula. An age-old one, really. Assets for credit."

Chas stared at her, his brow furrowed.

"The way you undoubtedly see it, you've extended me lots of credit, Chas. I live in your house, work in your office, am dependent on your financial plan. I borrow your car."

"Cecy—"

"And in exchange, I have put up—or should I say put out?—my *assets*, which you have fore-closed upon. But now it's time to unload them onto the market, isn't it, Chas? Oh, it's just business. Nothing personal. I understand."

"No! That is not what's going on, here. Just—"

"Don't feel bad, Chas. It's the age-old chauvinist bargain. Protection for pooty. Cash for tush. Diamonds for delight." Cecy could hear the tremor in her voice now, and willed it to go away.

"Why should you think I have any integrity? Or pride? I'm just a dim little piece of fluff, after all. Only smart enough to snare myself a nice Buckhead boy as a meal ticket." Her voice was now shaking.

"Sweetheart, I was only trying to—"

"*Don't* call me that. You can take your sexist terminology and shove it where the sun don't shine, Buchanan. Along with your outdated notions of women. I'm sorry I'm not perfect. I'm sorry I screwed up my life. But it's only temporary—just like you are." Cecy was choking on her emotion, now, but she was *damned* if she would let him see a single, solitary tear. She sucked in enough breath for her finale.

"Did you like having the tables turned on you, Buchanan? Did you like how it made you feel, you patronizing son of a bitch? Why *don't* you go out with Christian? After all, he's great-looking, successful, and rich. Why don't *you* suck his dick for your dinner? Because *I* don't operate like that."

Chas stared at her with horrified anguish.

"I'm moving out," she told him, tossing the scrub brush she clenched into the sink. "I'll be back for my things in the morning."

The door slammed behind Cecy. Chas cursed, spewing imaginative filth in new and improved combinations. He couldn't get over what an incredible dick he was. He had hurt Cecy beyond belief, and hadn't even realized his actions were damaging. Hell, he hadn't seen that his whole thought process was abominable. Why did it take a woman, particularly *this* woman, to point that out?

But one thing was for sure—no matter how angry she was at him, he wasn't letting her walk anywhere in the middle of the night. It wasn't safe out there. She was on foot, and alone in the heart of Atlanta. Not even a crass, unfeeling Yankee like him could permit her to wander around in the dark.

Chas swept his Jeep keys off the cherry hall table and went after her. She wasn't far down the street, hadn't even passed the long grilled wall of the governor's mansion. Chas rolled down his windows to call out to her, and realized that two monstrous Dobermans growled and snarled through the fence at his petite blond quarry.

"Hah!" Cecy barked at them. "Bite me."

Chas was certain that they'd be only too happy to oblige. Though the dogs were restrained by bars of steel, they still made him nervous. He pulled up next to her. "Cecy," he said, with all the authority he could muster, "get in the Jeep."

She turned with a look that should have reduced him to ashes, had there been any justice in the world. "Suck wind," she said, distinctly. And kept walking.

Ah, Jesus. Chas followed her at two and a half miles per hour, with his head stuck out the window.

"Cecy," he tried again. "Be reasonable."

"Reason is for accountants, Buchanan. Not for little balls of fluff like me. If you're going to stereotype me, at least be consistent."

He gnashed his teeth. "Be smart, then."

"Again, flawed logic on your part. I'm just a tiny little blonde, clinging to a corner of a big Buckhead wallet, remember? Don't expect me to be smart—just manipulative."

His right eyelid twitched, and Chas gunned the motor. It didn't help his mood that his eyes swiveled with her hips at every outraged step she took. *Damn the woman.*

"Look," he ground out. "It's not safe for you out here. If you don't get into the damned Jeep, I'm going to follow you all the way to wherever you're going."

"You're going to look pretty stupid, then," Cecy returned, "because I'm *through* being beholden to you. Not even for a ride."

"Come on, Cecy. Please don't do this."

"Do what? Try to recover my self-respect? My pride? My life?"

"All that has nothing to do with getting into my Jeep."

"Oh yes, it does."

"How do you figure?"

"Look at it as a metaphor, Buchanan. I'm not accepting any more rides from you."

"Walking in the dark alone at night isn't about metaphors, Cecy. It's about muggers. Will you please get in? I'll take you wherever you want. You don't have to come home."

She swallowed the lump that appeared in her throat. She had no home. Why did he have to say things like that? She wished he would just go away.

But he didn't. He kept rattling along next to her. If the Bean Counter wanted to shadow her all the way to Inman Park, then fine. She couldn't think of anything to say that would make him go away.

Cecy glanced over her shoulder as bright, blinking red lights reflected off the high white concrete walls of another Paces Ferry estate. One of Atlanta's finest pulled up behind Chas's Jeep and flashed him to pull over. This should be fun.

A burly police officer got out of the driver's side door and approached them, leaving his companion in the passenger seat. "Ma'am? Is everything all right here?" He had warm chocolate brown skin and kind, rounded features. "Is this man bothering you?"

"I was worried about her, Officer," Chas broke in.

"Did I ask you anything?" The kindness disappeared from the policeman's expression.

"Er, no sir," said Chas. "But—"

"Is this man bothering you, miss?" The officer asked Cecy again.

She flashed Chas a smug look. "As a matter of fact, he is. He's following me."

"I'm trying to—"

"Step out of the car, please, sir. I'll need to see some ID."

"But—"

"ID! Which letter didn't you understand?"

Chas fished his wallet out and handed over his driver's license. "I live right down the street."

"That's not what it says, here." The officer flashed him a look which boded ill for Chas.

"Oh, that. I haven't gotten the address changed, yet—I just bought—"

"Have you been drinking, sir?"

"No! I mean, just a couple of beers. I just had a par—"

"I'd like you to come over here and take a breathalizer for me, please."

Cecy folded her arms, stood back, and watched the scenario unfold. Chas glared at her.

"I'll need you to breathe into this instrument, here, sir." The policeman pointed.

"Go blow, Chas," Cecy said sweetly.

Thank God he passed, and wasn't over the legal limit. The policeman grunted, and turned back to her. "Now, miss. How long has this man been following you? Is he stalking you? Are you afraid of him?"

Cecy chewed on her bottom lip, and Chas could see her debating on how much trouble she should cause him. He was going to jail tonight, for sure.

She sighed. "He's only trying to make sure I'm safe. No, he's not stalking me, and no, I'm not afraid of him. I just hate him, that's all."

Chas let out his breath in a whoosh. He was profoundly relieved that she'd decided to play fair and not manufacture trouble for him. A lot of women would have done it out of spite. But Cecy was . . . she was honest.

"Would it be possible for you to take me to Inman Park?" Cecy asked the uniform. "I really don't want to go with *him*." She jerked her thumb in Chas's direction, as if he were an unpleasant specimen of creepy-crawly.

"Well, miss, it's not something we ordinarily do. But if you'll wait just a moment, we'll take you when we're finished here."

Now, what? Chas fulminated.

"Sir," the officer said to him, "Your tags have expired, and your brake lights are not functioning. I'm going to have to write you a ticket."

"I'm overjoyed."

The officer gave him a sharp look. "I can always add a fine for disrespect, buddy."

"That won't be necessary, Officer."

"Good." He scrawled out the ticket and handed it to Chas with his driver's license. "May I suggest that you leave the lady alone? She obviously doesn't want your company, whether it's well intentioned or not."

He nodded in silence.

" 'Nighty 'night, Chazzy." Cecy blew him a kiss and climbed into the squad car.

Chas rattled back home in the Jeep, slammed the door as he got out, and stomped inside. Anger, guilt, shame, and poor judgment roiled in his stomach, as if he'd mixed several different varieties of alcohol in one evening. He needed some Pepto Bismol and a soft bed.

He passed through the dining room and gazed despondently at the table. He saw Cecy sitting in one of the chairs, lifting her delicate chin and announcing that she'd had the misfortune to fall in love with someone who obviously didn't consider her special.

Cecy was in love with him? The thought sent a warm "zing" through his body, until he repressed it. Cecy had *thought* she was in love with him, and Cecy wanted her problems taken care of. He was no sap.

Then why had she gotten so upset that he'd tried to set her up with Christian? He told himself that she'd already put in a lot of effort on one man, and so resisted having to start over with another. That was it.

But if she was that shallow and manipulative, then spite should play a big part in her personality as well. Out there on Paces Ferry tonight, she'd played fair. Hell.

Okay, so Cecy Scatterton was honest. She'd never taken money from the office, even when she was starving. She'd taken his cold, soggy, half-munched burger instead, and only when she knew he was through with it. That image still drove him nuts.

She'd moved into his office when she was homeless, but instead of hocking all the computers and equipment, she'd worked extra hours to pay for the window Barney broke.

Chas tunneled his fingers through his hair and dug them into his scalp. She'd accused him of stereotyping her as a devious little blond piece of fluff. Tom Barry had accused her of the same thing, out on the golf course. Why was that?

Perhaps because Tom had known Maria, too, and she'd affected their expectations of women. After the sweet goodness of Chas's mother, and the refreshing, nutty vitality of Grand, he hadn't been prepared to meet someone like Maria. He'd had no reason to distrust her.

So maybe he *was* guilty of stereotyping Cecy because of his past experience. All right. But that still didn't mean that she was really in love with him. How did he know she didn't just feel a sense of obligation to him? While the question was a definite slap to his ego, he had to consider it.

Maria hadn't thought him irresistible, after all.

Chas sighed, trying to sift through everything logically. Even if he gave Cecy credit for being intelligent enough to distinguish gratitude from love and sex, that didn't mean he was in love with *her*.

He looked around him at the lofty ceilings, tall windows, and hardwood floors of Grand's house. He wasn't about to put the house at risk for any woman. He'd worked too hard, and too long, to possess it.

He wished Cecy would get out of his head, but he kept seeing the damned squad car, brake lights glinting, with the last of her disappearing into it. That shapely calf stayed in his mind, that elegant little heel, those hors d'oeuvre toes.

Worse, though, the hurt in her voice echoed in his head. Whether he returned her feelings or not, he had no right to make light of them. He'd had no right to unload her so unsubtly. His actions had been crass. Thoughtless.

He didn't like that. He'd always been what people referred to as a "good egg." But was it better to be hard-boiled, or over easy?

19

"**B**ut I've signed a contract," said Cecy to Etienne and Sylvie, later that evening. "I have to work in his office for a year."

Etienne paced back and forth, his hands laced together on his paunch. "Bah!" He stopped to pluck a tuft of cat hair off his sleeve and toss it to the ground. "Zees eez barbaric! Eez monstrous!"

"Yes, *chéri*," Sylvie agreed, stooping to catch the tuft before it reached the polished floor. "But, a contract, eet eez a contract."

"Eh?" He waved his arms at her. "Peeg-wash! Mule-featherz! Bull-vomit!"

Cecy sighed. They were going to have to work on his idioms—but not tonight. What malice she could muster toward Chas had left her feeling exhausted and guilty. She squirmed. When she'd ladled the potato salad into the utility drawer and jammed the pork ribs down the disposal, she'd conveniently forgotten that she would have to face Chas at work. Ooops. Thank God she hadn't thrown the baked beans in the dryer, after all.

Then she chased away the guilt. He hadn't even apologized! Even though it had been written all over his face, he had not said the words, so he deserved what she'd done.

She refrained from mentioning her streak of vengeance to Etienne and Sylvie.

"You will stay here, ahve course, *chérie*," they said in unison.

Though they were very kind, she couldn't just exchange one Samaritan for another. It was time to stand firmly on her own size six feet, whether in three-inch heels or moldy sneakers. "You are wonderful to offer, but—"

"No bahts! Bahts are not permissible."

They argued about it for a while, and Cecy finally agreed that she would move into their finished basement, but would pay them three hundred dollars a month for the privilege. Barney would come with her.

She was relieved to find the basement space was tiled, and possessed a tiny bathroom. Sylvie had painted the walls a cheery yellow, and lace curtains hung over the small, high windows. At least she and Barney wouldn't be making friends with rats or creepy-crawlies.

"I do insist on working through the term of my contract with Buchanan, however," she announced, her tone of voice brooking no argument. "I signed an agreement, and I will not back out. He arranged a loan for me, based on nothing but my honor and integrity, and I won't compromise them."

They eyed her gravely. "Eet will be most—how you say—uncomfortable," Sylvie warned.

"You're telling me."

"But thees eez why we like you, Etienne and I. You have ze *je ne sais quoi*, the class, the integrity, eh? You are *someone*," Sylvie declared. "*Comprends-tu?*"

Cecy nodded slowly. What a compliment. She was *someone*. Someone, not nobody. She felt her face split into a big smile she hadn't dreamed she was capable of at this moment. "Thank you."

"*Zut alors*," Etienne waved his hand, "eet eez within *you*. Do not thank *us*."

"*Maintenant*," said Sylvie, "you will sleep, eh?" The older woman put an arm around Cecy's shoulders, and led her to the sparsely furnished guest room with a plain blue-cotton blanket on the double bed. Cecy already missed Grand's quilt, with the singing moose, belly-dancing elephants, and kissing monkeys.

Chas entered the big old black-and-white kitchen, Barney tagging after him. The cat sat on his haunches and yawned while Chas surveyed the party mess. Cecy seemed to have put away all the food except for the beans. He was hungry, and despite the fact that it was one o'clock in the morning, he stuck his head into the refrigerator in search of ribs. He felt like gnawing savagely on something's bones.

How curious. No ribs in sight—only chicken. He knew there had been plenty of leftovers. Where were they? He looked suspiciously at Barney, but the cat wasn't burping. Chas shrugged and made for the Ding Dongs Daisy and Pam had brought. He tore the package open and unwrapped one, taking a huge bite.

Most of the dishes were loaded into the racks of the dishwasher, which stood open. He added a few more cups and a plate while chewing, threw in the soap, closed it, then hit START.

He washed some mystery blobs and crumbs down the disposal, then noticed a small bowl of salsa, which had been sitting out since early that evening.

Chas poured the salsa into the disposal and ran water after it, then flipped the switch. A thunderous rumbling ensued, followed by a high-pitched whine, a couple of *thwacks*, and finally smoke.

Barney scrambled.

Chas jumped for the switch and turned it off.

He peered down into the black hole, then shoved his hand into it. His mouth turned down, his nostrils flared, and his brows snapped together in revulsion as he yanked out a slimy, veggie-speckled pork rib, and then another. And another.

Next he fished out a broken blade, followed by four more ribs. He flung them into the garbage and kept scrounging. Two more ribs emerged, one with another broken blade embedded in it. Once he had the disposal cleared, he flipped the switch again, but nothing happened.

Chas's jaw worked.

Then he began to choke on a guffaw.

The guffaw morphed into a gasp and a cough, and finally into a roar of laughter.

Barney peered cautiously around the doorframe as his host convulsed over the sink.

"Cat," Chas managed, "I'm guessing Cecy's *over* her sense of obligation to me."

Cecy chewed nervously on her bottom lip as she approached the door of Chas's office next morning. She took a deep breath, smoothed a nonexistent wrinkle out of her skirt, and turned the knob.

"Good morning," Chas said in jovial tones. He looked impossibly handsome in the eight o'clock sunlight. He was freshly shaven and clad in the usual knife-creased khakis.

Cecy blinked.

"And how are you? Like some coffee?"

"F-fine. No thank you."

"I know you're probably worried about Barney. He had a nice breakfast of scrambled eggs and Meow Mix in milk."

"Meow Mix in *milk*?" She wasn't sure she'd heard him right.

"I figured it was like cat Wheaties."

"Oh. Were the scrambled eggs necessary?"

"I thought so, for protein. He'd left the leg of a bird on my pillow, and I found the rest of it under the bed."

Cecy clapped a hand over her mouth. "Sorry! But it's really your fault—he starts with that if he doesn't have his toys. *You* scratched them off the list."

"Ah. I should have known it would work out to be my fault, somehow. I just figured it was a protein deficiency."

Cecy walked to her desk and dropped her purse into its drawer. "If it makes you feel any better, Barney only brings dead animals to people he likes." *Though why he likes you is unfathomable.*

"Yeah? I kind of like him, too. He possesses some very doglike qualities. How did you teach him to retrieve?"

She spun to face him. "He's been playing 'fetch' with you, too?"

Chas nodded.

Barney was developing particularly poor judgment. Cecy shrugged in answer to the question. "I just started him young, with a tennis ball. Then we moved down to a ball his size. He figured out that if he wanted me to throw it, he had to bring it to me."

Chas shoved his hands in his pockets. "Hey, I wanted to thank you for cleaning up the kitchen." His expression was bland—too bland.

Cecy narrowed her eyes at him. "No problem."

"You have quite a sense of humor," he added. "You really know how to rib a guy." He winked at her, then disappeared into his inner office, shutting the door gently.

She stared after him. Where was the Buchanan Bellow? She'd been left with no satisfaction whatsoever. And he *still* hadn't apologized. Damn the man.

Chas took a huge gulp of air once he was behind his door. He was so relieved, he was weak. *She had come to the office.* He told himself that he was so happy because he wouldn't have to train another assistant. But he knew damned well that he'd been eyeing those cute toes of hers in their pretty sandals. And those lips, which were plump, pink, and positively pouty this morning. The tips of her ears stuck through her tousle of hair, as usual.

If he looked closer into the labyrinth of his brain, he also discovered satisfaction that she didn't back out of a bargain even if it was emotionally uncomfortable. Cecy, once the poster child for irresponsibility, had become reliable.

He told himself that her moving out provided him with the best of all possible worlds. He'd

have her very competent services during the
day, while at night he'd have his house to himself. A man had to be able to retreat to his cave.

Unfortunately, his thoughts on this changed
at the end of the day, when he'd been treated to
enough cool civility to drive him mad. *Mr.
Buchanan? Mr. and Mrs. Koslow are here to see you.
Would you sign right here, Mr. Buchanan? Thank
you. This letter requires your immediate attention,
Mr. Buchanan.*

After work, she stopped by the house with
Sylvie to retrieve Barney and her few boxes of
things, and told him coolly that she'd see him at
the office next day. Fine, that was just fine, he
told her, and helped them pack her boxes into
Sylvie's car. It was the least he could do.

Chas paced all over the house, making notes
on a legal pad about improvements and repairs.
He flipped on lights and the television to combat
the dark silence, but the electric companions
weren't much comfort.

He cursed and dialed Tom Barry's number.
No answer. He tried his friend's cell phone.

"Hello?" Barry's voice was fuzzy. Music
played in the background, and a female voice
laughed. "Stop that, baby!"

"Er," said Chas. "I obviously got you at a bad
time."

"No, no! I'm having a great time," Barry
drawled. "But it's not the kind of thing I'd share
with you, even if you are my buddy."

The female voice giggled again, then shrieked.

"Is that Pam?"

"None other. Mind if we catch up tomorrow, Buchanan?"

"Not at all." Chas hung up the receiver and glared morosely at the paper wad he'd hung on a doorknob with fishing line. The ugly, broken-tailed beast wasn't even here to play with. This sucked.

His head ached, and he trudged up the stairs to the bathroom to find some aspirin. Once he'd taken a step inside, he closed his eyes. The small room smelled of Cecy—the fragrances of her hair, her body, her subtle perfume. Peaches and hydrangea.

He blinked rapidly and gazed toward the tub. She'd removed everything from the vanity and other surfaces except for the bottles of bath oil and body lotion he'd bought for her. They stood in a corner, under a towel rack.

Chas wasn't sure why, but the sight of those bottles was like a punch to the gut. She'd thrown his small gifts back in his face.

He inhaled the scent of her once again, and wondered if he could really blame her. The towels she'd used to dry her body with only yesterday morning mocked him. He drew one of them slowly off the chrome bar and buried his face in it.

Still clutching the towel, he turned and

walked into her room. She'd left it immaculate—the pillows plumped, bed made, Grand's quilt spread evenly over the frame. He went to the closet and opened it. Wire hangers hung silently with nothing draped over them. The shelves over the wooden rods were bare. Not a sweater, not a scarf, not a single T-shirt remained of her. He backed out and was closing the door when something in the far corner caught his eye. Something red, peeking from behind an empty cardboard box.

Chas bent and reached for it, and held it in his hand with a wry smile on his face. It was a high-heeled scarlet-leather sandal. He could see the light imprint of her foot in the lining, and he rubbed his thumb over it affectionately. What a fitting memento for her to leave behind. He took it into his own bedroom and set it on his teak dresser.

It perched incongrously next to a silver bowl filled with cuff links and a small humidor. He shook his head and left the room.

As he descended the stairs, running his hand down the smooth mahogany banister, he looked left toward the portrait of his grandparents. Was it his imagination, or did Grand look irritated, instead of serene? He shook off the thought, and went to do the couch-potato thing in front of the television. He grasped the remote and felt the power surge through him. He was now in control, and that was as it should be. He could manipulate all the images on the screen, zapping them away when he didn't like what the characters did. Unpleasant emotional scene? Click. Sappy women cooing at a baby shower? Click. Rugged man in the Rockies, expounding upon his hemorrhoid cream? Click.

Forget women and dogs. A man's best friend was his remote control. With it, naked women came hither, beer was always a hot topic, and he could watch some sort of sport almost every minute of the day.

His phone rang just as he'd surfed all sixty-odd channels for the third time. "Hello?"

"Chas, you sexy thang. I was just thinking about you," a plummy male voice purred.

His heart did a backflip into his stomach, where the digestive enzymes and acid kicked in and had a party with it. "Christian?"

"Mmmmmm hmmmm."

Chas stared at the little holes in the mouthpiece of the phone as if each one would birth a rattlesnake at any moment. "Uh, hi. It was good to see you again after so long."

"I never figured you for the shy type, Chazzy. But then, I never figured you for the alternate lifestyle type, either. You're so macho, so . . . sort of *growly*, you know? Such a delightful surprise."

"Listen, Christian, about that—"

"Cecy told me that it's been rough on you, facing up to it and all. It was agonizing for me, too."

"There's something about Cecy that you

should know," Chas said. "She's rather angry at me right now, because—"

"I know, I know. You've *been* with her, and she had hopes, but you couldn't get it up because you prefer men."

"She told you that!" gasped Chas.

"She was angry about it initially, but she assured me that all is forgiven, and she wants only to be your friend."

"Oh, she does, does she?" He was going to grab her by those cute little ears and shake her 'til the teeth rattled in her head. Then he was going to string her up by those hors d'oeuvre toes. "Listen, there's been a big mistake here. Let me clear it up before this gets any more embarassing."

"I have tickets, first-class, to Grand Cayman. We can clear up anything you like over martinis on the plane. Bring your trunks, a lot of skin, and . . . your sports equipment." Christian laughed softly. "I'll provide everything else."

Chas shuddered. "Cox. Buddy. Thank you. *But I'm not gay.*"

A long silence greeted this statement. "But Cecy was so definite . . ."

"Cecy," he said evenly, "was being malicious because I was going to set you up with *her*. Not realizing, of course, that you'd gone through . . . changes."

More silence.

"Christian," Chas continued, "I have the utmost respect for you and wish you all the happiness in the world, with whoever is out there for you, but that person is *not* me."

"Oh, my God. The little vixen. I'm so embarrassed."

"Don't be. You were set up, good and proper, and so was I. The problem is that I deserved it, but you didn't. She and I are going to have a talk about that."

"If only I were into spanking *women*."

Chas choked. "Yeah, well. You stay in touch, okay? Let me know how business is going."

"Absolutely. Bye."

He threw the receiver back into its cradle and heaved a sigh of relief, feeling his heart squeeze itself back through his intestines and up into its proper place. Why was it that this whole experience had him feeling off-kilter? He didn't believe he was prejudiced against any minority, but being slavered over by another man sent shivers up his spine.

God—he felt like such an *object*, a piece of *meat*. Was this how a woman felt, when she entered a bar alone? Hell. Was this how he'd made Cecy feel?

Chas resolved never to look a woman up and down again. Well, not in an embarrassing way, anyhow. He was human, after all. From now on, he would treat the world's women with the utmost respect. Though he still wanted to strangle one of them.

He wasn't even sure Cecy Scatterton still qualified as a woman in his mind. She was a demon, a Jezebel, a shrew. She had told Christian Cox that *he couldn't get it up*. The more he thought about it, the more he stewed.

Maybe he'd deserved having the tables turned on him, but Christian hadn't deserved being embarrassed like that, and she had no right to call Chas's manhood into question. He had a primitve impulse to stride out into the neighborhood, beating on his chest and emitting Tarzan howls. How dare she? She knew his equipment was in perfect order, and that the blood ran red and hot through his veins. He'd proved it to her, and he'd prove it again. He'd boink her into the next century—by God, he would.

Cecy got to the office early next morning, and started the coffee. Another day of professional courtesy lay ahead of her. *Blek*. The dark liquid oozed and dripped through the filter, landing with a muddy splat in the bottom of the glass pot. It reflected her mood.

She'd slept poorly the night before, flopping about like a landed fish in Etienne and Sylvie's guest room. Tonight they would move her things into the finished basement, where she'd have a door of her own to the outside, and the tiny half bath next to the washing machine and dryer.

Cecy frowned and dug into the pocket of her cardigan. Thinking of Etienne and Sylvie had reminded her that a friend of theirs, who owned a

French restaurant, needed accounting help with the American tax laws. She'd just pulled out the scribbled name and phone number when she heard the main office door slam, with a force that rattled the cabinet doors in the tiny kitchenette.

Khaki-clad thighs brushed together furiously with a *whish, whish, whish.* Loafers clomped across the carpet, and a large index finger suddenly hovered like a bumblebee two inches from her nose.

"Top of the morning to you, Mr. Buchanan," said Cecy calmly. "Would you like coffee?" *He must have found the potato salad.*

"Don't give me that crap." Chas dumped his briefcase and blazer in a chair and stood arms akimbo, his chest puffed out.

"I'll take that as a 'no,' " she murmured, and poured herself a steaming cup of the brown liquid. "Now, why are we all scowls and growls today?"

Chas snatched the cup of coffee out of her hands and plunked it on the counter.

"Hey!" Cecy protested.

His big hands grasped her shoulders, burning through the thin layers of silk shell and cardigan. "We're all scowls and growls, as you put it, because I got asked out on a date last night. By Christian Cox."

She smirked at him. "So?"

He gritted his teeth and tightened his hold on her. "So, I discovered that a mutual aquaintance of ours had told him a pack of lies."

Her smirk widened. "Oh, *I* know what you're upset about."

He towered over her, the pupils of his eyes dark and heated. She could smell the soap on his skin, the detergent in his shirt, the clean, woodsy scent of his hair. She closed her eyes briefly, and could smell something else, too—a peculiar, pulsing male challenge coming from every pore of his body. It was a warning, and as she registered it, she opened her eyes—a second too late.

His mouth descended upon hers and devoured her catty little grin, making mincemeat out of it. She opened her mouth to ask him what the hell he thought he was doing, only to have all her impudence driven out by his tongue and then melted into a little moan in the back of her throat.

His hands moved down her back to cup her bottom, and then to ruck her skirt up around her waist. In a single smooth movement, he lifted her onto the edge of the sink, where the metal basin divider chilled through her panties. The hormones in her hive buzzed out in an excited swarm.

He stood between her bare legs and rubbed his hardness into her cleft until she gasped and strained against him. He ran his hands up under her top and scooped her breasts out of their lace nests, teasing her nipples with his thumbs.

Cecy squirmed at the incredible sensations

ripping through her, and wrapped her legs around his waist. She wanted the feel of his lips on her, wanted his dark, sexy razor stubble burning her everywhere.

She wanted him naked, driving and pulsing inside her until she was nothing but a pool of melted butter.

Sensation started whirling, but not fast enough for her. His hands still toyed with her breasts, but he'd pulled himself away from the core of her, and she felt hot, wet, aching and empty. She opened her eyes in a daze, and murmured, "Please . . . please, Chas. Oh, please."

His eyes were heavy-lidded, his masterful tongue caught between his teeth, and he stared into her eyes. It obviously took an effort for him to speak, but he managed. "Please what, sweetheart? Take you now? Ravish you like a wild boar?"

She flushed.

"I'm afraid I can't do that. You, of all people, should understand . . ."

No, he can't be about to say this, do this. I'll kill him a hundred times over.

". . . that I can't *get it up*! After all, you told Christian so." Chas's lip curled as she panted, half with passion and half with humiliation and rage. Knowing that she deserved this made it all the worse. Paybacks were a bitch.

Chas backed away from her, an enormous bulge tenting his khakis. At least he was as frustrated as she, damn him. He gave her a last hot, male glance and walked awkwardly into his inner office, adjusting himself.

Cecy jumped from the sink and landed with a wobble on her heels, pulling her skirt down. She reached with a shaking hand for her coffee and choked some down, before setting it aside and straightening her bra.

After a couple more gulps of coffee, her brain resumed control over her body. *Two can play at this game.*

She stepped out of her panties and shoved them into her skirt pocket. Bare to the air under her skirt, and wearing three-inch heels, she felt deliciously wanton. As she walked back to her desk, she felt like the most depraved creature. This was probably illegal. It had to be, or it wouldn't be so much fun.

She sat in her chair and got to work, though her concentration was admittedly poor. She bided her time, and Chas eventually got up and went to the bathroom. Now was her moment.

Cecy crept stealthily into his inner office and slung her panties over his desk lamp.

20

A man could take only so much temptation, even in the name of revenge. The tiny pale blue panties had moons and stars printed on them, and they sent Chas into orbit. He picked them up gingerly on one finger and twirled them around.

Cecy typed away at her computer, seeming not to notice. There she sat, her legs primly crossed at the ankles, looking as calm and professional as you please. And under that clicking keyboard, under that simple navy skirt, sitting in that tweedy office chair, was her bare naked ass. Not to mention other delightful things.

Chas hardened so fast he hit the edge of his desk with an audible thump, and winced. He had to have her now, or go stark raving mad. He glanced at his watch and saw that it was now 8:48 A.M. He had twelve minutes until his nine o'clock appointment with Mrs. Trudy Wallace, a sixtyish widow. Twelve minutes to divide and conquer. Twelve minutes of sexual nirvana with the woman of his . . . nightmares.

He sprinted to the door and locked it, then dashed to the miniblinds and adjusted them. He turned to find Cecy lounging in her chair, elbows on the desk, fingertips steepled together. "My," she drawled, "aren't we in a hurry about something. Could it be that you need me for . . . *dick*-tation?"

"Could be," said Chas, advancing on her. He threw the panties down like a gauntlet.

She leaned forward on her elbows and uncrossed her ankles, shifting her feet about a yard apart under the desk.

His lungs froze.

She quirked an eyebrow. Slowly she slid her arms back and up before linking her hands behind her head. She rolled a few inches away from the desk, and then propped one toe up on the edge.

The vision before him was dusky and forbidden.

Cecy watched his eyes pop out of his head, grinned, and decided to go for it. She swung her other leg up and propped her heel on the flat surface, drawing the first toe to rest on her knee.

Dear Heavens, what a slut she was! But the feeling of power was intoxicating.

Chas had apparently stopped breathing, and his expression was blank and glazed.

She smiled in delight. She'd reduced him to a blithering idiot. How utterly wonderful.

Just as she'd reached this conclusion, Chas rounded the desk and tackled her, knocking the chair flying. They crashed to the floor and rolled, lip-locked.

"You *Jezebel*," he said, briefly coming up for air. They rolled again, and he slipped his hands under her blouse and sweater.

She gasped. "You pompous *preppie*," she retorted.

He wrapped his lips around a nipple and drew it into his mouth to suck, hard.

She moaned.

"She-cat in heat," he taunted her.

"Chest-pounding primate," she shot back, wrapping her hand around the bulge of his manhood.

They ripped the clothing off one another, and that was the end of foreplay. Chas spread her legs and drove home into her hot core. He filled her over and over again, driving her to the brink of blinding light. She would have sworn one of her feet was on the South Pole, the other on the North Pole, and the whole delicious world was between her legs.

He took her like a madman, in a wild ride to

the borders of sanity and back again. They climaxed together, shouted together, then lay trembling together.

"Jesus Christ, Cecy," he mumbled into her damp hair, "move back in with me. Please, sweetheart."

She stared at him, opened her mouth to answer she-didn't-know-what, and then the doorknob jiggled. "Hello? Hello? Mr. Buchanan . . ." called a quavering voice.

They scrambled like cartoon characters for their scattered clothes. He jumped into his boxers and khakis, tripping in his haste. She tried with shaking hands to turn her skirt right side out. Finally, she grabbed all of her clothing she could find and ran like a rabbit for the bathroom, leaving Chas to answer the door.

Mrs. Trudy Wallace had entirely too many grandchildren, Chas decided. Not that they weren't cute, but there were *dozens* of them. When she spread their photos out across his desk, all he could think about was all the great practice sessions her children must have had to make that many kids.

Jesus. He was most definitely a goat. How could he have such a thought in front of this sweet grandmother?

Chas pulled himself together. "Now, which one plays the saxophone and will be going to Juilliard?"

"Thomas," said Mrs. Wallace, with affectionate pride. "He's only eight, but I can tell. So we must make sure he has adequate college funds."

"Right," said Chas. "And it's little Trisha who wants to study the world's animals from a hot-air balloon?"

Mrs. Wallace nodded. "And I know those balloons are expensive. We've got a lot of smart investing to do, young Chas."

"Mmmmm." He scribbled it all down on a legal pad. "Now, Tabitha, Michael, and Donald want to form their own circus. They'll need start-up capital to pay for trapezes and elephants."

"Horses, too. And basic payroll for the other performers, like the sumo wrestlers. Oh, and dear heavens, the *lion*. I understand that they're dreadfully expensive to import, not to mention the liability insurance once they're here. But little Donald insists that lion tamer is the only role for him."

"Does he." Chas wrote it all down. Good thing Mrs. Wallace was a multimillionaire.

They covered the rest of her needs at an agonizingly slow pace: a Learjet for dear Timmy, and medical degree from Harvard for Samantha, who gave her teddy bears injections with such competence. And last, but not least, a publishing company for ten-year-old Thea, who wrote the most marvelous fairy tales. "We can't have her suffer the agonies of rejection, can we, young Chas?"

"No, indeed." He was going to have to turn Mrs. Wallace's three million into several billion, at this rate. He prayed that as her grandchildren grew up, they would adjust their expectations a little.

"Well," he said, at the end of the list, "let me see what I can do. We're going to have to adjust your current investments, that's for sure. I'll draw up a plan and we can look over it in a week or so."

"That would be lovely, sweet boy." Mrs. Wallace put on her white-lace gloves and rose, at last, to leave. "I haven't seen you at the club in years, dear."

Chas knew she meant the Cherokee Town and Country Club. "I don't, ah, frequent the place anymore."

"That Maria—well. I probably shouldn't bring it up, but you might be interested to know that she's had quite the ugliest baby I've ever seen. Worse than a monkey, and bad-tempered to boot. It actually *bites* people."

"Good God," said Chas, walking her to the door.

"Yes, can you imagine? She and Dr. Thing are being sued by one of the golf caddies who made the mistake of being friendly to it . . ."

After Mrs. Wallace had left, Cecy crept out of the bathroom fully dressed, stared at him, and giggled.

"What?" he asked.

"Come here, silly." She started to unbutton his shirt.

"Cecy, we can't do that again right now! William Eubank is due any minute."

"Your shirt is buttoned crooked," she retorted. "I can't believe Mrs. Wallace didn't notice."

"She wasn't wearing her glasses, and she was focused entirely on her grandchildren and their brilliant futures."

"There," Cecy said, in tones of satisfaction. "Now you're presentable."

He caught her hands in his and looked down at her. "Thank you."

"You're welcome."

"Cecy." He took a deep breath. "I really meant it when I said I wanted you to move back in."

She pulled her hands away and folded her arms across her chest. "Why?"

"What do you mean, why?"

"I mean *why*?"

He opened and closed his mouth several times. "I—ah. Um. I don't know."

"I'm sorry, but that's a less-than-compelling reason for me to go through all the hassle."

"Well," he said, reaching, "it would make it a lot easier for you to get to work."

"That's pretty lame."

"Okay ... see, the thing is, I've gotten kind of used to your cat. I miss him."

"You miss Barney?" Cecy's voice was incredulous. "No, I'm sorry. I don't buy that. What are you really trying to say, Buchanan?"

"Fine. All right. If I must be blunt, you and I have great sex together—you have to admit that.

And it would be so much more convenient if you were back on Paces Ferry. Don't you see?"

"Yes," she said, in dangerous tones. "I see very well." She was silent for a moment. "You son of a bitch! You have the gall to tell me that I should move back so that you can have a *convenient boinking buddy*? You should get down on your knees and thank God that you were born with numbers skills, Buchanan, because you sure as hell weren't blessed with an iota of tact!"

Too late, Chas realized how he'd sounded, and smacked his forehead with the heel of his hand. But how did he say what was running through his mind? *Cecy, I found your red high-heeled sandal and put it on my dresser. I stared at it from my bed in the dark last night until I was slobbering insane. I missed the sound of you in the bathroom down the hall, washing your face, brushing your teeth, and gargling in that adorable way.*

Hell—only pussies told women things like that. *Sheesh.*

Cecy retreated again to the bathroom and slammed the door in his face when he tried to apologize. "Go away!" she shouted.

"Oh, come on. I didn't mean it that way, and you know it. Please, open the door." Chas leaned his forehead against the raised center panel.

"I hate you, Chas Buchanan."

Were those tears he heard in her voice? He scrambled for something, *anything*, to say that would make it better. He hated knowing he'd made her cry. "Cecy," he said, and then swallowed. "I found your red high-heeled sandal last night and put it on my dresser. I stared at it from my bed in the dark until I was slobbering insane. I missed the sound of you in the bathroom down the hall, washing your face, brushing your teeth, and gargling in that adorable way."

He heard a sniffle behind the bathroom door and then silence. "Go on," she said.

Go on? He'd already emasculated himself beyond all measure, and the woman wanted him to continue? This was hell, pure and simple.

"Uhhhhh. When you're in the tub, I want to be bathwater."

"Really?"

"Yeah. Well, as long as it doesn't have all that flowery stuff in it."

"Chas, isn't there anything else you'd like to say?"

He stared at the door suspiciously. This sounded like a trick question, one of those doozies women threw at men to grind them into the dust when they gave the wrong answer. "Can you give me a hint?"

She made a frustrated noise behind the door. "You said you missed the sounds I made in the bathroom. Is there anything else you miss?"

He frowned. *Sounds. The five senses. What were they, again? Sound, smell, touch, sight, taste.* Okay . . . "I miss the smell of you in the bathroom, too?" He thought of how he'd buried his face in the towels she'd used. "Is that the right answer?"

It sounded like she was beating her head against the door.

"Okay, okay. What else do I miss, let me see . . ." Then it hit him. She wanted to hear that he missed the whole enchilada, not just the cheese or the green tomatillo sauce. "Cecy, I miss *you.*"

The door opened abruptly and he almost fell in.

"You do?"

He nodded.

"Really?"

The look on her face was worth all the money he saved in a year clipping coupons—times ten. "Yeah. Really." She had mascara smudges under her eyes, and he took her face in his hands and rubbed the marks away with his thumbs. "You know I don't just think of you as a 'boinking buddy.' "

"You don't?"

"No. I care about you, Cecy. A lot."

She threw her arms around him, almost knocking the breath out of him, and buried her face in his shirt. Something about the gesture jolted his heart and caused a strange buzzing sensation in his chest. He held her for a moment, smoothing her hair. "So," he asked, "will you move back in with me?"

"No," she said to his left pectoral muscle.

"Huh? Why not?"

"Because"—she sighed, stepping out of his arms—"I want more than you can give, Chas. I'm in love with you, and you're not in love with me. You don't even trust me. You're still a victim of your divorce. That's just the way it is." She smiled at him, a brave smile that seriously screwed with his heart. And she walked back to her desk to sit down.

Chas opened his mouth to announce that he wasn't a victim in any sense of the word, only to have his next appointment walk in. "Mr. Eubank," he said blankly, "how are you? Come in, sit down."

Chas emerged from the meeting with William Eubank to find a note on his inner door. "Call this man," it said, in Cecy's handwriting. "He's the French owner of a restaurant. Needs help with American tax accounting laws. Friend of Etienne and Sylvie's. I've gone to lunch."

"Business office, Chez Suzanne," a receptionist's voice announced in a French accent, when he called. "May I help you?"

Chez Suzanne? Good God. Chez Suzanne was an entire *chain* of restaurants, strung all over the East and West Coasts. Chas asked to speak with the owner and identified himself.

"Very good, Mr. Buchanan. Hold, please, *un moment.*"

Chas did so.

The receptionst came back on the line. "Mr. Grenoble requests an appointment with you on next Tuesday at ten o'clock. Will this be satisfactory?"

"Yes, thank you." Chas hung up the phone, bemused. Had Cecily Scatterton, walking emergency, just landed him the client of his dreams? The client who could catapult him into a whole new business stratosphere? That would be truly ironic.

Cecy stood outside the business office of Christian Cox's chain of video stores, clutching a bouquet of yellow roses wrapped in tissue and clear plastic. God, this was going to be awkward. But she had to apologize to the man. Her conscience had been nagging her for days.

She took a deep breath and rapped on the door.

"Come in!" Cox's voice called.

Cecy bit her bottom lip and turned the knob. In scant seconds, she stood in front of his desk.

He was scrutinizing some papers, elegant little reading glasses perched on the end of his nose. His eyes flickered up at her and froze. He tossed the papers down. "Well, if it isn't Cupid herself."

She shot him a sickly smile and gazed around the room, gathering courage. The place managed to be both cheerful and elegant, a rare combination for offices, in her experience. Chairs were upholstered in bright patterns of red and yellow. Framed contemporary art posters hung on the walls.

"I came to apologize," she forced out. She

held the yellow roses out to him, and noticed too late that her hands were shaking.

He studied her for a moment, then accepted them. He took off his glasses and laid them on the desk. "I knew you were ballsy, Cecy, but now I know you have courage. You could have sent me a note, or called. Or simply avoided the issue and prayed never to see me again. That's what most people would have done."

Cecy twisted her toe on the carpet. "I just felt that I owed you a visit. I was really awful the other night, and I'm sorry. All I could think about was getting back at Chas."

Christian chuckled. "Well, I believe you accomplished your goal. The hairs on the back of his neck were bristling with phobia, though I assumed it was simple embarrassment at the time. I thought it was cute."

"I'm sorry, Christian. I didn't think about your feelings at all." Cecy looked straight into his hazel eyes, unable to believe she saw good humor in them.

He waved the yellow roses at her. "All is forgiven. Nobody's brought me flowers in a very long time. Now tell me, *where* did you get those shoes?"

Cecy brightened. "You know that little place just off of Roswell Road near the Prado? Well, they had the most fabulous sale . . ."

Cecy rushed back into the office, breathless. "Sorry I'm late! Christian took me to lunch, and then we had to stop in at this little boutique he knew of . . ."

Chas stared at her. "Christian *took you to lunch*? After what you did?"

She nodded, sheepishly. "Yes. We had such a good time, talking designers and fashion trends. Imagine, he's familiar with Bagdley Mischka, and Marc Jacobs, and—"

"Who?" Chas blinked.

"Never mind. It's not a straight man's hobby, generally speaking."

He cleared his throat. "I guess not. Hey, listen—thanks for giving me that French guy's name. Do you know who he *is*?"

She shrugged. "Owns some restaurant, Etienne and Sylvie said."

"He owns an entire, huge chain of restaurants, all over the country, Cecy. He's looking for tax shelters and extensive planning. This could be an incredible opportunity for me."

"Good," she said. "Glad I could help."

"Cecy, just out of curiosity, why did your French couple pass his name on to me? I wouldn't have thought I'd be on their list of favorite people."

"I told them you were the best," she said, simply. "I told them what you'd done for me, and that it wasn't your fault you couldn't fall in love with me."

He stared at her. She was the least vindictive person he'd ever met. It humbled him. And there was that "l" word again. It made him uncomfortable. "I haven't done that much," he muttered.

How could she casually make that statement in front of him—"I'm in love with you"—and then take a sip of coffee? Or smile at him? Or give him a referral? She really was the damnedest woman. A completely unique woman. A courageous woman. A woman he didn't know what to do about.

21

Chas went home that evening after waving good-bye to Cecy, and stared at the freakin' red shoe on his dresser again. He stared at it as he changed out of his business clothes and into a pair of jeans. He stared at it as he rolled the cuffs of his white shirt up and peeled off his dark socks. He was aware of it as he threw each sock up onto the ceiling fan and watched them be flung to the far corners of the room.

He flopped on his bed, barefoot, and considered the shoe some more. The silly thing was just like Cecy. It was elegant, beautifully designed, without being stuffy. The sandal straps flashed a little elastic here and there, for flexibility. Its height made it utterly impractical for walking, but the thing possessed a sturdy sole. The shoe was sexy, and it was fun.

I want more than you can give, Chas. I'm in love with you, and you're not in love with me.

Oh, Jesus. What was love, anyway? What were the ingredients in the great recipe of love? With Maria, they'd been coy and empty promises, heart-shaped boxes of candy, and diamonds. But had he ever really loved Maria? Or had he simply gone through the logical, linear steps of meeting, dating, and marriage?

With Cecy, nothing had been in the least logical or linear. They hadn't met in a normal way. He'd wanted to kill her almost immediately. She embodied nothing he looked for in a woman.

So why was he sitting around mooning at her shoe? Sniffing her towels? Asking her to move back in with him? Was he *nuts*?

And she'd said *no*, damn it. *No*. Not even "No, thank you." Just plain old, bald, no-nonsense "no." If he weren't a man, and a man with no need for feelings, his would have been hurt.

You don't even trust me, she'd said. He wanted to trust her. That disturbed him. Women always wanted something from you. Gold diggers abounded out there, hiding their little chisels in their bras and panty hose. They'd brandish the tools when a man was least expecting it. Hell, there were women out there who'd suck the gold caps out of a man's molars during the first good-night kiss.

But Cecy's not like that. If Cecy'd been a gold dig-

ger, she'd have asked you to pay her debts long ago. If she were a chiseler, she wouldn't have turned down an invitation to move back into his Paces Ferry house. Hell, she'd never have left in the first place. She would have found a way not to be insulted by what he'd done. Chas was forced to admit that Cecy was not after his money.

In fact, Cecy was after things entirely different than money. Cecy was after respect, and love, and affection. A place in the world. A purpose in life. Things that had no price, but were the most precious entities in the world.

Cecily Scatterton might have been raised with no parents, no permanent home, and no idea how to manage her affairs, but she'd somehow learned the right values. He marveled at that.

You're still a victim of your divorce, she'd said. What the hell did she mean by that? He was no victim. The word victim implied weakness, implied wounds, implied a lack of control. None of those things were true of him. He was strong, and cynical, and at the helm of his business and his life.

Chas swung his legs off the bed and trudged downstairs, leaving the blasted shoe on his dresser. Maybe finding something to eat would take his mind off Cecy, or at least help him figure out exactly what he *did* feel for her.

He wrinkled his nose as he walked into the kitchen. *Ugh. Something must have died in here.* What was it? He'd just taken out the garbage this morning, but he checked under the sink to see if something had fallen behind the trash container. Nope. *Whew.* Whatever it was, it smelled truly gruesome. Absolutely disgusting. Beyond description.

Chas opened the refrigerator and looked around for a likely culprit. But he'd cleaned the damned thing before his ill-fated party, and nothing seemed blue, green, or hairy.

Perhaps a rat had died in the wall? Or a squirrel in the attic? Chas went to fetch a ladder so that he could peer up into the crawl space. Many curses and cobwebs later, he was forced to admit defeat.

He put the ladder back in the garage, and began to prowl the kitchen nose first, like a wolfhound. He lost the scent the farther he moved away from the kitchen sink. He opened cabinets, hunting for a rodent carcass. Nothing.

His nose finally isolated the scent in the area of the cabinet under the utility drawer. He pulled everything out of the space, every last can and box of crackers and pasta. Nothing. The smell was still so strong that he had to hold a paper towel over his nose.

Chas frowned. Still holding the paper over his nose and mouth, he slid open the utility drawer—and staggered back, gagging. The foulness all but blew the hair off his head.

There, splatted on top of his good screwdriver set, was a mass of blue-green-black-brown *some-*

thing. It was chunky and oozing. It was definitely man-made, and had never been any type of animal. Furthermore, it had been put there deliberately, if the large serving spoon next to it was any indication.

The last time Chas had seen that particular serving spoon, it had been in the potato salad on the night of the party. He peered at the stinking mass through slitted eyes and fantasized about how satisfying it would be to give Cecy Scatterton a swirlie in it.

Whatever his feelings for her might be, they certainly didn't encompass love.

Or did they? Chas lay in bed in the dark, hours later, staring once again at that confounded shoe.

He'd tied a dish towel around his mouth and nose and emptied the whole kitchen drawer into the garbage can in the garage. By the time he'd used the fireplace tongs to extricate his screwdriver set, hosed it off, and sprayed a whole can of Lysol into the drawer, he'd begun to laugh. The whole maneuver was just so . . . *Cecy*. Who else would get Machiavellian with sliced vegetables and mayonnaise?

Did he love the only woman in the world capable of using potato salad as a dangerous weapon?

Chas began to laugh with helpless abandon. He laughed until tears ran down his cheeks.

Great—the woman had now reduced him to giggling madly in the night, alone with her shoe.

"I give up," he gasped, "I love her, God help me. I don't know why, but I love her." Chas sat up in bed, and shouted it to the shoe. "I *love* her!"

22

Cecy perused the Georgia State course catalogue with growing excitement. The certification courses looked interesting, spanning subjects from multiculturalism to psychology to advanced teaching techniques. The plan for practical training in the classroom was extensive. She'd do a lot of student teaching before she was finished.

She would send in her application fee now, and if accepted, could start classes in January. In the meantime, she'd do some studying on her own, continue to tutor, and plan her future.

A sense of satisfaction swelled within her. She had a road map for her life now. Goals, and a purpose, and an inner conviction that teaching was the right choice for her. After all, Etienne was now saying "hogwash," instead of "peeg-wash," and "horse feathers" instead of "mule-feathers." Sylvie had learned to make it clear in any restaurant that "greets" were not a welcome addition to her plate.

Cecy closed the catalogue and laid it next to her on the little bed in the finished basement. All of these plans, in addition to her work for Chas, would keep her from getting all sappy about him. She frowned. *Will you move back in with me?* His words echoed in her mind.

Oh, how she'd wanted to say yes, especially after he'd made it clear that he cared about her, missed her. But caring about someone was a long way from loving them. And when he found that potato salad, she doubted very strongly that he'd want to write poetry in her honor, or stare deeply into her eyes. Cecy screwed her mouth into a wry twist.

Mama Sue would have scolded her for wasting food. Starving children roamed barefoot on the earth, and she'd filled Chas's utility drawer and disposal with a perfectly good meal or two. She resolved right then and there that when she got out of debt, she would spend some free hours working in a soup kitchen. She also had a bad feeling that she probably owed Chas a new disposal. Why did her plans for revenge always backfire on her like this?

Cecy scooped together a white-plastic basket of hand washables and walked into the small half bath with it. She stoppered the drain on the sink and sprinkled a little soap into the cold running water. She swished her blue-silk camisole and tap shorts around in it, rubbing here and there to make sure it got clean.

When you're in the tub, I want to be bathwater. Now, how was she to interpret that, exactly? Did he want to be lukewarm bathwater, soothing her? Or steamy, hot, sexy bathwater? Or frigid, cold, get-on-with-your-life bathwater? Men were so cryptic and confusing. Given that he'd said he cared about her, she decided that he wanted to be bathwater of the warmer variety. She frowned.

So? Bathwater was nice while it lasted, but it eventually wrinkled the skin—most unattractive—and one eventually opened the drain and washed it away.

Cecy draped her wet camisole and tap shorts over a hanger. This she hung on the door, letting the fabric drip onto the tile floor. She decided that though Chas was brilliant when it came to numbers, he wasn't altogether competent with metaphors.

As she scrubbed and swished a black-silk blouse in the sink, she heard Barney begin to cough and hack in the main room. She dropped the blouse into the water, dried her hands on a towel, and walked out to examine him. He'd been listless and apathetic lately, not his normal self, and she wasn't sure why.

He crouched on a small throw rug and tilted

his head sideways while he coughed. His normally expressive tail drooped behind him.

"Barney, sweetie, what's wrong?" She got down on her knees next to him.

He glowered up at her and emitted a weak "meow." Was it her imagination, or did one of his eyes seem swollen? He kept opening his crooked little mouth and letting his tongue loll out.

"What's the matter, baby?" She hated not being able to communicate with him. If he didn't seem better by tomorrow, she was taking him to the vet. In the meantime, she went upstairs to the kitchen and cut him a small piece of chicken from some leftovers in the refrigerator. She brought it down on a saucer, and put it in front of him.

He sniffed at it, and crept closer. His poor little tail jerked up in a thank-you maneuver, and he opened his mouth to take the morsel. But when he tried to bite down on it, he hissed and dropped the chicken back on the saucer. He shook his head and tilted it to the side, then emitted a long, lugubrious howl.

Cecy stared at him in consternation. "What is it, honey? Does it hurt you to eat the chicken?"

Barney yowled again, sniffed at it, and lay down next to it. Surely that was feline longing in his eyes, but he made no further move to take it. He opened his crooked little mouth again and hung his tongue out the side.

Cecy fetched him a bowl of water, but he didn't seem to want any of that, either. She heard prissy little kitty patters on the stairs behind her, and turned to behold Fleurette, Etienne and Sylvie's cat. She stood on the bottom step, her expression inquisitive, her whiskers bent forward. She wiggled her tiny pink nostrils as she took in the scents around her.

Then, slowly, she extended first one svelte, sleek paw, and then another, until she stood on all fours on the floor.

Cecy folded her arms and swallowed a laugh. Fleurette's attitude suggested that she really wasn't accustomed to visiting such lowbrow environments as basements, thank you very much. The little kitty sashayed over to Barney with cool elegance, curling her tail in come-hither figurations.

Barney didn't move a muscle; just eyed her with macho charisma. He had become the Lion King. He gazed at Fleurette, unblinking. Cecy could almost hear them exchanging lines from some old movie.

"I was merely in the neighborhood," she could picture Fleurette saying. "I . . . I wondered how you were."

"So, ya left your camel's hair coat to come slumming, did ya, little girl?" Barney growled. "This is no place for you. Go back to your cream, and your fancy windowsill overlooking the garden. That's where you belong."

"I cannot!" Fleurette cried, clutching the pearls at her bosom. "It means nothing, nothing without you!"

"That's what you think now, in the heat of the moment. But give you a few months without your featherbed, and your high-and-mighty Aubusson rugs, and you'd tire of me all too fast. Get outta here. Go, Fleurette." He coughed, and grimaced in pain.

"Barney, you're ill!" She flew to his side, sniffing him from head to toe, and then licked his cheek, his ear, his head. "I won't leave you. I won't, I won't!"

Cecy shook herself. She was squatting in a basement, dreaming up a script for a romance between two *cats*. She was crazy. Except that Fleurette really was licking Barney's head, and he gave every appearance of being soothed. What was going on here while she was at work? They'd hissed up a storm at each other when they'd first met.

She got up, her knees protesting, and returned to the bathroom to finish her hand washables. When she checked on the cats again, Fleurette had curled herself around Barney, and both were asleep. The piece of chicken sat untouched in the saucer, defying everything Cecy knew about cats.

Fleurette and Barney were in much the same position when she awoke in the morning and went upstairs to get her coffee. She brought two bowls of wet, stinky Ocean Delite cat food down for them. Fleurette got up and gracefully accepted hers. Barney tried to do the same, but again, when he opened his jaw to take the food, he hissed and shook his head. Fleurette licked him, but he walked away from her, tail twitching, and hissed again.

Cecy noticed that one of his eyes had swollen to a squint, and real worry assaulted her. What was wrong? She couldn't let him remain in pain; it was out of the question.

She showered in a hurry and jumped into her clothes, then called the vet before Sylvie took her to work.

The veterinarian was not the woman she normally saw, but a young man who had recently joined the practice. "What happened to your cat's jaw?"

"I think he must have gotten hit by a door as a kitten," she answered. "The jaw never mended right, and has always been twisted to the side like that. He was that way when I found him near my studio apartment in college. It's never seemed to bother him before."

The vet began to examine Barney, who let it be known that he was not enjoying himself—especially not when the young man touched the area around his mouth and eye.

"Hush, sweetie," Cecy soothed him. "He's trying to help us."

"He's got a lump, here, which could be a tumor. But I'm not sure what's going on with his eye . . ."

Cecy tried to ignore the dreaded word "tumor," without much success. Lots of tumors are benign, she told herself. She blinked rapidly.

The vet took Barney's temperature, which the cat did not appreciate. "He's running a slight fever."

He finished with Barney and turned to wash his hands before facing her again. "I'm going to recommend," he said seriously, "that you take him to Athens, to the University of Georgia, so that they can look at him there. I've never seen anything like this before. They'll almost certainly need to do a biopsy, to determine what's happening with that lump. I think my partner would agree with me, but I can have her call you later today if you'd like to check with her first."

Cecy hugged Barney to her chest with growing horror. *No. Please, no. Please let there be nothing really wrong with him, please God. He's all I have left. He's not just a cat to me; he's my friend.*

"Ms. Scatterton? Do you want her to call you?"

She realized that she'd said nothing, but didn't trust her voice. She shook her head.

"Do you want me to set up an appointment for you in Athens?"

She nodded, dumbly.

"Okay." He laid a hand on her arm. "Don't look that way. He may be just fine." The vet led the way out to the reception desk. "There's no charge today, since I'm just sending you on to UGA."

"Thank you," she whispered.

"What's your schedule like?"

"I'll take him anytime. I don't care." Her voice came out reedy and thin.

When the vet had made the call and handed her a card with a date and time on it, she accepted it like a robot. She blinked at his reassuring smile.

"Everything will be fine," he told her.

"Sure. Yeah, I'm sure it will."

Cecy said nothing to anyone about Barney. Perhaps if she didn't speak the possible disaster aloud, it wouldn't come true.

The following Monday, Chas appeared in front of her desk and hovered. He stood there, big and somehow awkward. He shoved his hands into his pockets. "Cecy, I—"

She looked up inquiringly at him.

He ran a hand through his hair. "I've been doing some thinking."

"Hence the smell of burning rubber around here," she teased.

"Very funny. It's got to smell better than that potato salad you dumped in my utility drawer."

She blanched. "Oh my God. I wondered when you'd find that. I'm really, really sorry. Sometimes I do stupid things on the spur of the moment, and—"

"Nah. Not *you*."

"It's like I can't help myself, even when I know it's not a good thing to do, and that it will blow up in my face later, and I know I owe you a new disposal and—" She stopped and registered that he was grinning. *Grinning*. "Aren't you mad?"

"Nope." He continued to display all of his very white teeth.

"Yes, you are. You have to be somewhat mad."

"Huh-uh."

"A tiny bit angry?" She held up her thumb and forefinger, just a bare inch apart.

He shook his head, still smirking.

Irrational disappointment swirled through her. "Oh, but I *insist*. You must feel at least somewhat irritated."

"No," he said firmly, "I do not."

"But," she stammered, "that's not rational. It doesn't add up."

He quirked an eyebrow at her. "Seems to me that you've reminded me many times that emotions aren't linear, or algebraic. Not even the emotions of an accountant."

"Oh, come on, Chas. Potato salad plus one week's degeneration equals horrific smell equals pissed-off guy."

"Perhaps. But take pissed-off guy, and divide him by sense of fair play and ability to see humor in strange things. Then multiply him by agonies of unfamiliar feelings toward donor of degenerated potato salad, and solve for 'x.' "

"What do you mean, solve for 'x'?" Cecy was now thoroughly confused. "I don't get it."

"It's okay, sweetheart. I don't get it either, although I have managed to solve for 'x.' "

Cecy closed her eyes and chewed on her bottom lip. "What is 'x'?"

"What is 'x'?" Chas mused, aloud. " 'X' definitely does not conveniently mark the spot." He shoved his hands farther into his pockets, as he dug further into the definition they were both seeking. " 'X' is a word, which is really a sign, for quite another entity—an emotional entity, which is much better defined by those who deal in literature rather than those who deal in numbers. Don't you agree?"

Cecy released her frustration in a long, piercing scream.

"I love making you scream, baby." Chas was grinning again.

She leaped to her feet, stamped both of them, and clenched her fists. "What is 'x,' you big . . . baboon?"

"It's a four-letter word, Cecy. You find it scrawled on sidewalks, buildings, and overpasses. In bathroom stalls."

She racked her brain for suitable candidates. There were many, but they didn't seem to fit the puzzle in quite the right way. She went back over the original phrasing of his bizarre equation.

. . . *take pissed-off guy, and divide him by sense of fair play and ability to see humor in strange things. Then multiply him by agonies of unfamiliar feelings toward donor of degenerated potato salad, and solve for "x."*

Agonies of unfamiliar feelings toward donor of degenerated potato salad . . . Was Chas saying, in the most oblique, obfuscated, obnoxious way, that he had feelings for her? Why then, solving for "x" must mean . . . that "x" was "love"! But no. No way. When a man loved a woman, he just *told* her that, in any one of several conventional ways.

He said, "Gee, baby, I dig you," if he was into wearing fringe and beads and peace signs.

He said, "Darling, let's merge over martinis," if he was the corporate shark type.

He said, "Lookee here, Sweet Pea, let's get hitched," if he was the country bumpkin type.

But never, *ever* in her experience did a man say anything to do with potato salad and solving for "x" if he was trying to communicate tender feelings to the woman of his choice.

Irrational disappointment surged through her once again. "Buchanan," she said, looking at him askance, "you are one strange man." She picked up a pile of letters that were ready to be mailed. "We need stamps. I'm going to the post office."

She grabbed her purse and left. And he thought *she* was nuts?

23

That evening, Chas strode around his house on West Paces Ferry Road and looked at it dispassionately for the first time.

The place held a lot of memories for him. Memories of the whole family gathering around the Christmas tree and ripping into presents. His mother, bringing hot cocoa to him and Hal, with real whipped cream on top. She would kiss the ends of their noses and make sure they didn't burn their hands on the cups.

His father and Grandfather Chastain had argued about politics in wing chairs on opposite sides of that very fireplace. Grand would fly through and drop some conversational bomb into their midst, and then disappear into her garden to collect pinecones for some odd project.

All of these snippets of the past were wonderful, and he wanted to keep them intact forever. He was glad now that it had taken him so long to be able to buy the old place. The divorce would have forced him to sell it, if he'd bought it during his marriage, and that would have killed him. But Maria wasn't representative of all women.

Should wanting to hold on to the past prevent him from creating a meaningful future? Should fear of losing the house in a divorce settlement prevent him from getting married again? He thought briefly of a prenuptial agreement, but they didn't always stand up in court. And they were hardly romantic.

Would tying the knot with Cecy jeopardize his dream, or would it actually cement the building of future memories in the house?

Chas ran his hand across the carved wainscoting in the foyer, then walked outside to the back patio. He needed fresh air to think. He sat in one of the wrought-iron chairs at the patio table and gazed about, more memories crowding his thoughts. Grand had planted mums and pansies out here, in an assortment of odd containers. Once she'd deposited English ivy in an old train case of hers that she'd primed and painted.

He stared at the trio of plants that Cecy had arranged around the marble birdbath, and realized what it was about her that drew him so.

Cecy, with her nutty approach to life and her whimsical charm, reminded him of Grand. They were two of a kind, even if they'd come from wildly different backgrounds. Grand, like Cecy, would have thought nothing of raising a bromeliad in a toy fireman's hat. She, too, would have planted blue daze in an old Tonka truck.

Grand, reduced to the same circumstances as Cecy, would doubtless have starved stylishly, as well. He had no difficulty picturing his grandmother set up at a card table, hawking her Limoges and Baccarat to buy food for herself and that damned farting dog. She would have done it with her chin held high and a twinkle in her eye, no matter what old Atlanta thought of her.

Not that Grandfather Chastain would ever have left her in such circumstances. He'd been a planner, like Chas, a quieter, more solid personality.

He couldn't remember Grand ever pulling anything like the potato-salad stunt, but he did seem to recall some story about her switching her husband's mouthwash with his aftershave when she'd been angry with him. Chas chuckled.

He stood up and stretched, looking at the mellow cream stone of the house, the wide expanse of windows, the warm glow of the porch lights. It was such a beautiful old place. Too beautiful to have no laughter, no warmth, no trust inside. Without that, the house would never be a home to him, no matter how many memories it held. They'd simply float about like dust motes and settle onto the polished wood surfaces.

Cecy exuded that quality of life. She wasn't a planner, she didn't know jack about finances, and she drove him crazy in more ways than one. But she was vibrant and glowing and she made him feel complete, somehow. He felt necessary to her—just as she was to him. He was earth to her ocean, canvas to her paint, bread to her wine. He needed something about Cecy.

Cecy held Barney in her lap and stroked him, trying to make him understand that she was leaving him at the University of Georgia teaching hospital for only a few days. "These are nice people, sweetie. They're going to do some tests on you. They're going to fix your jaw and find out what's wrong with your eye and see if that tumor is a mean one. Okay?"

Barney backed as far as he could into her stomach and the crook of her arm. He meowed his disgust at the smell of this place, the white shiny floors, and the strange people who kept poking at him. The invasive maneuvers they performed upon his various orifices were completely unacceptable. He would probably pray to the Big Cat in the Sky that they, too, would have to undergo a fecal exam before their despicable lives were over. He would also ask the Big Cat to ensure they were infested with fleas.

"My poor baby," murmured Cecy into his fur. "Everything's going to be all right. It has to be." She rained kisses all over Barney's head, and placed him reluctantly inside his pet carrier. "I'll see you in a few days, Fuzzy One."

A technician carried her cat through a door and away from her, and she stared after him in dejection. She turned to the receptionist. "You'll take good care of him?"

The girl nodded. "Of course. They'll do a biopsy on his jaw, and we should have the results back in a couple of days. If the news is good, and they find no cancerous cells, they'll operate." The girl hesitated, and looked into Cecy's eyes with sympathy. "It's hard for me to say this, and harder for you to hear it, but you need to be prepared for the worst-case scenario. If they find cancerous tissue in his jaw, it's better to put him down than force him to live in pain."

A lump the size of the Jeep rose in Cecy's throat, defying any attempts to swallow it. She simply could not imagine her life without Barney. The thought of sleeping without him sprawled across her feet was impossibly painful. The idea of never seeing him stoned on catnip again, or retrieving one of his toys, or clacking his teeth at a bird—she couldn't take it. *Please, God, leave me Barney. I got through my brother's death somehow. Don't take my friend, too. I don't know how I'll bear it.*

"An opthamologist will look at his eye, which

is a whole different matter," the receptionist continued, "and unfortunately, a separate charge."

Cecy managed to draw some air around the lump and into her lungs. "How . . . how much is all of this going to cost?" She didn't have any idea how she was going to come up with the money to pay for Barney's treatment.

The receptionist looked inside a manila folder and did some calculations. She cleared her throat. "With the X rays, biopsy, diagnosis, surgery on the jaw, and separate surgery on his eye, it could cost as much as eighteen hundred dollars."

Cecy dug her now-natural nails into her palms. The lump in her throat began to swell, squeezing all the available oxygen out of her windpipe. "Eighteen hundred dollars."

She wrapped her arms around herself and locked her knees so she wouldn't sway with the shock of it. "I see. Okay. Thanks." Somehow she made her way out the glass doors, down the concrete steps, and across the tarmac of the parking lot. She unlocked the Jeep and sat inside it without moving. "Eighteen hundred dollars." She leaned her head back against the seat and stared, dry-eyed, through the flattened bugs on the windshield. "Sure. No problem."

Chas muttered to himself as he crunched some numbers on a spreadsheet for Mrs. Wallace's investments. The freakin' phone rang again, to his irritation. Cecy had requested a half day of personal time and wasn't there to answer it for him. "Buchanan Financial," he growled. "Buchanan speaking."

A high-pitched, warbling chirp greeted him, signaling a fax transmission. He punched star-five and slung the receiver back into the cradle. With its customary groan, the fax machine began to roll.

Chas turned back to his spreadsheet and tried to concentrate, but Cecy's face kept swimming in front of the numbers. She'd been very quiet lately, her face pale and pinched. He wondered what she'd needed personal time for. She hadn't seemed open to questions, and he hadn't pushed the issue, wrapped up as he was in his conflicting emotions about her. Admitting he loved her was one thing. Marrying her was another. He was pretty certain that if he just sat her down and used the dreaded "l" word, she'd move back in with him again, and they could just live in sin. That way they avoided any messy legalities, and—well, his house was safe. Bottom line, it was far less of a commitment, but still a big move on his part. She'd be a recognized girlfriend/lover/Buchanan-official-woman, not just a temporary roommate. Really, it was a big plus for her.

The fax machine grumbled to a stop, and Chas looked over to see what kind of advertisement had come through this time. A restaurant lunch special? A trucking company's special rates?

The thin, shiny paper was smudged with toner, as usual. He was going to have to cough up the dough to replace the machine.

He walked over to it and ripped the page out. It was barely legible, but with concern he made out the word "hospital" in the heading, and the end of Cecy's last name: "—erton." The fax was almost solid black on the left side of the page, but with growing horror Chas sifted through a lot of medical mumbo jumbo and came upon the words "tumor" and "calvarium of the skull."

He sat abruptly in his chair and threw the paper to the floor. Hospital? Tumor? Good God. Cecy had a tumor, and hadn't told him? He grew cold at the thought.

Was a malignant cancer growing under her streaks of butter and gold and chestnut hair? Under her pink, downy scalp and between those little ears that poked through the mass of blond?

A python was wrapped around his entrails, squeezing the life out of them, and the buzzing in his ears drowned out everything else.

Chas stared at the wall in front of him until he realized he wasn't breathing. He vacuumed a huge lungful of air into his chest and continued to stare. Cecy's brother had died of leukemia.

A terrifying image of Cecy flashed before his eyes. She lay waxen white and stiff in a coffin, wearing her short bathrobe and the red high heels. In one hand she clutched her useless credit cards, and in the other a photo of Barney. Chas began to hyperventilate.

He imagined a funeral procession to a burning pyre, where Barney, all lugubrious yowls, tried to throw himself upon her coffin before Chas caught him just in time.

Stop it. Get ahold of yourself. Do something useful. Thoughts somersaulted and tangled in his mind.

How could he help Cecy? How could he make sure she got the best care available? She only had very basic health coverage, and no money. He wanted her to have the finest care money could buy—the best doctors and treatments.

Cecy couldn't die on him. She couldn't. He loved her—he wanted to spend the rest of his life with her!

With shaking hands, he retrieved the fax from the floor and scoured it for the phone number. By some stroke of luck it appeared at the bottom right of the page, still legible between smears.

He grabbed the telephone receiver and threw it on the desk in front of him, punching in the numbers on the telephone with cold, stiff fingers.

He knew it was no use inquiring about her status—they wouldn't tell him anything, since he wasn't a relative. All he could do was ensure her bills were paid so that she wasn't sent to some quack-in-a-box who wouldn't take care of her properly. Then it occurred to him. He could *become* a relative. He had good insurance, and if Cecy became his wife, coverage would extend to her, too.

He could hear the faint babble of a woman's

voice answering the line, but Chas wasn't sure he could trust himself to speak. Slowly, he lifted the receiver to his ear, as she said, "Hello? Hello?"

"Don't hang up," he managed. "You have a woman on record with the name of Cecily Scatterton. I want to make sure all her bills are paid, in full. Here's my credit-card number."

24

Cecy covered her mouth with her hand and stared at poor Barney. He stared back at her, mute. He'd lost at least twenty-five percent of his body weight. His left eye was stitched closed. The whiskers on that side of his face had been cropped to a one-inch length, and though his jaw was properly aligned, he now retained only one of his large bottom incisors.

Barney looked like . . . FrankenKitty.

Her small feline monster held his head cocked to the side, and his tongue lolled out of the right side of his mouth, as if to compensate for the missing whiskers. He was the most dreadful, pathetic vision. She had to get him home.

The girl at the reception desk, Andrea,

spouted Greek to her. "Barney had exophtalmos of the eye, along with an indolent ulcer. The CT showed that the ramus of his mandible was pushing into the globe of that eye. It also displayed a bony proliferation that looked like it extended into the calvarium of the skull."

Cecy nodded. "Uh, right."

"They removed half of his mandible . . ." The girl went on to give instructions for his care, and these were extensive. She handed over a typed sheet of reminders.

Cecy braced her hands on the counter. "About the bill," she began. "I know it's sizable. Enormous. And I'm prepared to pay it in full, of course."

Andrea opened her mouth, but Cecy rushed on.

"I've just had some financial . . . setbacks lately, and I don't have any credit cards anymore."

"Ms. Scatterton—"

"I could do a payment plan," she blurted, "but it might take me a long time. So I was wondering if I could do something in trade. I'll clean out cages. I'll walk dogs, or give flea dips, or whatever you want."

"Ms. Scatterton—"

"I'm a hard worker. I know I should have mentioned all this before, but I couldn't stand for Barney not to get the care he needed. He's my baby, you see, and—"

"Your bill is already paid."

"—so I know it was borderline unethical for me to do this, but—" she stopped. *"What?"*

"The bill's been paid in full."

Cecy's ears rang. "B-but that's not possible."

Andrea pointed to a carbon from a credit card. "Seventeen hundred forty-nine dollars and twenty-five cents. Paid this morning, by phone."

Cecy opened and closed her mouth. At last she said, her voice weak, "Who?"

"Chas S. Buchanan is the name on the card."

Chas had paid the bill? *Chas*, who'd never hidden his dislike of her cat? *Chas*, who clipped coupons religiously and could pinch a penny until it turned blue in the face, then silver, and was reborn as a dime?

"I need to sit down for a minute," she said. "Are you sure you got the name right? It doesn't say Charles Somebody, and the slip got attached to the wrong bill?"

"I'm positive."

"Oh." Cecy stared at Barney, who glowered back at her with his one eye. "Did he seem lucid? He wasn't babbling about pink elephants or anything?"

"Not that I know of."

"As long as you're sure." Cecy's mind reeled. He was crazy. Once again, she was in debt to the man. She cast her eyes heavenward and visualized herself at age ninety-seven. An ancient crone, with a beard and several warts, she was still typing with gnarled fingers and cackling into his phone, "Buchanan Financial, may I help you?"

Cecy shuddered. It was a scenario too grue-some for words, since warts and all, she'd still be in unrequited love with the man. She tried to picture what he would look like in seventy years, and failed. Through any future paunch or tuft of ear hair, she would still see a tall, broad, gloriously stubbled god in a pair of cowboy boots. She was cursed.

As she took a cab back to Etienne and Sylvie's, she tried to make sense of the thoughts rushing through her head. Chas had paid her bill, and paid it with plastic. So unless he had that amount of cash lying around, he was also going to pay interest on her bill for a couple of months. It was so wildly uncharacteristic of him.

Had she done more damage with the abacus than she'd realized? Head wounds were tricky, and he'd been badly concussed. She didn't know what else to make of it.

The double yellow lines in the center of the road burned into her eyes and looped into ques-tion marks in her mind. Chas had been acting very weird lately—smiling at her, touching her affectionately, and striding around with an enigmatic smile tugging the corners of his mouth.

Of course, she had turned him on to a major account, thanks to Etienne and Sylvie. Perhaps paying Barney's bill was his way of saying "thank you"? If so, he'd forked over one hell of a commission.

Come to think of it, how had Chas even known about Barney's problems? She hadn't mentioned them to him—not once. Had he become a psychic, as well as a financial planner? This was all too weird.

The cab pulled into Etienne and Sylvie's driveway, and Cecy carefully eased Barney's carrier off of the seat. "We're here, little love. Let's get you inside and make you comfy. Then Mama's got a little jar of pureed baby beef for you. A special treat for the One-Toothed among us."

Chas urged the Jeep at breakneck speed through chinks in the wall of traffic. When he couldn't find a chink, he created one. With every traffic light, every miserable lowlife left-turner, his anxiety grew into an irrational wrath. How could Cecy not have told him something this momentous? What was he, just her boy-toy to be tossed aside when she didn't need service? How could she grow a tumor behind his back? What kind of a woman was she? And dying on him was simply out of the question. He wouldn't permit it.

At last he made it through the forest of bumpers and turned into Inman Park. By the time he pulled up outside Etienne and Sylvie's house, he was propelled by a volcanic mixture of fear and adrenaline. He slammed the door of the Jeep, surged up the front steps, and punched the bell.

Several sweat-trickling moments passed before Cecy swung open the chestnut oak door. She was holding a jar of baby food and a spoon. "Chas!"

"For God's sake, Cecy, why didn't you tell me?" he thundered at her. He focused miserably on the pureed beef she held. A delighted baby grinned at him from the label, and his stomach twisted. He wanted one of those. With Cecy. And sweet Jesus, she was already reduced to eating pulp, not real food. He passed a hand over his face.

She blinked. "I . . . didn't think you'd really care that much."

Chas goggled at her. "You didn't think I'd *care*? You must think I'm one cold-hearted son of a bitch!"

"Thank you for taking care of the bill. But are you nuts? That's so much money, Chas. I'm going to pay you back every penny."

"How can you even talk about money at a time like this? Money versus a life? Money versus proper medical care? Cecy, I'm made of flesh and blood, not . . . not . . . *turnips*!" He grabbed her arm, heedless of the pureed beef. "We're going to get married right away, so you'll be on my insurance plan. Get your purse."

"Huh?" Cecy's hand pressed down hard on the handle of the spoon, which was still stuck in the jar, and bent the utensil almost double. The baby still radiated professional cuteness from the label. *Baby, baby, baby.* He and Cecy could have had such adorable babies together. Maybe it was still possible. They just had to beat this thing, this tumor that was threatening to swallow their world.

"I said, get your purse."

"Buchanan, have you lost your mind? I'm not getting anything but a good shrink for you. Married? Insurance?"

"Cecy, I know you only have the most basic coverage. All the tests and treatments are hideously expensive, and won't be in your plan. We've got to get you on mine. *Now.*" He wouldn't even mention babies to her. She was already overwhelmed. No use tormenting her with thoughts of a future they might never have—no! He was going to think positively. He was going to do what strong men did best: take care of things, in order of priority.

"How is getting me on your insurance plan going to help—"

"I can't even stand to talk about this. Let's just go." It sounded like a hundred pounds of gravel had gotten mixed into his larynx, and something was rising up in his throat and choking him. Chas squeezed his eyes shut right before his face somehow . . . cracked. He opened his mouth and gasped for air, but it was hot and devoid of oxygen, and he had to gasp again. Jesus, someone had thrown burning grit into his eyes, too.

He felt Cecy's small body pressed against his, and an arm wound around his back. He pressed his face into her hair, inhaling deeply of peaches and hydrangea. And pureed beef.

"I had no idea you were so attached to Barney," she said.

He froze.

"But it's okay. He's going to be fine. You can forget all this marriage and insurance stuff, Chas. I mean, sure, we could prove he's a dependent, but if they wanted a photo it would blow the whole scheme right away."

Chas slowly drew himself up and set her away from him. Her blue eyes gazed earnestly into his. She still clutched the smelly little jar and spoon, and the baby's sunny smile morphed into an evil smirk. "You're telling me," he said carefully, "that it's *Barney* who has the tumor?"

"Had," she corrected. "They cut it right out and—" She covered her mouth with her hand, eyes wide. "Oh, no. You thought it was me who was sick?"

Chas suddenly discovered why unlucky schmucks declared that they didn't know whether to shit or go blind. He'd never really understood the phrase before.

"You thought *I* had the tumor?" Cecy asked, again.

He nodded, bereft of speech. A maelstrom of emotions hurled themselves about his inside track, vying for first place. In the lead was a relief, that felt like astringent on the pores of his soul. A nose behind that was a black cloud of fury at her for scaring him. And third, only by a length, was a great, woolly, sheepish embarrassment at his own reactions.

Chas inspected his knuckes. Curious that they weren't dirty, since they'd been dragging the ground ever since he'd met Cecy.

"Oh, Chas . . ." she murmured tenderly.

He refused to look at her.

"You were going to marry me to get me good insurance?" She sighed. "That's heartrendingly sweet."

He perked up. So maybe his dignity was shot to hell, and he'd spent two thousand bucks on a ball-snacking rodent. But "sweet" was a good term, in Woman-Speak. She would overlook the embarrassing parts of his behavior and marry him anyway. Then they could have babies much cuter than the one on the jar.

"But Chas, you of all people should know that they wouldn't cover a pre-existing condition."

He stared at her. She was right, of course. In his panic he'd overlooked it. He felt like an even bigger idiot.

"You don't have to marry me, Chas," she said. "I'm quite healthy, and I have a decent job, and I'm going to have a great teaching career. You're off the hook. But thank you."

No way! She was turning him down?

"But Cecy, I *want* to marry you."

She reached up and patted his cheek. "No, you don't. You're just saving face because you asked me before. It's okay. Really."

Before he knew what had happened, he was standing outside the door of Etienne and Sylvie's house, and they were pulling into the driveway, effectively putting an end to personal conversation.

What did strong men do, in order of priority, when their love was mistaken for charity?

25

Cecy sought solace in her wet pillow that night, burying her nose in it like an aardvark searching for ants. Her shoulders finally stopped shaking convulsively, and she figured it was about time to spit the hair out of her mouth. She couldn't breathe at all this way.

She struggled to an upright position and sniffled blearily. "Barney," she wailed.

Her cat squatted in the corner of the room, tilting his head as if still unable to get accustomed to only one set of whiskers. He blinked at her.

"Barney, he p-p-proposed to m-me for *insurance* reasons. Have you ever heard of anything so dastardly? He only wanted to m-m-marry me because he thought I was *dying*, and wouldn't be around long enough to pester him."

She stumbled into the little bathroom to splash some water on her face. She looked like an overripe tomato with bad hair. "A pity-proposal, that's what it was. In fact, it wasn't really a proposal at all. It was a command, an announcement, a *growl*."

She marched back into the main room, hands on her hips. "Get your purse," she mimicked to Barney. "Sign on the dotted line. I don't think so!"

Barney squinted his eyes at her, as if to say, "You're overreacting."

"Yes, it was sweet of him. And good of him. And . . . *charitable* of him." Her face crumpled again. "But I don't want to be a charity bride," she sobbed. "I w-want him to love me, not pity me."

By morning, she was more collected, if still a little leaky. The swelling in her face had gone down, but not the redness, so that she now resembled a chili pepper with bad hair. A shower and blow-dry helped with that, as did a new affirmation, repeated twenty times into the mirror. "I, Cecy, am nobody's charity case, but a strong and independent woman."

This kept her head high until she arrived outside Chas's office building for work, and remembered that she, Cecy, was a strong and independent woman who now owed him eighteen hundred dollars for her cat's medical adventures. Oh, God. Was there no end in sight to her debt?

She ratcheted her chin into the air, adjusted her jacket, and walked with a fraudulent poise into the office.

Chas lounged behind his desk, hands clasped behind his head, not even pretending to work. "Hello, Beautiful," he said.

That brought her up short, and she gazed at him suspiciously for a moment. Then, nodding good morning, she launched full steam ahead. "Okay, Chas. We have something to discuss. You've been very sweet, and paid Barney's bill, but I now owe you piles of money, which of course it's going to take me some time to pay off. At this rate, I'm going to be your indentured servant for life."

He ran a hand over his jaw and paused. Was that a hint of a smile? What was wrong with him today? "Well, maybe," he drawled, "but that's a very old-fashioned way of looking at things."

"Huh?"

"Not to mention a cynical viewpoint. I mean, I don't expect you to scrub the floors, cook all my meals, and do exactly as I say."

"Well, that's a damned good thing," Cecy said in dangerous tones. *Courtesy*, said her conscience. *You owe him courtesy*.

He pursed his lips. "I would prefer that you sleep with me," he mused, and she gasped.

"But we don't have to make it a law."

Cecy choked. "A *law*?"

"I will ask, however, to see you naked at least once a day."

Cecy took a deep breath before she surged toward him and stabbed him in the chest with her index finger. "I'll scrub toilets at the bus station if I have to, to pay off what I owe, but I am not forming any kind of sick, perverted agreement with you!"

Chas wore a puzzled expression. "But people do it every day—"

"Not me!"

"—in churches, and city halls, and parks."

"This is an age of freedom for women, not bondage."

"It is true that some feminists look upon the arrangement as a form of legalized, monogamous prostitution, but I think that's a little extreme, don't you? And hardly romantic."

"You," Cecy stabbed him again, her finger now shaking, "are not fit to say the *word* 'romance.' Do you understand?"

"Ouch," said Chas, now openly grinning. He reached behind him for a long, narrow box, and placed it gently in her arms.

"What—" spluttered Cecy. Inside the box lay a dozen long-stemmed roses in tissue. "No! Not even! Don't begin to think you can give me these after your disgusting—"

Chas put his finger up to her lips, as if to shush her. She was mad enough that she bit it.

"Ouch! Look, Cecy, there's something I want to say to you."

"Well, I have *nothing* to say to you, Chas Buchanan! You're the worst kind of creep—"

He took her arm and led her to one of the reception chairs. "Just listen to me for a minute."

"Absolutely not, you—you—"

Chas rolled his eyes, plucked three of the thornless roses from the box, and jammed them between her teeth. "Cecy, shut up for a minute." He pushed her gently into the chair and held her hands. "Just let me speak, okay?"

"Aaaaaaahhhhggg." She shot sparks at him from her eyes. Roses, she discovered, tasted a lot like dirt and grass. It was just her luck that the one time a man gave her roses, he stuffed them into her mouth as if she were a horse. It only fueled her outrage.

"I really meant for this scenario to be quite different, but you're not cooperating."

She rolled her eyes and snorted.

"That's my baby," Chas told her tenderly. "Now listen to me. I was only teasing you earlier. Maybe that wasn't such a good idea."

She glared at him.

"I'm trying to propose here! Will you give a guy a break?"

Cecy involuntarily bit down hard on the rose stems. She goggled at him. Propose?

Chas took the roses out of her mouth, and while she wiped her lips, he put them back with the others and handed her the whole box. "Let's start over," he suggested. "Cecy, these are for you."

"I'm speechless."

"You should give a glad little cry, now, and throw yourself into my arms, kissing me all over."

Cecy narrowed her eyes. The man was a loon. "Let's pretend I already did that."

"Well, okay." He sighed. "None of this is turning out the way I'd planned it, but then, you're not the sort of woman anyone can plan around." He ran a hand through his hair.

"I'm a bean counter, Cecy, not a poet. I'm not always articulate about my feelings. I wasn't trying to make some kind of sick sex bargain for your cat's bill. Maybe I paid it by mistake, but I want you to know I'd pay it ten times over just to see a smile on your face, just to know you weren't worried about Barney anymore."

She felt her lip trembling. "Ten times?"

"Twenty," he said. "The thing is, Cecy, when I asked you to marry me yesterday I botched things completely. I was frantic—I thought you were going to die on me. I didn't ask you out of pity, you crazy woman. I asked you because I *love* you. I asked you because if you were sick, I wanted to spend every possible moment taking the best care of you that I could."

Two fat tears blurred Cecy's vision of Chas.

He stuck a hand into the pocket of his knife-creased khakis and pulled out a small black-velvet box.

Cecy covered her mouth with her hand as he opened it. Inside sparkled the symbol of his love: multifaceted and precious like Chas himself.

"Will you marry me, Cecy? I love you."

In her mind, she pirouetted into his arms and breathed, "Yes, my darling. You are my new dawn." In reality, she sat paralyzed and emitted a sound similar to a goose honk.

"Excuse me?" The man of her dreams raised a brow.

She finally found her voice and her motor skills. She rose and wobbled toward him. "Oh, Chas, I love you, too."

He cupped her face in his big hands and kissed her deeply, thoroughly. Then he gathered her close with one arm, lifting up the ring box with the other. "So . . . do you like it?"

"I love it. It's beautiful."

He released her and took it from the box. "You can only have it if you agree to marry me."

"Well," said Cecy, now that she'd recovered, "that's a lot to ask. I'll have to think about it."

Chas went straight for her ribs and tickled her into submission.

"Yes!" she shrieked. "Yes, I'll marry you."

He slipped the ring onto her third finger, and it fit perfectly. She blinked down at it, tears in her eyes. "Chas?"

"What, baby?" He kissed her again.

"*Why* do you want to marry me?"

He lifted his head and looked into her eyes. "Something about you, Cecy, makes me love you. Something about you is so right, so rare. You've just got something that I can't live without."

Epilogue

Cecy wiggled her toes and posed for yet another formal wedding photo. Chas had insisted that she wear the high-heeled red sandals under her white gown. Since this was the South, everything had to coordinate, so she'd chosen red roses for her bridal bouquet and worn deep red lipstick.

Impatient with the endless boring poses, she jammed a pair of white-plastic sunglasses onto her nose, plucked three roses from the dozen she held, and slipped them between her teeth. She beckoned at the photographer to shoot, and he did so, accompanied by Chas's broad grin and several gasps from proper ladies among the guests.

Then her new husband pulled her into his arms. "Cecy," he murmured into her ear, "what else matches your shoes?"

She smiled wickedly at him. "You'll just have to wait to find out, won't you?"

"You're a cruel woman, Mrs. Buchanan."

"Yes, and unusual, too."

"That's the part I like best. And I've been wondering," Chas murmured, between lip-locks.

"About?"

"If perhaps we could have a baby, as well as a cat."

Cecy pulled back from him and tucked her hair behind her ears. "It's a definite possibility. You've, uh . . . already made a deposit into my account."

"I have?"

She nodded. "Yes. And all the interest is compounding. Based on my calculations, your principal should be enormous in about eight months."

"That's quite an investment." His dark eyes reflected joy, and he kissed her tenderly again.

"The only thing I'm worried about is the rate of inflation," Cecy told him.

"You'll be beautiful pregnant," Chas reassured her. "I wish all my investments were front-end load."

Dear Love Doctor,

I'm a man who has it all—a thriving business, power, and women just fall all over themselves to get next to me and with all I've got to offer I can't say as I'd blame them! But there's something missing from my life . . . could it be love?

Sincerely
Self-Made Man

How would you answer a letter like that?
Discover what columnist Daffy Landry gives
out as advice to Hunter James in

Dear Love Doctor

by

Hailey North

Coming next month
An Avon Contemporary Romance

Coming Soon from
HarperTorch

CIRCLE OF THREE

By the *New York Times* bestselling author of
THE SAVING GRACES

Patricia Gaffney

Through the interconnected lives of three generations of
women in a small town in rural Virginia, this poignant,
memorable novel reveals the layers of tradition and respon-
sibility, commitment and passion, these women share. Wise,
moving, and heartbreakingly real, *Circle of Three* offers
women of all ages a deeper understanding of one another, of
themselves and of the perplexing and invigorating magic
that is life itself.

"Filled with insight and humor and heart,
Circle of Three reminds us what it's like
to be a woman."
Nora Roberts

"Powerful . . . Family drama that is impossible
to put down until the final page is read."
Midwest Book Review

"Through the eyes of these strong, complex women
come three uniquely insightful, emotional perspectives."
New York Daily News

0-06-109836-1/$7.50 US/$9.99 Can

COT 0401